SWORD OF DARKNESS

THE CHRONICLES OF BRIANNA BOWERS

Billy Stancil

Sword of Darkness: The Chronicles of Brianna Bowers
© 2023 Billy Stancil
ISBN# 999

Published by TaylorMade Publishing
Jacksonville, FL
www.TaylorMadePublishingFL.com
(904) 323-1334

TaylorMade Publishing

"God's goodness is so abounding, that He can even turn the most heinous tragedies of life around for our good and His glory."- Brianna Bowers (the real one)

To James and Nathan

The joy of the Lord is my strength.

For Jerry and Carolyn Winkler

The hands and feet of Jesus

I know a man in Christ who fourteen years ago was caught up to the third heaven. Whether it was in the body or out of the body I do not know--God knows. And I know that this man -- whether in the body or apart from the body I do not know, but God knows—was caught up to paradise and heard inexpressible things, things that no one is permitted to tell.

2 Corinthians 12: 2-4 NIV

Be alert and of sober mind. Your enemy the devil prowls around like a roaring lion looking for someone to devour.

1 Peter 5:8

[i]

For our struggle is not against flesh and blood, but against the rulers, against the authorities, against the powers of this dark world and against the spiritual forces of evil in the heavenly realms.

Ephesians 6:12 NIV

And I will ask the Father, and he will give you another advocate to help you and be with you forever—the Spirit of truth. The world cannot accept him, because it neither sees him nor knows him. But you know him, for he lives with you and will be in you.

John 14: 16 & 17 NIV

But the Advocate, the Holy Spirit, whom the Father will send in my name, will teach you all things and will remind you of everything I have said to you.

John 14: 26 NIV

INTRODUCTION

CHARLOTTE, NORTH CAROLINA

Caleb and his wife, Kortney, had only been living in their new house for a few months. They moved to North Carolina from Florida and absolutely loved the idea of finally having seasons. The young couple, having met in college, and marrying shortly after, had both landed dream jobs in Charlotte. Caleb was a software engineer for a major tech company and Kortney was teaching fifth grade science at a pristine private school.

Another dream that Caleb had recently made come true in his life, was owning a motorcycle. A brand-new Harley Davidson Fat Bob 114, to be precise. He couldn't believe that Kortney had been okay with him getting a bike. "You've worked so hard to get to where you are, baby," she'd said, after he'd cautiously brought up the subject. "You deserve to have something nice for yourself. Besides, I know you're a responsible driver." A week later, he'd gotten his motorcycle license and his new bike in the same day. He was presently giving said bike a good cleaning in his driveway on this beautiful, sunny day.

"How's Fat Bob?" Kortney asked, as she brought him a bottle of water and a slice of watermelon.

"You tell me," he replied, stepping back for her to look it over.

"Very nice," she said, reaching out to touch the mirror. He quickly grabbed her hand to stop her.

"You're a married woman, Mrs. Fagen," Caleb said with a smile. "You shouldn't be getting Fat Bob excited by touching him."

"Did you really just stop me from touching your bike?" She put her hands on her hips. "Seriously?"

He twisted his hand towel as a threat to pop her with it. "Just step away from the bike, Ma'am."

Just as she went to give him a good pop with her hand, a horn blew from the street. They looked over to see Amber, their neighbor, from across the street. She was waving at them as her window slid down. "You love birds are so cute!"

"He won't let me touch his precious bike!" Kortney yelled and snatched the towel from Caleb's hand. Caleb proceeded to chase her across the yard.

"The bike looks nice, Caleb!" Amber said. "Michael is so jealous of it."

"Thanks, Amber!" Caleb replied. "Let him know he's more than welcome to watch me ride it anytime." They all laughed.

"Hey, Ms. Kortney!" the adorable little blonde girl called from the backseat of Amber's car.

"Hey, Megan! How are you doing, sweetie!?" Kortney replied.

"I'm good!" she replied, holding up a stuffed animal. "I got a new puppy, and his name is Charlie!"

"Hey, Charlie!" Kortney said with a wave. "Welcome to the neighborhood!"

[iv]

"You guys should join us for hot dogs later!" Amber said. "We can get in the pool!"

"That sounds great, text me with a time and let me know what we can bring!" Kortney said as Amber waved and pulled into her driveway. She parked in front of the garage door and got out.

"Why did you agree to that?" Caleb asked in a whisper. "You know I'm trying to eat healthy. I have to look good for my sexy wife, you know." He grabbed the towel from her and chased her into the garage. She screamed the whole way. Instead of popping her with the towel, he grabbed her and gave her a big kiss.

"It'll be fun," Kortney said. "I'll make something with veggies." She looked over and saw Megan running across her yard making her puppy fly. Amber must've taken the first load of groceries inside, because the back door of the car was still open. Megan giggled and said something to her puppy. Kortney smiled at the thought of her future children playing in the yard.

"You aren't getting any ideas, are you?" Caleb asked, noticing her watching Megan.

"What if I were?" She lightly shoved his chest.

"I just got a motorcycle! Give me at least a few months to live dangerously before you make me a daddy!"

Hearing the way he said that made her giggle. "I can live with that…just don't live too dangerously." They fist bumped and he pulled her in for a hug.

"Who's that?" she asked, looking toward Amber's house, where a black hot rod had just pulled up in front of the house. A young white man with scraggly hair got out and walked around his car.

Caleb looked. "Don't be a nosy neighbor, dear." He attempted to tickle her, but she pulled away.

"Stop, Caleb!" she snapped and stepped out of the garage, sensing something wasn't right. "Can we help you!?" She called to the man as he walked back around to his open driver's door.

He only waved and shook his head. He slid into the front seat, and his car growled as he pulled away. At that exact moment, Amber came outside talking on her cell phone. She glanced back and forth for Megan.

"Caleb, Megan's gone! Oh my God, her puppy is on the curb!" Kortney yelled, sprinting across the street. "That man took her! Oh God, Amber, that man snatched Megan!" Amber dropped her phone and screamed. Before Kortney could get across the street, Caleb's motorcycle came to life. He slid on his helmet and peeled out of his driveway. His helmet had built in speakers and microphone for his phone. He dialed fast before he hit the end of his road.

"911, what's your emergency?"

"A little girl has been kidnapped," Caleb said calmly. He hit the gas and made it to the entrance of his neighborhood in record time. He looked left and saw the car about two blocks away. "The kidnapper is driving a newer model black Dodge Challenger."

"Sir, what is your location?" the dispatcher asked.

"I am on a motorcycle, just exiting Crimson Oaks neighborhood onto Grayson Blvd. I'm heading South." He punched it again.

"Do you have a license number for the Challenger?"

"Give me about ten seconds and I will." He got into the center turn lane and quickly caught up with the Challenger. "There's a 'lost tag' sign on the back." Just then, the driver must've realized he was being followed, because he made a sharp, tire squealing turn. Caleb followed. "We just turned onto a side road, and I didn't see the name!" Caleb quickly caught up with the car.

"Sir, do you know the child that has been taken?"

"Yes, her name is Megan, she's four or five years old. She's our neighbor's daughter. My wife and I witnessed the kidnapping." The Challenger made a sharp left onto another road and punched it. "Does this punk really think he can outrun me?"

"Do you know the name of your neighbors, sir?"

"Michael and Amber Duncan."

"Okay, sir. Thank you. We have the girl's mother on another line."

"Well, let her know this punk is not getting away. I'm on Casper Road, by the way. It looks like we're heading for the expressway. I'm going to try and head him off."

"Sir, please don't try anything, just keep your distance. I have officers in route to you."

"Well, they better hurry." Just then Caleb heard sirens. He smiled. "That's right, punk! You're going away for a long time." He saw blue lights ahead. Just then the driver slammed on the brakes and the black Dodge slid off the road and into someone's yard. Caleb cautiously passed the yard. He had to assume that a child abductor would most likely have a gun. He came to a stop about fifty feet away, just as the guy jumped out of the car and ran around the house. Caleb parked his bike and flagged down the officers. He pointed in the direction the guy had run.

The officers stopped and several of them withdrew their weapons and made chase on foot. Another officer circled around the block in his squad car, while one stayed behind and cautiously approached the Challenger. The stereo in the car was blaring loud music. He told Caleb to stay back. With gun drawn he stepped up to the car and swung open the back door. A little blonde girl was lying in the back seat screaming.

"It's okay, honey. I'm a police officer." He reached for her hand. She jumped into his arms, sobbing.

"I want my daddy!"

Caleb came running over. "It's alright Megan, we're going to get you to your daddy." The officer handed her to Caleb, and she held onto him tightly.

The officer radioed it in that the child was safe. He turned to Caleb with tears in his eyes. "You, my friend, did an amazing thing! These things almost never have happy endings."

Caleb had tears of his own as little Megan clung to him for dear life, sobbing her eyes out. This precious little girl's life had almost been destroyed. "It's okay, baby." He squeezed her tighter. "My God," he thought. "Do I really want to bring a child into this world?"

CHAPTER 1

BERLIN, GERMANY

Brianna sat in the back of the police van as it made its way through the dark Forst Grunewald. There were three vans and six patrol cars making their way to the river, Havel. There were no lights flashing or sirens blaring…they were being as quiet as a church mouse. Several times she wanted to ask how much longer it would be, but none of these officers seemed to appreciate the fact that she was the reason they were out all night following a hunch. A hunch? Her tips had led to the release of over 300 victims of human trafficking and the arrest of 37 suspects, thank you very much. They were lucky to have her, if she did say so herself.

The twenty-nine-year-old Brianna Bowers was a beautiful woman from America. Her dark brown hair was just below her shoulders. She had often been teased for being so short, at just five feet tall, but that had never kept her from doing the things she needed to do. She was single, though her life choices pretty much guaranteed that…at least that's what she told herself. She was a sold-out Christian. She loved Jesus more than the air she breathed.

She spent hours a day on her knees in prayer…mostly for the victims of human trafficking that she hadn't found yet. She made it a point of reading and studying her Bible at least an hour a day. She was also the head of Das Menschenhandel Ministerium, or the DMM, which in English stood for The Human Trafficking Ministry. Yeah, Brianna definitely did not have time for a man.

"We will be there…few moments," the officer in the passenger seat said in his broken English. Another reason they didn't care for Brianna was that she spoke very little German. Pretty odd for a woman that had lived and worked in Germany for five years, but she had just been too busy since she'd gotten here. Brianna took out her laptop and pulled up the information she had. According to her "source", there would be several semi-truck trailers ready to be picked up. They would be parked in the forest near the river. "Remember…you stay…here." He pointed toward the floor of the van.

Brianna smiled and nodded. These guys were a part of the German Federal Police called the Bundeskriminalamt or the BKA. They were working with Interpol in catching a crime ring of human traffickers. Interpol had been after these guys for almost a decade. If this played out like she hoped, it would be huge. Their van came to an abrupt stop and Brianna's laptop almost hit the floor. They pulled to the side of the road, and everyone got out except Brianna and the driver.

"Is this the place?" Brianna asked the driver, though she suspected he did not speak English. He did not respond. There were no windows in the back of the van, so she had no idea what was going on out there.

The side door slid open, and a tall thin man peaked inside. "Good evening, Ms. Bowers," he said in a thick French accent. "I am Chief Inspector Toussaint."

"Ooh, I love your accent," Brianna smiled at him. "Toussaint? Is that like the famous wax museum?"

The older man gave her a grim look. "That is TussAUD…not Toussaint." He glanced at someone beside him that Brianna couldn't see." This was apparently something he'd

~ 2 ~

been asked before. "We have located the trailers. My men are positioning themselves around the perimeter to be sure it is safe before we investigate the contents." He nodded to the driver, who quickly unbuckled and exited the van, walking away toward the action. Junior Detective Skutnik here," he said and stepped aside for her to show herself. She was young, even younger than Brianna. Her smile was beautiful as she held out her hand to Brianna.

"Please, call me Nadia," she said in what Brianna guessed was a Russian accent. "It is a pleasure to meet the famous Brianna Bowers. Thank you for the work you do. You…"

"Junior Detective Skutnik will now be taking you to a safe location," the Chief Inspector said, interrupting Nadia and closing the door. A moment later, Nadia was in the driver's seat, pulling away.

"So, Nadia Skutnik? Is that Russian?" Brianna asked.

"Nadia IS a Russian name, but I am Romanian," Nadia replied.

"Well, it's a beautiful name," Brianna said. "And thank you for being nice to me…I'm not very popular with most of your coworkers."

Nadia pulled off the road and into a field about a mile away from where they'd been. She put the van in park and unbuckled. She turned to face Brianna with a serious look on her face. "I am from the city of Mangalia in Romania."

"I've heard of it," Brianna responded. "We rescued several young girls from there."

Nadia nodded. "You rescued my little sister," her eyes teared up as she spoke. "My sweet Ana was six years old when she went missing. We thought we would never see her again." She wiped her eyes. "My parents spent everything they had looking for her. I joined Interpol so I could look for her." She stopped talking and seemed to be remembering something. "It was my last day of University. I was in the middle of a final exam in Criminology when a student entered the Hall where I was. He walked right up to me and handed me a note…a small yellow paper. 'Your sister is found, call mama'." She smiled at Brianna.

"My sister told me how you held her and told her everything was going to be okay. She said she clung to you as if her breath depended on it." She wiped her tears again. "Nice to you? I owe you everything, Brianna Bowers." She reached back and took Brianna's hand. "I've followed your work ever since. You are my hero."

Brianna wiped her own tears. "That is so awesome," she said, squeezing Nadia's hand. "Thank you for sharing your story."

"Everyone be alert!" came the cry over the radio. "We have visitors coming in from the South. Five cargo trucks."

"So, I have to ask you Brianna Bowers," Nadia said quite awkwardly.

"Please, just call me Brianna."

"Brianna, who is this so called "source" that you always say tells you where to find these girls?"

Brianna smiled, having been asked this question a million times. Some had accused her of being involved

somehow. How else would she know such precise details? "You wouldn't believe me if I told you."

"So, tell me so I can have a good laugh," Nadia replied.

"God told me," Brianna said, expecting a different reaction than she got.

Nadia had a slight smile on her face. "I half suspected that's what you would say. I told you I've followed your work. Every time you mentioned your "source", you smiled. That told me that it was someone you cared about. Your parents live in a small town in Florida and your sister lives in California.

I seriously doubt any of them are giving you inside information on human trafficking. You're not married or in a relationship, so that leaves out a partner with connections. Your best friend is that famous church singer who travels around with that televangelist with the Irish name." Brianna smiled at her description of her best friends. "I mean, they tour the world and meet lots of people, but I didn't really think they were your source."

"And you're only a Junior Detective?" Brianna asked. "Girl, you got skills."

"Junior Detective Skutnik, bring Ms. Bowers to the sight!" Chief Inspector Toussaint said over the radio.

"Right away, sir," Nadia replied into her radio. She started the van and pulled out into the road.

"Do you believe in God, Nadia?" Brianna asked.

Nadia was silent for a moment before answering. "No, I don't…but sometimes I want to."

~ 5 ~

"I understand," Brianna replied. "Just know, He believes in you…and He loves you very much."

After a moment of silence between them, Nadia cleared her throat. "Everyone says that whole experience you had as a teenager was a hoax, you know? Some kind of trick photography."

"I know," Brianna replied, remembering that crazy night in Gateway, Florida sixteen years ago. "But trust me…It was very real." Brianna closed her laptop and prepared herself for what she was about to be doing. "I'm not asking if you believe what you saw on television. I'm asking if you believe there is more to this life than being born, living your life, and dying…because there is, Nadia. So much more."

The van came to a stop on the side of the road. There was a lot of commotion outside. Lights were now flashing; people were hustling around. There was even a helicopter flying overhead and shining a spotlight on the activity. The side door slid open. It was Chief Inspector Toussaint. "Fifteen suspects have been taken into custody. Two were shot and killed in an attempt to escape. Only one of our agents was injured, but he'll be fine." He looked from Nadia to Brianna. "It appears that your tip was quite useful, Ms. Bowers. I and the rest of Interpol thank you. This arrest will hopefully lead us to bigger fish."

"What did you find in the trailers?" Brianna asked, fearfully.

The Chief Inspector looked down. His demeanor changed. He stepped back so Brianna could get out of the van. "Out of the forty-seven children that were in the trailers…only thirty-one were still alive."

Brianna closed her eyes and took a deep breath. The horrors those children faced. "Those poor babies."

"Twelve have been rushed to the hospital," he added. "There is no telling how long these children have been without food and water." He led Brianna and Nadia over to where the children were being taken care of. "Their ages range from about four years old to fourteen. There are six boys. They and the suspects are all Vietnamese."

Brianna walked over to where a young girl of around six was crying as the medical team tried to set her up with an I.V. Brianna sat down beside her and set her in her lap. She wrapped her arms around the little girl and began to pray quietly in her ear. She immediately calmed down and relaxed into Brianna's arms. Brianna continued to pray out loud as the medical team examined the young girl.

After several moments, someone tapped Brianna on the shoulder, and she looked up to see a woman smiling at her. She nodded to the sleeping girl in her arms. Brianna smiled and handed the child over. The woman placed her in the back of an ambulance. "I am happy… you speak Vietnamese," the woman said to Brianna in the best English she could muster. "It helped to calm her down."

"What are you talking about?" Brianna asked. "I don't speak Vietnamese."

"Well, you do now," the E.M.T said with a laugh as she went to help another child.

Brianna looked over and Nadia was watching her suspiciously. She shrugged and went to see if she could be useful elsewhere. Seeing a young, teenage girl sitting in the

back of one of the vans hugging her knees and hiding her face, Brianna climbed in and sat down beside her.

"She won't let anyone touch her," one of the officers said.

"Just give me a few minutes with her," Brianna replied. The officer walked away. Brianna leaned back in the seat beside her and began to pray silently. She asked God for guidance in dealing with this girl. After a few minutes, she opened her eyes and looked over. The girl had lifted her head and was staring at Brianna. "Hi," she said and held out her hand, palm up. The girl looked at it and reached out and placed her hand on Brianna's. She began to cry and wrapped her arms around Brianna. She sobbed into Brianna's shoulder and held her tight.

"You're like a wizard with these kids," Nadia said from the open door.

Brianna smiled at her. "It's all God."

"The Chief Inspector needs to see you when you are done here," Nadia said. She walked away but continued to look back at Brianna interacting with this young girl.

Brianna pulled out of her hug and put her hands on both sides of the girl's face. "You are going to be okay; do you understand?" The girl nodded. "God has you in His hands." She hugged the girl one more time and then led her to the medical team so they could examine her.

"Brianna!" Nadia called to her from under a small canopy they'd set up near the river. She waved Brianna over. The Chief Inspector, Nadia, and three other men were standing next to a table where a laptop computer was open. Brianna approached them.

~ 8 ~

"Brianna Bowers, I would like to introduce you to the Secretary- General of Interpol, Gunther Schmidt." Chief Inspector Toussaint pulled Brianna over to face the screen where a good-looking, forty-something man sat at a large desk wearing a very expensive looking suit.

"Hi," was all Brianna said.

"Hello, Ms. Bowers, it is good to finally meet you," the Secretary-General said in a thick German accent. "First of all, I would like to personally thank you on behalf of all of Interpol for your help in bringing down this human trafficking ring. Granted, it isn't over yet…but we are closer than we've ever been…thanks to you."

"Oh, um…you're welcome, sir," Brianna replied. "It is my pleasure and honor to help these children in a time where nobody else can."

"Forgive me for getting straight to the point, Ms. Bowers, but I am a very busy man. I would like to throw a party, here in France, in your honor…if you would allow me," the Secretary-General said.

"Oh, wow, that is so not necessary, sir." Brianna replied. "Seriously, I do what I do for the glory of God, not…"

"Balderdash!" he said, interrupting her. "I've already ordered the cake." He smiled. "Besides, we Germans need but an excuse to celebrate victory. I insist, Brianna Bowers. Nadia has been given charge of you. This weekend I want to personally shake your hand and place a medal of honor around your neck." Before Brianna could object, the screen went black.

~ 9 ~

"Isn't it exciting!?" Nadia said with a little too much enthusiasm. She grabbed Brianna's arm and led her out from under the canopy. "They are throwing you a party!"

"Nadia why are you…" Brianna started to say, but Nadia shushed her.

Once they were far enough away from everyone, Nadia let go of her arm and faced her. "Something is wrong."

"What do you mean?" Brianna asked.

"This new Secretary-General Schmidt…I don't like him. He's bad, I just know it."

"Bad? What kind of bad?"

"I just think he has a different agenda than that of most of Interpol," she said, looking around to make sure nobody could hear her. "I'm usually pretty good at reading people," she whispered. "And I'm rarely wrong." She looked around again. "I wouldn't be surprised if he was somehow involved in…" she let her eyes say the rest by looking all around.

"You think he's involved in human trafficking!?" Brianna asked in a loud whisper. "Nadia, that's huge!"

"Ssshhh!" Nadia put a finger over Brianna's lips. "It's just a thought." Again, she looked around. "That said, you need to be careful. If he IS involved, then his reason for your "party" could be a way of…"

"Stopping me from interfering," Brianna continued for her. "Probably for good."

~ 10 ~

CHAPTER 2

CLARKSTON, GEORGIA

Travis Scott was a twenty-six-year-old good for nothing, loser. He had a police record as long as his arm and an extreme gambling debt that kept him involved in a life of crime. He'd started off stealing cars, selling drugs, and breaking into homes. He was your basic white trash, with his long, shaggy hair, body covered in tattoos, and incessant knack for staying in trouble.

Presently, he was sitting in his small trailer, furnished with a dirty mattress and a cooler full of warm beer. He had no electricity or running water. He sat on the floor, leaning back against the wall rocking back and forth, as the drugs he'd taken to calm his nerves began to wear out. "IDIOT!" he screamed at himself. "STUPID IDIOT!" He couldn't believe how close he'd come to getting caught. He would've gone away for a very long time.

His latest string of crimes was something he never thought he was capable of doing. In fact, he hated himself for getting involved, but the money was incredible. It had been about two months earlier when he was approached by a man, Jack Watson, who knew he was drowning in debt. He told Travis that if he did a job for him, he would help him pay off his debt.

Travis thought it was a dream come true until Jack had told him that he'd be snatching children. No way he could do it. After struggling with the idea for several days, he decided to just look at it as a job. Nothing more and nothing less. He just couldn't think about it. After the first job, where he'd grabbed a seven-year-old girl from a Target in Macon, he'd thrown up all over the dash of the van he'd been driving.

He'd been miserable, listening to her scream and cry. He'd almost let her out of the van. Then he'd seen the payoff. Jack had paid off $10,000 of his gambling debt. It was probably for the best that Jack paid it directly because Travis would've just gambled it away and made his situation worse. Since then, he'd taken two more little girls, each one in a different town. His $240,000 in gambling debt was starting to go down.

Then, he'd decided to go to Charlotte. He couldn't stay in the same town long; he didn't want to draw attention to himself. He'd been driving around all day looking for a good opportunity. Driven through countless neighborhoods and parking lots. Then he'd seen her. That little unsupervised white girl playing with her stuffed animal in the front yard. It had taken him mere seconds to get her in the car, and then he heard the lady across the street. Nosy neighbors. He'd been seen. "STUPID!!!" he screamed, slamming his hand against the wall.

He'd been so excited to finally have a target, that he hadn't checked his surroundings. That guy had a motorcycle too. No car could've caught him. He'd had to ditch it without cleaning his prints off. "Stupid, stupid, stupid." He'd run into the woods behind that house, found a creek, and ran as fast as he could.

Eventually he'd come to a culvert and hid under a railroad track for hours. That's when Jack had called him. It was apparently all over the news and Jack was calling to see if it was his work. He'd told Jack everything. After calling him every bad name in the book, several times, Jack had told him to find

a way to get back home. He'd waited until dark, stolen a car from a Walmart parking lot, and headed back to Georgia.

Just then, he heard a vehicle pull up outside his trailer. He jumped up and looked out the window. "Oh, no," he mumbled a few curse words and slammed his fist into the wood paneling, making a hole. "Can't I even get a second to unwind!?" The large black Escalade with the solid black tinted windows let him know that Jack was not wasting any time in punishing him for his screw up. What was going to happen? Yell at him? Slap him around? Break bones? Or…worse?

The inevitable knock came at the door. Travis slung it open like peeling off a band-aid. Just get it over with. The large dark-skinned man before him would have to duck down to come through the doorway. He wore a black suit that looked like it cost more than the Escalade. He also wore black shades even though it was almost nighttime.

"Mr. Watson would like to see you," the large man said in a deep, serious voice that told Travis this wasn't a suggestion.

"Okay, let me grab my…wallet," Travis said, knowing his wallet was in his back pocket. No way he was going with these guys right now. The pain in the pit of his stomach told him this was the end of the line if he did. He went down the hall and quietly opened the back door. As he went to step out, he was greeted by a second large individual. A white man with his long blonde hair in a ponytail, wearing the same expensive suit.

"Why don't you come with me, Mr. Scott?" he said, taking Travis by the arm and leading him around the trailer. The other man opened the back door of the Escalade for him, and he looked in and saw Jack sitting on the other side.

~ 13 ~

"Travis!" Jack said. "Climb on in, our employer would like to speak with you." Jack was a big man himself. He looked like he would be more comfortable dressed in jeans and flannel, with his full blonde beard and puffy red cheeks. Arms the size of tree trunks and a chest as big as a rum barrel. He wore, instead, a pair of khaki pants and a burgundy-colored polo style shirt. His blonde hair was slicked back with what looked like motor oil.

Very little was said on the drive to Jack's mansion in Buckhead, an upscale residential district in Atlanta. Travis was led into what appeared to be a media room in the basement of the house. He was made to sit down in a cushy recliner next to Jack. The two muscle men left the room at the same time a beautiful, thin Asian woman of about twenty-one or so entered on the other side.

"Ah, Tien!" Jack said, smiling as he eyed the scantily clad beauty. "Pour us a Scotch, won't you?"

She nodded with a smile and went over to the bar.

"Listen, Mr. Watson," Travis said. "I'm real…"

"Mr. Watson?" Jack replied, interrupting his guest. "I thought you called me Jack."

"I'm sorry, Jack," Travis answered. "Please, let me explain."

Tien brought their glasses over and handed them to the men. She bowed and excused herself.

"Ten-year-old Scotch, Travis," Jack said. "Cost more than a used Toyota!" He started laughing at his own joke. "Take

a sip and enjoy it, son. Let it burn its way down your throat. Smooth and silky."

Travis took a small sip, noticing that his hands were shaking. He held the glass with both. He began to cough, and Jack started laughing.

"Goes down different than warm beer, huh?" Jack said with a chuckle. He reached over and picked up a small black remote and clicked the television on as Travis continued to choke on his whiskey. "Now don't go dying on me just yet, son. You haven't even met Joshua." The enormous screen on the far wall came to life. There appeared to be an older Asian woman facing them, as if she were right in front of the camera. "Hello, Chi! Is Joshua nearby?"

"Yes, Mr. Watson," she replied. "He has been expecting you to call." She stepped away from the screen.

Travis was quite impressed with this technology. He'd heard about video calls but had never been fortunate enough to see one. He set his glass down and leaned forward in his seat. "Where are they?"

"It's a secret location," Jack replied. "Sit up straight when he comes on!"

"Perfect timing, Jack!" came a man's voice from off screen. "Everything is just wrapping up here at the new location," he said in what sounded like a European accent. He stepped in front of the screen and Travis saw a tall, good looking man with olive skin, black hair, and eyes as green as Tennessee grass. He wore a loose fitting, thin button up shirt and looked richer than God. "Ah, I see you have brought a friend!" He added with a big smile. "You must be Travis."

~ 15 ~

Travis only nodded; he was too intimidated to speak.

"Say something, dummy!" Jack whispered loudly.

"Yes, sir!" Travis swallowed hard. "I'm Travis."

"Well, Travis, I am Joshua, your boss' boss, so to speak. You can now join me on a tour of our brand-new facility," he said, motioning for someone to pick up the camera or computer or whatever they were using. "We are presently three floors underground."

Travis was impressed. The lighting made it look like they were above ground with windows open. Now that he looked though, the light in the windows were not sunlight, they were just lights. "Wow, that's so cool," he said out loud.

"Just listen," Jack said.

Joshua took them down a long corridor with lots of small bedrooms. Each of them had a bed, a dresser, and a sink. There was also a large bathroom at the end of the corridor. He then led them to a large kitchen and dining hall. Everything looked brand new and state of the art. "All three of the underground living floors are identical. Other than that, there's the warehouse and the bidding arena. I have spared no expense." He began walking over towards a large silver door that Travis could see in the distance.

As Joshua approached, it slid open to reveal that it was an elevator. "Now, I want to introduce you to the crew that made all this possible." The elevator doors closed, and Joshua took the camera or whatever it was in his hands. "You see, Travis, we were forced to relocate our housing facility because our last one was discovered and raided by Interpol and the

C.I.A. If I ever find out who their informant was…God help them.”

“I’m sorry, sir, what is it a housing facility for?” Travis asked, feeling quite confused as to why they were showing him all this.

“Did you really just ask that question, son?” Jack said in unbelief. Joshua just had a look of pity on his face. That’s when it hit Travis. They kidnapped children. This was where they kept them.

“Never mind…I got it. Sorry, brain burp.” Travis hung his head in embarrassment.

“You’re killing me, dude.” Jack added. “Just sit back and shut up!”

“It’s okay, Jack,” Joshua said with a slight smirk. “Our young friend is new to the business.” He exited the elevator into what appeared to be a cave. The walls appeared to be made of stone. There were lights built into the walls, but they were quite dim, like candlelight. Joshua moved along at a quick pace. “We need to hurry, the men are awaiting their bonus!” He laughed and stepped out into the sunlight.

“My friends! Can we get everyone over here by this beautiful tree for a picture? I want to remember this momentous occasion for years to come!” Travis could see about forty or so people, mostly men, moving over toward the big tree. They appeared to be mostly construction workers. “Perfect! Now, Jerry if you could get everyone a little closer! Yes, that’s it! Stay right there! Now, he held up his phone. “Can you say, really big bonus!?”

Some of them laughed, some of them nodded, some of them started to say, "Really big…" But it was at that instant that from somewhere above Joshua, a loud vibrating chainsaw sound came. Then, to Travis' horror, the people getting their picture taken, began to drop, scream, and try to get away, as they were being mowed down by a large automatic weapon.

Travis immediately threw up right on Jack's white carpet. The sight before him was horrific, as each person was cut down. He tried not to look but couldn't turn his head. When the gun ceased firing, all that was left was a bloody pile of body parts, severed by bullets. Travis sat there in shock. He looked over at Jack, who took another sip of his Scotch, and grinned at the scene. "What the…"

Joshua slowly turned around and faced the camera. "I know what you're thinking, Travis. How could I? These men and women have done nothing to deserve this." He turned and looked at the carnage. "In fact, their work for me had been sheer perfection…but I could not allow them to leave, you see…they were the only ones, other than those closest to me, who knew where my facility was located.

Yes, each of them had signed a nondisclosure, agreeing to never reveal the location to anyone, but we both know that would never last. Someone would say something to someone. It was a secret too rich to contain. Unfortunately, they had to die. Don't worry, their families will be compensated."

As he spoke, Travis noticed several men behind him were pouring gasoline on the bodies. "We will say there was a gas explosion or something, and everyone was killed…Chi will work out the details. I will, of course, pay off the local law enforcement, and that will be that." He took the camera and

walked over closer to the bodies, just as a match was thrown in. They lit up like a bonfire. Travis could only imagine the smell.

Joshua zoomed in on the bodies and Travis threw up again. Jack only shook his head. After a moment, Joshua turned the camera back on himself. "Travis Scott, I want you to listen to me…and listen good. These men and women were good to me. They did everything they were hired to do. Yet their bodies burn because of what they knew." He turned the camera towards the fire again. It was a nasty sight, and Travis heaved again.

"You, however, have failed me. You got clumsy. You were almost caught and although nothing about you getting caught would have led to Jack or me or this vast empire I have created, you would have brought our industry to the surface. You HAVE brought our industry to the surface. The story of that biker saving that little girl is on the news and social media all over the world! Do you know what that means?"

Jack only shook his head, as he wiped his mouth with a napkin.

"It means that mothers will watch their children more closely. They won't step away at the grocery store. They won't leave them unattended in the yard. They will be extra careful in everything they do with their children. Install cameras, alarm systems, and probably even use those stupid kid leashes, as if their children were animals!" He stepped back and calmed himself. "All because you didn't pay attention to your surroundings. I need you to…WHAT DO YOU WANT!?" he screamed at someone off camera.

"Sir, we have a problem." The screen went black.

~ 19 ~

Travis leaned back cautiously in his seat, scared to look over at Jack, who probably had orders to put a bullet in his head. He closed his eyes.

"It sucks to be you, dude," Jack said, as he stood up.

"Why?" Travis asked, trying to sound innocent.

"Because Tien is going to kill you when she sees what you did on her carpet." Jack stood up and walked toward the door. He opened it and motioned for his big henchmen to enter. "You can return Travis to his home," he said, smiling at Travis. "You'll be hearing from me soon."

Travis stood and walked toward the door where the two hulking men stood. They walked out in front of him. He passed Jack thinking he'd really gotten out of this easy. Just as he passed through the doorway, Jack slammed his head into the door jam and pressed into him hard. "Dude!" He tried to wiggle free, but Jack was crazy strong.

"Listen to me you little punk," Jack's spittle hit his cheek. "You screw up again…your last moments will be found screaming as I feed you, feet first, into a wood chipper…do you understand me?"

Travis nodded. "Yes, sir!"

"You have one week to deliver three little girls to me…ONE WEEK!" Jack released him and walked back into the room. "Travis!"

Travis straightened his shirt and turned to look at Jack.

"You're my only guy for this in the southeast. You do your job, and you can move up to homeless teens," he said with a smile. "They're much easier prey."

CHAPTER 3

SAN DIEGO, CALIFORNIA

Jonah Westbrook is a hard-working man. He is the Structural Engineer for Maitland Construction, a company out of Denver, Colorado. He's thirty-one-years-old and single, though there are several women in his life that would love to change his Facebook status to "Married." He's 6'2" and ruggedly good-looking, with dark brown hair, blue eyes, and a well-trimmed beard. He lives just outside Denver, in Henderson, though he is rarely home. His job has him traveling all over the world at times.

Presently, he's in San Diego, having just flown in last night. He'd received a call from his sister, Jaclyn, yesterday, telling him that his father had suffered a massive heart attack. He'd notified his site boss and jumped on the first plane out of the city he was working. He now sat in the waiting room at Preby's Cardiovascular Institute, waiting on word from his father's surgeon. His mother was not handling this well at all. She'd been the one to find him unconscious, on the kitchen floor. She'd called 911 in a panic, telling them he was dead; and not for their quick response, he would've been. She sat between Jonah and Jaclyn, crying and ranting about how everything can change in an instant.

Jonah's cell phone dinged with a text message, pulling him out of his thoughts. He took it from his pocket and saw that it was Lacey, his ex-girlfriend. He hadn't spoken to her in years. They'd been high school and college sweethearts, who were supposed to get married, have two and a half kids, a dog, and three cats…according to her. That was all fine, but Jonah had not wanted to go to work for her father, who owned his own construction company. He'd wanted to go out on his own and that had not fit into Lacey or her father's plans. "I want to be my own man!" he'd argued in their last fight. "Not somebody your father can control and mold into his little puppet!"

"Daddy only wants the best for you!" she yelled. "The best for us! You could eventually take over his company!"

"Well, too bad I have NO intention of living in San Diego ever again!" he'd spat back at her. It had been the first time he'd mentioned THAT to her. He'd lived in San Diego his whole life and absolutely hated it there. In fact, he hated California and wanted to get as far away from it as he could. She had stormed out of the room crying and he had packed his bags, throwing away a six-and-a-half-year romance. They hadn't spoken since, and that was ten years ago.

He checked her text, surprised that he remembered her number. "Hey, it's Lacey! How is your dad?"

He debated with himself as to whether he should reply, then decided it best to be civil. "Hey, Lacey! He is in surgery right now. Waiting to hear something."

"Is there anything I can do for you guys?" came the response.

"We're fine. Thanks." He hit send and looked over at his mother with the tissue pressed against her eyes. "Mom…did you tell Lacey I was in town?"

His mother looked away. A true sign of guilt. "You could do worse than that girl, you know." She straightened up in her seat. "You two were a perfect couple. You had all the same wants and desires."

~ 22 ~

"Except where I wanted to spend my future and what I wanted to do with my life!" He couldn't believe this. His own mother was trying to set him up with the woman he'd spent a decade trying to forget.

"Jonah, it's not always about you," she huffed back. "Sometimes you have to sacrifice for what others want."

"Mama, what I want to know is, where, in the midst of all that's going on with Daddy, did you find the time to contact Lacey?" She'd been a complete wreck ever since he'd arrived. There was just no way she'd had the presence of mind to let Lacey know he was coming.

"I had your sister contact her," she said, matter-of-factly.

"Jaclyn!" he glanced over at his younger sibling who was doing her best to avoid this conversation. "What the heck!?"

"Sorry, Bro," she said without looking up from her phone. "It seemed important to Mama, and at the time, making her happy was priority."

"What did she say, Jonah?" his mother asked, looking towards his phone. "What did Lacey text you that was so horrible?"

"That's not the point, Mama!" he replied. "I have managed to avoid speaking to her for …"

"The doctor's coming!" Jaclyn said, sitting up in her seat.

A very tall, barrel-chested, middle-aged man wearing a long white coat over blue jeans and what appeared to be a

Randy Travis t-shirt, approached them. He held out his large hand to Jonah. "You must be Jonah…I'm Dr. Reed."

"Pleasure to meet you, sir," Jonah responded, shaking his hand.

"How is he, Doctor?" Jonah's mother asked, sounding more feeble than he'd ever heard her.

"Well, I'm not going to lie, Martha," Doctor Reed replied. "We almost lost him…in fact, a couple of times, we did." He saw her horrified expression and gave her a grim smile. "But he's alive! Though the next twenty-four hours are going to be critical." He knelt in front of Jonah's mother and took her hands in his. "He's not out of the water, Martha…I don't want to give you a false hope." He squeezed her hands. "His heart took a big hit…and even if he makes it through this…he's got a lot of changes to make in his life."

She nodded. "I tell him, and I tell him to leave that red meat alone. It'll kill you, I say."

Dr. Reed smiled at her and stood up. "It's more than just food, though. He's going to really need to start taking it easy and relaxing more."

Jonah's phone dinged again. He looked down to see that it was Lacey again. He ignored it and listened as the doctor told them what to expect in the next twenty-four hours. He also told them they'd need to wait at least two more hours before they could go see him. Jonah's phone dinged again, and he reached down and muted it. Dr. Reed told them a nurse would come and let them know when a room had been assigned. Jonah's phone buzzed in his hand. "Good grief," he said. "This woman…oh, it's not her." He saw that it was his boss, telling him to call.

~ 24 ~

"Excuse me," he said to his mother and sister. He headed for the courtyard to make his long distant call.

"Jonah!" his boss said. "You're here every day for the work and don't get to participate in the celebration! We finished the job an hour ago!"

"That's great, Jerry!" he said excitedly. That meant he wouldn't have to fly back out there. He was officially on vacation for the next week. "Has the owner seen it yet?"

"Yes, and he's ecstatic!" Jerry replied. "He's telling us to hang around, he's having food catered in. The guys are ready to get home, but he mentioned giving each of them a special bonus, so that peeked their interest."

"Awesome!" Jonah replied. "So, can you make sure all my tools and stuff find their way back home?"

"Yes, I already had Kevin pack it all up!" Jerry replied. "How's your dad?"

"He's out of surgery and so far, so good."

"Hey, Jerry!" Jonah heard someone in the distance call to his boss. It sounded like a European accent, so it was probably Joshua, the owner. "Can you get all the men together for a picture? It would mean so much to me!"

"Yes, sir!" Jerry responded. "Hey, Jonah, I need to go! I'll let you know when I find out something about this bonus!"

"Alright, Jerry, You guys enjoy your flight home!" He clicked off the call and went to put his phone in his pocket when it rang again. Without looking, he answered it. "Forget something, Jerry?"

"Jonah?" it was Lacey's voice. His heart raced. He hated that he'd answered and was tempted to click it off. "Are you there?"

"Yeah, Lacey, what is it?" He didn't mean to sound so harsh.

"Have you heard anything about your dad yet?" she asked, innocently.

"Yeah, he's out of surgery," Jonah replied, feeling bad for being rude. "We can't see him for a few hours."

"Well, I'd really like to see you, Jonah. Can I buy you lunch? I can meet you somewhere near the hospital."

"I'm sorry, Lacey," Jonah said. "It's not a good time…my mom needs us here."

"Actually, she's the one who suggested it…just now."

"Dear God, that woman!"

"I'm sorry," Lacey said, sounding almost in tears.

"No, it's just…" Jonah started. "I asked her to stop meddling."

"It's just lunch, Jonah," she replied. "We don't ever have to speak again, if you don't want."

He ran his fingers through his hair and sighed. "Okay," he replied, looking at his watch. "Let's meet at Preston's in a half hour?"

"I'll see you there," she said and hung up.

Jonah went back in and told his mother he'd be back in time to see his father when he was checked into a room. She

asked him where he was going but he refused to give her the satisfaction of knowing the truth. He headed to the bathroom in a lame attempt to freshen up. Moments later, he emerged with his hair finger combed and his face and hands washed.

He walked the three blocks to Preston's and got a table. Just as he'd asked the waiter to bring him a cold beer, he looked up to see her coming in the door. A blue baby doll dress, with black heels. Her blonde hair was shoulder length and partially covered her right eye. All the air in his lungs escaped. His palms began to sweat. She'd always had that effect on him. He stood as she approached. "Lacey," he said with a smile. "You look beautiful."

"Jonah," she replied, giving him a big hug. "Handsome as ever." She sat across from him just as the waiter brought his beer.

"What may I bring you, ma'am?" the waiter asked.

She eyed Jonah's bottle. "Just bring me a glass of water with a lemon, please." She smiled at Jonah. "I'm sure I'll be drinking pretty heavy tonight after you break my heart again."

"Always the optimist," he replied with a grin.

"So, what are you doing now? For a living, I mean," she asked, as the waiter set her glass down and walked away. "That's odd that he didn't take our orders."

"I took the liberty of ordering for both of us already," Jonah replied. Seeing her curious look made him smile. There was a time when he would do whatever it took to get that look from her. She was such a smart woman; it took quite a bit to throw her off her game. "Anyway, I'm the Structural Engineer

for Maitland Construction out of Denver…but I'm sure my mother has already told you that."

She ignored his last statement and smiled at him. "That's awesome, Jonah. I knew you had great potential. Maitland is huge. You probably get to travel the world."

He nodded, knowing she probably knew more about where he'd been than he did. "I've been a few places."

The waiter came and set a plate of sizzling crab cakes and grilled asparagus in front of them both. She barely had time to be impressed before he set a bowl of lobster mac & cheese down. "Enjoy," he said with a wink to Jonah.

"What was that for?" she asked.

"I told him I was trying to make a good first impression."

"Well, mission accomplished!" she replied. "I can't believe you remembered this was my favorite!"

"I was in love with you for over six years, Lacey," he responded. "If I couldn't remember what you liked to eat…" He saw the look in her eyes when he'd said that and backed off. "Sorry…let's eat."

Just then, his cell phone buzzed on the table beside him. He looked down to see the area code of the town he'd been working. "That's odd…would you excuse me? I think this is work related." At her nod, he answered the phone. "Jonah Westbrook."

"Mr. Westbrook, my name is Chi," a woman said in a thick European accent. "You may have seen me around the job site a time or two. I am Mr. Coff's assistant."

"Yes, Chi, I remember you," Jonah replied. "How may I help you?"

"Well, Mr. Coff has given a special bonus to all of the men on your crew, and we realized that you were not here."

"Yes, Jerry mentioned that earlier, he said he would let me know about it later."

"Well, Mr. Coff would like to send your bonus to you by mail…not by third party. I would need to get an address."

"Sure, I'll be here in San Diego with my parents for a while," he said, and gave her the address.

"Thank you so much, Mr. Westbrook," she replied. "You can look for your special bonus to arrive in just a few days."

"Thank you, Chi," Jonah said. "You have a nice day." He realized she had already hung up. He smiled at Lacey. "Where were we?"

"I was enjoying these amazing crab cakes," she said through a mouthful of crab cakes.

CHAPTER 4

The Cessna carrying Brianna was presently somewhere over the English Channel and heading from Berlin to London. She had been invited by her best friend to speak at a Christian Youth Conference at Wembley Stadium. Seeing how Nadia had been instructed to stay with her until she was in France on Saturday, Interpol had arranged to transport her to her destination.

She was sitting in her window seat pondering all the things that had happened recently. The men who had been caught, and those innocent children…rescued…what a blessing. She thanked God for His mercy and grace and found herself wondering how someone could be so evil as to take children from their homes and make them into slaves for sex or servanthood. So sad.

"Schwert der Dunkelheit," the older, gray-haired gentleman sitting beside her mumbled.

"What was that?" Brianna asked out loud.

"Schwert der Dunkelheit," he repeated.

Quickly she pulled out her phone and using a translation app, repeated the words into her phone. It was apparently German for sword of darkness. What did that mean? She looked up the word sword as used in the Bible. Ephesians 6:17 says sword of the Spirit, which she knew to be the word of God. In Matthew 10:34, Jesus said that He didn't come to bring peace, but a sword. Out of the thirty-something references, there was no sword of darkness. "What does it mean?" she asked the man. He was silent though. That's how he was sometimes.

"Are you talking to yourself?" Nadia asked in her thick European accent, walking up and sitting in the empty seat next to Brianna.

"Just praying," Brianna replied. "Does the term sword of darkness mean anything to you?"

"No," Nadia replied. "Should it?"

Brianna shrugged; she would wait until later to give it more thought. "Thanks again for the lift to London. This is super nice." She looked around the cabin at the beautiful jet. Tan leather seats, wood paneling on the walls. Small television/computer screens on the backs of each of the seats. A bar where you could get various drinks, fruits, or snacks.

"Honestly, I was shocked when Interpol offered it," Nadia replied. "They must really want to keep an eye on you?"

"Yeah, I have a bad fee…" Brianna started, but Nadia held up her hand.

"Let us just enjoy our flight," Nadia said, placing a finger to her lips to shush Brianna from talking about what they had discussed before. There was always a chance you were being listened to, especially while on an Interpol jet.

Brianna pulled out a pen and pad. "Have you learned anything new?" She wrote and handed the pad to Nadia.

"No, but this whole thing is suspicious. Interpol never acknowledges their informants…NEVER!" Once she saw that Brianna had read it, she tore off the paper and slid it in her pocket.

~ 31 ~

Just then, the pilot turned on the seat belt sign. They both buckled up, just as one of the flight attendants came out and instructed them that they would be arriving in London in twenty minutes.

Forty-five minutes later, a van pulled up to get Brianna and Nadia. A blonde woman about Brianna's age, jumped out of the back of the van and wrapped her arms around her in a big hug. "Oh my gosh, it's so good to see you, girl!" Gabi Morgan, Brianna's lifetime best friend, said. "It's been too long!"

"Yes, it has!" Brianna replied. "You look so beautiful, you internationally famous worship leader!"

"Save some of that hug for me!" Gabi's tall, sandy-blonde haired husband said, climbing out of the van.

"Hey, Scotty Morgan!" Brianna squeezed him tight. "You guys are a sight for sore eyes!"

"Hi," Gabi said to Nadia, who stood awkwardly nearby. "I'm Gabi!"

"I'm sorry, Nadia!" Brianna said. "Guys, this is my friend and escort, Junior Detective Nadia Skutnik."

Nadia held out her hand to Gabi and Scotty, "please, call me, Nadia."

"It's a pleasure, Nadia!" Gabi replied. "Will you be joining us at the convention tonight?"

"I have orders not to leave her side," Nadia replied. "So, yes, I will be there."

"I love your accent, Nadia!" Scotty said. "Where are you from?"

"Thank you, I am from Romania." She handed their luggage over to the driver and they all got into the van.

"So, exactly what crime did you commit to get an Interpol escort, Brianna?" Scotty asked, and everyone laughed.

"I'm just that important," Brianna replied, giving Scotty a light shove. "But seriously, be praying about this whole thing." She shared a look with Gabi that said they would be discussing it later.

Over 75,000 people, mostly teenagers, were gathered at Wembley Stadium for the annual Dragon Slayers Youth Convention. It only had three stops in Europe, so people had come from all over. The entire event was being broadcast around the world in over thirty languages. There was quite a bit of excitement in the air.

As Brianna sat in her backstage room going over her notes, she could feel the ground shaking from the beat of the music. There was a video monitor to her right that she had muted while she prepped. She looked up to see several stagehands getting things set up. There was a knock at her door and Gabi poked her head in.

"Is Nadia in here?" Gabi asked.

"No, she's at her seat somewhere up high and away from the crowds," she laughed.

Gabi pulled a chair over next to her and sat down. "So, what's going on?"

~ 33 ~

"Well, I have been giving Interpol and other law enforcement agencies…tips on where to find some of the missing children from trafficking…"

"Okay, that's awesome," Gabi replied. "Were they legit tips? I mean, did they find any kids?"

Brianna nodded. "Lots, and plenty of arrests were made. Now, the Secretary-General of Interpol, wants to have a big…party in my honor."

"And this is a bad thing?" Gabi asked, thinking it would be an amazing opportunity to give God the glory.

"Well, the thing is, Nadia thinks that Secretary-General Schmidt is dirty. That he might even be involved with the trafficking…therefore having an ulterior motive for bringing in the girl who keeps messing up his operation."

"I see," Gabi replied. "You don't think he'd try and kill you, do you?"

"I don't know, but I do have a very bad feeling about the whole thing," Brianna said, standing up and walking across the room. "The Holy Spirit hasn't told me not to go, but I also don't have peace."

"Let's pray," Gabi held out her hand to her friend, who graciously took it. "Father God!" Gabi said, with authority. "Brianna Bowers is YOUR child! She is doing YOUR work! I pray right now that you would give her the wisdom she needs in going forward with this Interpol party. That your Holy Spirit would guide her every step in this!"

It was at that moment that Brianna felt a large hand on the center of her back. Her eyes filled up with tears as a warm oil seemed to be poured down her spine.

"I pray for protection! I pray for peace! I pray that YOUR power fill her to overflowing and evil be defeated in the name of Jesus Christ!"

That very hand slid up and squeezed her shoulder. "Fear not," was spoken into her ear. Brianna's knees buckled and Gabi caught her as she dropped.

The two women were sitting on the floor crying when there was a knock at the door.

Gabi wiped her eyes, "Come in!"

A young man with short brown hair, a pair of khakis, and a red button up shirt, poked his head in. "Um…everything okay?"

Brianna looked up and smiled. "Mark McGee, you come over here and give me a big hug!" He helped her up and she cried into his shirt as they hugged. Mark was probably the most amazing man she'd ever known. He was the one who headed up this whole event. It was him who had been the original dragon slayer.

"Oh, Brianna, God has been putting you on my heart all week," Mark said. "Are you okay?"

She looked up at him and smiled. "I am now." She looked at his shirt where she'd just cried on it. "I'm sorry, Mark."

He smiled down at her. "Tears from my hero? I'm not sorry." He hugged her again and she felt safe.

~ 35 ~

"How's Maria and the boys?" she asked.

"They're amazing, let me tell you…" he began.

"Mr. McGee?" a tall, teenage boy called from the doorway. "They're gathering for prayer."

"Thanks, Ricky," Mark said, and looked down at Brianna. "Are you ready to start a revival in England?"

She nodded, smiling at his attitude. He took her and Gabi by the hand and led them down the hall to a larger room where all the staff and volunteers were gathered in a big circle, holding hands.

"Okay, everybody!" Mark said, leading Brianna into the middle of the circle. "This is one of the best friends I've ever had, Brianna Bowers…she heads up a ministry that fights child trafficking." Everyone smiled and nodded to her. She saw her old friends Matt, Eddie, and Andy, each grinning from ear to ear.

"God bless you, Brianna!" someone yelled out.

"I know her!" a female voice said.

Brianna looked up and smiled at her old friend. She hadn't seen her in so long. Her eyes teared up through her smile. "Yvette," she could barely get it out before crying into Mark's chest again.

"Thanks, Yvette," Mark said. "She hadn't cried all over me enough." Everyone laughed. Mark lifted his face to the ceiling. "Holy Spirit! We NEED you tonight! Without you, we are empty vessels!" There were several amens. "Make your presence known in this place, we ask. There are tens of

thousands of people out there searching for the cross…let your fire light their way!"

"Yes, God!" Gabi cried out.

"And Holy Spirit!" Mark added. "Pour yourself in, on, and through my friend Brianna." He squeezed Brianna's shoulder. "Give her even more of you than she needs…everybody said…"

"AMEN!!!" Everyone in the room yelled.

"Okay, guys!" Gabi said. "Armor on! Let's go slay some dragons!" They each headed for where they were supposed to be.

The tall teenage boy, Ricky, walked over to Brianna. "Ms. Bowers, if you would, come with me." He led her back to her room to gather her things. Then they headed to a small waiting area directly behind the stage.

Within minutes, a countdown started on the screen and the crowd was screaming. Brianna watched it all on a monitor. As soon as the final ten seconds ended there was a massive explosion of pyrotechnics that put the crowd in a frenzy. Then…the video of that night 16 years ago began to play.

"This is Denise Morrison, of Fox Jacksonville, here in the small town of Gateway, Florida." You could see the stage in the background, and it looked like Yvette was speaking. A large crowd was gathered in seats and standing along the sidelines. "There has been a recent string of mysterious deaths here in Gateway, starting with a bus crash just weeks ago and…" Denise looked off camera as if someone was notifying her of something. "Well, it seems there is a sports car heading straight for the football field."

The camera panned down the street in the distance as a small, red sports car traveling at a very high speed was heading straight for the festivities. There was a police car about a hundred yards behind it. "Oh, my God! It doesn't seem like they're going to stop!" The car sped through the stop sign and just as it hit the fence, a bright light from out of nowhere flashed in front of the car, sending it into the air and over the people gathered near the fence. It hit the ground and rolled to a stop just before hitting the back row of chairs. It seemed everyone had frozen in place. "I'm not sure what caused that flash of light…perhaps the police had set up some kind of protection, but…" Just then, the ground began to shake.

Brianna looked at the crowd in Wembley Stadium. Every single person was on their feet watching the video. Although this particular video had been banned in most countries around the world, everyone seemed to know what was coming.

The ground shook violently, so much so that the cameraman lost his footing and fell over. The football field began to split, and people were running and screaming. Chairs and debris were falling into the crack that was opening up in the middle of the field. Then…the roar.

It was later dubbed the roar heard 'round the world. It was terrifying. Just moments later, the ground exploded upward, and a massive, black, scaly dragon burst out of the hole and sprayed the crowd with fire. And then, as if the cameraman knew where to aim the camera…an enormous hand emerged from the crack. Then, thirteen-year-old, fifty-foot tall, armor wearing Mark McGee stood up out of the hole in the earth.

Brianna was brought to tears as the roar of the crowd in Wembley Stadium was deafening. People had their hands lifted in worship. Others were crying as Mark lifted his sword and struck the dragon.

"I'm not sure if what we're seeing is real or some elaborate cinematography out of Gateway Middle School," Denise said. "But that is one large teenage boy!" The dragon knocked Mark back, and just then, thousands of black, scaly demons emerged from the ground and began attacking the fleeing crowd.

"Maria Sanchez," Brianna's old friend whispered in her ear, causing her to jump. "She's about to be taken…pray for her mother." Brianna looked around.

"No!" she started to cry. "Holy Spirit, please don't let her be harmed!" Ricky watched as Brianna fell on her knees and cried.

"Pray for her mother," he said firmly. "She will need your prayers."

On the screen, Scotty, Gabi, Brianna, and Jason emerged from the hole as large as Mark. They fought the demons as Mark battled the enormous dragon. In the end, Mark and his cousin, Jacob…who was also as big as Mark, took off the head of the dragon.

The crowd was so loud, you could hardly hear yourself think. People were screaming, shouting, and praising God. The dragon had been defeated.

Brianna was lying face down behind the stage, pleading with the Holy Spirit and fighting her own dragon.

As the band took their places, Mark McGee walked out to center stage. "Alright, Dragon Slayers! Are you ready to praise Jesus!?"

CHAPTER 5

JACKSONVILLE, FLORIDA

Carmen pulled into Sheffield Elementary parent pick up lane behind about twelve other cars and waited for the bell to ring. She was grateful that her boss allowed her to leave for lunch a little early each day to get her daughter. Carmen worked such long hours at the warehouse that this was their time to hang out. They would have lunch and then Carmen would take Maria to stay with her Tia Raquel, where she would pick her up later that night.

Carmen Sanchez, a twenty-six-year-old single mother of one, had shiny black hair that fell just below her shoulders. She wore very little makeup and had stopped caring about how she looked months ago. She had been made a widow at a very young age after her husband, Jorge, was killed by a roadside bomb in Afghanistan. She was pregnant with Maria at the time.

The military had helped her out a little, but for the most part, it had been up to her to make ends meet. She'd worked two and sometimes three jobs at a time over the past seven years to give her child a decent life. The downside was that she rarely got to see her eight-year-old. Still, Maria was her world…and she looked just like her daddy.

The bell rang and within seconds, children were being led out the doors. Those poor teachers were doing their best to corral those kids. It was almost comedic. They wanted to run and find their parents or their bus, but had to stay in line, so they could be checked off a list to show they'd been picked up properly. After several minutes, Maria's class shuffled out and she saw her little brown-haired daughter in her blue jeans and pink Hermione Granger t-shirt. It was her favorite. "Don't get us killed, or worse…expelled!" was the quote across the front.

That girl loved those Harry Potter movies. She was talking to her best friend, Chelsea, and not even looking for her mother. After a moment, her teacher tapped her on the shoulder and excused her to go get in the car. She threw her backpack in the backseat and climbed in the front. "Hello, beautiful!" Carmen said, sliding Maria's hair behind her ear. "How was your day?"

Maria shrugged. "It was okay, third grade is boring."

"You're just too smart," Carmen replied. "That must be the problem."

"Where are we going to eat?" Maria asked. "Chelsea's mom is taking her clothes shopping. I wish you didn't work so much." She buckled her seat belt.

"Maybe we can go clothes shopping on Saturday," Carmen said, pulling past a minivan full of kids. "I'm off by four."

"Can we go to Town Center!?" Maria asked excitedly. "That's where Chelsea's going!"

"We'll see," Carmen replied, knowing they were not going to Town Center. She bought Maria nice things, but she was not going to pay those prices when she could get them way cheaper at a Target or something. "Actually, there IS a Target at Town Center."

Maria sighed and sat back in her seat. "So, where are we eating lunch?"

"How does Subway sound?"

"Like that's what we had yesterday," Maria responded. "How about the Chinese place. I love their food!" Carmen smiled, knowing that her daughter had technically already had lunch, and would be eating very little. Still, this was their time together.

"Chinese does sound good," Carmen said, and pointed her Corolla in that direction.

Ten minutes later, they were standing in line at New Moon Palace, trying to decide what they wanted. "What are snow peas, Mama?"

"A vegetable," Carmen replied, still perusing the overhead menu.

"Duh!" Maria exclaimed. "What kind of vegetable?"

"They're like regular peas…in a blanket."

"What kind of blanket?"

"It's actually a pod, the peas are in a pod," Carmen said. "Have you decided what you want yet?"

"So, that's what Abuela means when she calls us two peas in a pod?" Maria asked, excitedly.

"Yes, baby, tell the lady what you want," Carmen said, nudging Maria in front of her.

"I want an egg roll," Maria said to the lady. "No, two egg rolls and a…can I get a can of Coke, Mama?"

"All you're eating is two egg rolls?" Carmen asked her daughter. "Are you sure?"

"Yes, ma'am, Chelsea and me shared our lunches and I ate a lot."

"Chelsea and I," Carmen said and then placed her order. Unlike her daughter, she was starving. She paid and they found a table where they would wait for their food to be brought to them.

"Can I play a game on your phone, Mama?" Maria asked.

"First, I need you to go wash your hands," Carmen checked her phone for any messages. She had a text message from a coworker needing her to call. She quickly dialed Alexa's number. "Hey, girl, what's up?"

"Hold on, let me step outside," Alexa said. Carmen could picture her sneaking out the back entrance where the smokers went during breaks and lunch. She probably had some juicy gossip that Carmen couldn't care less about but listened just so Alexa could vent. She didn't have an adult to converse with when she got home either. "Girl, I know you're with your daughter, so I'll be quick. So, have you seen what that little, you know what, Brittany, is wearing today?"

"I don't think I've had the privilege," Carmen replied.

"She had the audacity to wear a tight little skirt that rides all the way up to Canada, to her job in a warehouse!" Alexa said. "Got every man in this place sniffing around her like a bunch of coyotes in heat."

Carmen laughed. "I'm pretty sure it's the females who are in heat."

"You know what I mean, girl!" Alexa said. "Even Derek's been sneakin' a peak!" Alexa had been crushing on Derek ever since he'd started a year ago. She'd put out every hint she could think of to snag that man, but he'd never been anything but a gentleman around her.

Maria was coming back from the bathroom, wiping her hands on a paper towel. "Listen, Alexa, I have to go. It sounds to me like you need to put that girl in her place."

"Oh, Ima say somethin' to Bruce, you can count on it!" Alexa replied, talking about their floor supervisor. "That skirt HAS to be against policy!"

"Alright, girl, I'll be back soon!" Carmen ended the call and smiled at her daughter. "Have I ever told you how beautiful you are?"

"Only every day, Mama!" Maria replied. "Now, can I play a game on your phone, please?"

"Not now, Maria," Carmen replied. "The food is coming." Just then, the lady from behind the counter walked over and set their plates down.

As they sat there eating their egg rolls and fried rice, several people came and went. Carmen and Maria played a game of hangman on a napkin after Maria finished her two egg rolls. Carmen loved to hear her daughter's laugh when she couldn't figure out the phrase. Of course, the chance to hear that sweet laugh was why she could never quite figure them out. Carmen glanced down at her phone and realized she needed to get back to work.

"I'm going to run to the washroom, Maria, watch Mommy's purse for her."

"Yes, ma'am," Maria replied, picking up Carmen's cell phone.

Carmen headed into the bathroom to wash her hands. She looked at her pale face and tired eyes in the mirror. She desperately needed a vacation that she knew she would most likely never get. Unless, of course, she won the lottery…which she never played…so…she splashed some water on her face and headed back out into the dining room.

She rounded the corner and was about to try and sneak up on her daughter, when she noticed that Maria was not at the table. She saw that her purse was still sitting in the seat and her phone was on the table. She scanned the dining room where only a couple of people had decided to sit and eat. No Maria.

Carmen walked over to the front window and looked out. Leave it to Maria to spot a friend and just run out to say hi. She didn't see her daughter anywhere. She stepped out the door and looked around. No Maria. Panic started to set in. "MARIA!!!" she screamed into the parking lot. No one even looked her way.

She ran back into the restaurant and made a bee line for the men's room. Maybe she couldn't hold it and decided to go in there. The room was vacant. She ran back around to the counter where the checkout girl was on the phone taking an order. "Excuse me! My dau…" The girl held up a finger for her to wait.

Maria spun around and scanned the room again. No clue as to her daughter's whereabouts. She turned back around and grabbed the phone base that sat on the counter and slid it abruptly onto the floor. "My daughter! Did you see where she went!?" she asked the shocked looking girl behind the counter.

The girl shook her head and appeared to be trying to remember. "No ma'am."

"She was sitting right there," Carmen said, pointing to the table where her phone still sat. "DID YOU SEE WHERE SHE WENT!!!??? I just stepped into the bathroom for a second!"

"No ma'am, I didn't see anything!" The girl was starting to look scared.

An older woman walked up from the back and said something in what Carmen assumed was Chinese to the girl. The girl responded to her and headed for the back.

"MY DAUGHTER IS MISSING!!!" Carmen screamed to the older woman. "Do you have cameras?"

"No ma'am, no cameras," the woman responded. "You call police!"

Fifteen minutes later, the area was crawling with police officers. They were questioning everyone that was in the restaurant. Sergeant William Bernard of the Jacksonville Sheriff's Office was attempting to question Carmen, who was frantically attempting to give orders to every officer there. "Ma'am, I'm going to need you to calm down and focus. You are not helping us find your daughter in this state." He gently took her by the arm and led her over to a seat in the restaurant. "Now, how long would you say that you were in the restroom?"

"How is knowing how long it took me to pee going to help you find my baby's kidnapper!?" Carmen said through gritted teeth.

"It could help us determine if he was watching you…waiting for you to walk away," Sergeant Bernard replied. "Now, how long would you say?"

"Less than three minutes," Carmen replied, tearing up again. "I was gone for less than three minutes, and my baby is gone!"

"Now, I need you to concentrate," he said, placing his hand on hers to calm her. "Was there anybody in the restaurant when you left to go to the bathroom that wasn't here when you returned?"

"My daughter!" she screamed, pulling her arm away from him. "Why aren't you out looking for her!?"

"Ma'am, right now we have absolutely nothing to go on," he replied. "Nobody in here, including yourself, saw anything. I have no description of a suspect, no vehicle…all I have is a description of your daughter wearing blue jeans and a pink Harry Potter t-shirt." He saw the look of hopelessness in her eyes. "Is there anything else you can remember that would help us?"

She shook her head slowly and looked up at him. "I didn't know I needed to be paying attention to anything."

Just then another officer came in the door. "Hey, Sarge," he said, panting as if he'd been running. "Check this out," he said, setting a small laptop on the table in front of Sergeant Bernard.

"What is it!?" Carmen asked, looking up.

"It's video footage from the bank across the parking lot," the officer said. He hit a button as Carmen stepped around behind them.

It was showing the bank parking lot, but you could see all the way over to the restaurant's front. What appeared to be a black car drove slowly along the front of all the shops and stopped in front of the restaurant.

"That's it," the officer pointed. "He sits there for about five minutes." He hit a button to fast forward it.

A young-looking white man in all black, including a baseball cap exited the car and walked rapidly into the restaurant. He was inside for just a few seconds and came back out, clearly leading a child in a pink shirt to his car. Carmen gasped. "MY BABY!!!" she screamed, as the man forced the girl into the backseat and made his way around to the driver's side. He slowly pulled away.

A female officer that had been talking with the owner, walked over to comfort Carmen.

"Play that again," Sergeant Bernard said. "What is that? A Dodge or a Camaro?"

"Hard to tell," the officer said. "Definitely a larger sports car."

"See if there are any other cameras that caught anything down each of the streets," Bernard said. "We don't even have enough for an Amber Alert."

CHAPTER 6

Directly after the conference, Brianna was whisked away by Nadia. She'd hoped to spend more time with Gabi and the gang, but Nadia had been summoned to Interpol headquarters as soon as possible.

During the flight to France, she'd tried to remember how the conference had gone. She'd spoken about her ministry and how God was helping her to find trafficked children all over the world. She'd even shown a video of one of the rescues. At the end, Mark had come out and taken up an offering for her ministry, and then given an amazing altar call.

Hundreds of teenagers had responded. She could vaguely remember it all though. Her mind had been on the Maria Sanchez situation. The Holy Spirit had put this poor woman, who was about to have her world turned upside down, on Brianna's heart.

Because she'd had to leave so fast, Brianna hadn't gotten to talk to Gabi about it. When she'd gotten on the plane and settled in, she had texted Gabi. "Please pray for Maria Sanchez's mother. Maria is about to be kidnapped. The HS said to pray for her mother." Gabi responded within moments. "I will. I know your heart, Brianna…are you okay?" She hadn't known how to respond. She trusted God but she didn't like this part.

Sometimes the children don't make it out. She had a flashback of her last trip to India and seeing four- and five-year-old girls in cages behind shop windows. "No," had been all she'd sent. "I will be praying for YOU as well. I love you, girl!"

"Thank you, Gabi! I love you and thirst for your prayers more than you will ever know!"

Brianna closed her eyes to pray and felt nothing but darkness. It seemed as if her friend was not near. She knew he wasn't gone, but sometimes she had to willingly pursue him. It helped her to focus on him and not her problems.

"I'm sorry I had to rush you away from your friends, Brianna," Nadia said as she sat down next to her, holding a large cup of coffee. "I have no idea what they need me for, but I'm rarely told anything until I need to know it." She smiled at Brianna. "Are you okay? Have you slept?"

Brianna smiled a big cheesy smile and shrugged her shoulders. "No to both questions. How about you? Have you been sleeping?"

"I have not," Nadia replied, looking away. "I have been taking care of some business."

"Well, we're both going to be pretty tired when we get to our hotel," Brianna said.

"A luxury I will not have for quite some time," Nadia replied. "I'm to get you checked in and then report to headquarters as soon as possible."

"Oh, Nadia, you need your sleep!" Brianna said. "You won't be any good to anyone!"

"That's why I'm on my fifth cup of arbore de cafea!" she replied with a laugh, making Brianna smile.

"Well, don't overdo it," Brianna said. "You don't want to crash in the middle of a meeting."

Nadia leaned in close to Brianna and lowered her voice. "I have contacted a friend to watch you while I am not able to be with you."

"An agent?" Brianna asked.

"A friend."

A voice came over the speakers informing them that they would be landing soon. Brianna looked out the window and saw what she assumed was the city of Lyon, France. "I'm going to need my friend as well," she whispered to herself.

CLARKSTON, GEORGIA

"SHUT UP!!!" Travis screamed toward the back room of his trailer. He couldn't take it anymore. The crying, moaning, and attempts to scream through the duct taped mouths. He threw an empty beer bottle against the door and popped the top off another bottle. In less than six seconds he'd downed his fifth one. These girls were going to be the death of him. His nerves were shot.

He'd ditched the Mustang in the woods just off Interstate 75 after getting back to Atlanta from Jacksonville. In three days, he'd managed to grab three girls. Two white ones and a Hispanic one…she was Puerto Rican or Cuban or something, he could never tell the difference. From Nashville to Macon to Jacksonville. He'd hit Nashville first. She'd been left in the car at a gas station while daddy went inside to play the lottery.

In less than five seconds he'd grabbed her and been on the road. He'd taken six-year-old Allison to an abandoned

warehouse just North of Atlanta and tied her up while he drove to Macon. There he'd found his next victim in a rest area bathroom. Her mom had left her outside the stall waiting while she took care of business. Jessica was the youngest of the three at only four years old. He'd returned to the abandoned warehouse, tied her up, and headed for Jacksonville. He'd spent all morning cruising around the Northside of Jacksonville, until finally finding Maria, the oldest of the three, just sitting alone in that restaurant after her mother had gone to the back.

He'd walked in and asked her quietly if she'd seen his little brown puppy that was lost. She'd willingly walked outside with him, but he had to sedate her for the long ride back. Now he had all three girls tied up in the back room waiting for Jack to send someone to pick them up. Travis had been waiting for hours and was at his wits end.

Finally, there was a loud knock on the front door. Travis slung it open. "It's about time!" He said, his voice shaky. He was trying not to appear drunk. To his surprise, it was Jack himself who walked in.

"You're drunk!" Jack said, pushing past Travis and scanning the room. "That's sloppy and unprofessional!" Jack slapped him across the cheek. "What if I'd been a cop or a nosy neighbor? Huh?" Jack slapped him again and Travis almost fell over. "You need to be alert!"

"I'm sorry, Jack!" Travis managed. "It's just…they've been crying and screaming all day." He hung his head, not making eye contact with his boss. "I'm on edge."

"Where are they?" Jack asked.

"In the back bedroom," Travis pointed down the hall.

~ 53 ~

Jack stared at him for several seconds. "Well, go get them, you idiot!" He smacked Travis on the back of the head as he walked past. "I don't have all night!"

Travis went into the bedroom and snatched the girls up off the floor. "Get up and be quiet!" he yelled. "If you cry or scream, I swear I'll…"

"Come on, Travis!" Jack yelled down the hall. He opened the front door and motioned for someone to join him inside.

Travis led the three girls into the living room and made them stand in front of Jack as one of Jack's big goons came into the trailer.

Jack squatted down in front of the girls and slid Jessica's hair out of her eyes. "You done good, Travis," he smiled. "You done very good."

"This is Maria," Travis said, pointing to the Spanish girl. "This is…"

"I don't care," Jack said, standing back up and turning to his henchman. "Put them in the van." The girls were led outside, sobbing and looking terrified.

Travis watched them disappear into the night as the front door closed. "What happens now?"

"Now," Jack said, looking back at Travis. "You get paid. $30,000 will be paid toward your gambling debt and here's a little something for you to get yourself cleaned up with." He reached into his back pocket and handed Travis a thick envelope. "Don't be stupid with it. Lay low for a

~ 54 ~

while…I'll be in touch." Jack opened the door and within seconds the van was pulling away.

Travis stood there staring at the closed door for several seconds and then ran into the kitchen and threw up in the sink. What had he done? Taken three sweet children from their parents forever. Sent three innocent children to a life of absolute hell. He slid down the counter, crying a bitter, sloppy cry. Eventually he fell asleep right there on the kitchen floor where he had dreams of small children being led into a furnace by a large monster…with a face that looked a lot like him.

SAN DIEGO, CALIFORNIA

Lunch with Lacey had been uneventful. Jonah had managed to be a gentleman while not making any further plans with her…though she'd tried. He'd been firm when he'd told her that he was there to make sure his mother was taken care of while his father recovered, and that unless his father took a turn for the worst, he would be gone in less than a week.

She had thanked him for lunch and said she would be in touch with him, but he had not commented. Lacey was a beautiful, intelligent woman, but he would not let her sink that hook in him again. If there was one thing that Jonah Westbrook loved about his life, it was his freedom.

After lunch he'd gone back to the hospital just in time to go in with his mother and sister to see his dad, who was still sedated and hooked up to several machines. The nurse had told them that he would remain under for the rest of the night, and they would be running tests the next morning. His mother had sat next to his father for several hours, crying and talking to

him, even reminding him of various chores that needed to be done around the house.

"Mom," his sister said. "Even though he's unconscious, you should probably not stress him out with all that. Besides, Jonah can do those things."

"Thanks, sis," Jonah said with a smile, as he made a note of each project in his phone. His mom had given Jonah the key to the house and told him to go stay there for the night while she stayed at the hospital. He'd walked his sister, Jaclyn, to her car and told her to say hi to Ryan and the kids for him. Maybe he would see them tomorrow. He'd jumped into his rental car and drove to his parents' house.

Presently he was standing in his old bedroom that he hadn't lived in since high school. It was almost like a shrine that hadn't been touched by human eyes in over a decade. He couldn't believe his parents hadn't made it into a hobby room or something. He was so shocked to see his old posters on the wall, his baseball trophies on the shelf, even pictures of him and Lacey taped on the wall by his desk. Nothing had been touched.

He sat down on his old twin bed with the Bob the Builder blanket and sheets, (as a joke, Lacey had bought them for him, since he'd always loved to build stuff) and took off his shoes. He remembered something and grabbed his phone from his pocket. Jerry had never called him back. It went straight to voicemail. They must still be in the air. "Hey Jerry, call me when you land…tell me about this bonus!" He clicked off the call and headed to the bathroom.

Fifteen minutes later, he was climbing into his old bed and sliding under the covers. "Did you miss me, Bob?" It had

been a long day and it didn't take long for Jonah to drift away into dream world.

Several hours later, Jonah woke up, having to pee. It was pitch dark in the room and for a second, he had no idea where he was. "Oh yeah," he mumbled to himself. "Old bedroom…parent's house." He stood and made his way to the bathroom across the hall. There was a small solar nightlight that came on in the dark next to the sink, so he didn't have to turn on the light.

Jonah flushed, washed and dried his hands and left the bathroom. As he stepped into the bedroom, he heard a noise downstairs. Stopping where he was, he stood still to listen. A clicking sound and the infamous squeaking sound the back door made when it opened. He made a mental note to lubricate it in the morning.

"Decided to come home after all huh, Mom!?" he said into the darkness. "I told you those hospital chairs weren't comfortable!" There was nothing but silence. "Mom!?" He stepped out into the hall. "Mom, please respond to me or I'm coming down with Dad's gun!" Silence. He walked backwards to his parents' room, keeping his eyes on the stairway. He quickly stepped over to his father's nightstand and punched the code into his handgun safe. He pulled out the 9mm and made sure it was loaded. Still, he heard nothing downstairs.

Hopefully it had just been his mind playing tricks on him. He chambered a round and stepped back into the hall. "Okay, if someone is down there, I have a gun!" He immediately heard the backdoor open again and then close shut. He took off running downstairs and into the kitchen, gun pointed low. He swung the backdoor open and stepped onto the

back deck. No sign of anybody. "That's right, punk," he mumbled, stepping back inside and closing the door. "You better run."

That's when he heard it. Something had moved inside the pantry. Almost like a can being slid on the shelf. Cans didn't slide on the shelf all by themselves. Jonah lifted his pistol toward the pantry doors just as they exploded open and someone large jumped toward him. He fired the gun as he jumped back, and they dropped to the floor like a sack of potatoes. A large knife slid across the floor.

Jonah kept his gun trained on the motionless man on the kitchen floor with one hand and reached for the light switch with his other. His heart was racing. He'd just shot someone. The light revealed a very thick, muscular, white man. He wore all black, from the knit hat on his head, to the black military grade boots on his feet.

Jonah slowly knelt down to check for a pulse and noticed the growing puddle of blood. It was then that he saw that he'd shot the man directly in his right eye. "Well, I'm going to assume you're dead." Quickly he ran back upstairs and grabbed his cell phone. He dialed 911 as he came back downstairs.

"911, what's your emergency?" the dispatcher asked.

"Ye…" Jonah cleared his throat. "Yes, I've just shot and killed an intruder in my parent's home." That's when the thought hit him. What if his mother had been home alone? What if she'd come home and he'd stayed at the hospital?

"Sir? Are you positive the intruder is deceased?" the dispatcher was asking as his brain hazed over with those thoughts. "Sir? I'm going to need your address."

"Yes, he's deceased," Jonah replied, looking down at the body on his mother's kitchen floor. He gave her the address and clicked off the call. Immediately he called his sister.

"Jonah?" she answered in a groggy voice. "Is dad alright?"

"Yeah, Sis," Jonah replied. "But you aren't going to believe what just happened at mom and dad's house…"

CHAPTER 7

LYON, FRANCE

After getting checked into the hotel, Nadia led Brianna to her room. "Your name is Evelyn Hanson, by the way," Nadia said over her shoulder. She handed Brianna an envelope filled with papers. "You'll need to burn your current passport and identification."

"Say what?" Brianna asked, rushing to keep up with her long-legged friend. "Burn them!? Isn't that a bit dramatic?"

Nadia used a key card to let them into room 316. They both entered the large suite, and she closed the door. "Brianna, I am ninety-nine percent sure that Secretary General Schmidt means to silence you," she said, walking over and looking out the window. She pulled the curtains closed tight. "If I am correct, and you know, I am…you will not be safe anywhere in the world." She checked all the rooms and closets. She took the room phone apart to check for bugs. "It seems we are good for now….GO!" She pointed toward the bathroom. "Take your purse and empty it of anything that identifies you as Brianna Bowers!...here!" She handed Brianna a lighter. "Burn it all in the sink."

"Okay…you're scaring me, Nadia." Brianna said, in exasperation. "Why did you bring me here if you're that positive they want me dead?"

"Because I had to work out a plan to get you off the grid without implicating myself," Nadia replied. "And if you had simply turned down the invitation, they would have found another way to kill you…hand me your phone."

"Hey, I need my phone!" she replied in a panic. "All my contacts and…" she stopped talking when she saw the look Nadia was giving her. She handed over her phone.

Nadia retrieved a small electronic device from her jacket. She scanned it over Brianna's phone and then scanned it over another phone just like Brianna's. She handed Brianna the new phone. "This phone is in Evelyn Hanson's name but has all your personal information still intact."

"Really? That's so cool," Brianna said, turning it on. All her contacts and pictures were still intact. "Thank you, Nadia."

"Be careful who you contact, Evelyn," Nadia said. "After you disappear, your friends and family will be watched."

"Evelyn…" Brianna pondered. "It's a beautiful name."

"It was my grandmother's name," Nadia replied, seeming to be remembering her. "She was a beautiful woman." There was a knock at the door causing both women to pause and look in that direction. Nadia reached into her jacket and produced a small pistol. She held it out to Brianna. "This is the safety, slide it over and pull the trigger." Brianna smiled and nodded, for her father had taught her how to handle a weapon when she was young. "Just in case." There was another knock at the door. "Stay here," Nadia said, and disappeared down the hall.

Brianna stared down at the gun in her hand. Could she really shoot another person? She tried to imagine a scenario where she would be able to take someone's life. She definitely knew there was evil people in the world and would never judge anyone for killing them, but she just didn't think she could do it…and hoped she never had to find out. She lit all her papers on fire. It seemed Brianna Bowers was no more.

It's okay, Bria…Evelyn!" Nadia called from the living room. "It is my friend!"

Brianna walked into the front room where Nadia was speaking Romanian with a young, good looking guy of average height. He had black hair and a neatly trimmed beard. He smiled at her as she entered. "Hello…Evelyn," he said in a very thick accent. "I am sorry, my English is not so good."

"Well, it's better than my Romanian," she said with a genuine smile that made him laugh.

"I am Cristian, and I am here to…how do you say…protect you."

"Protect," Nadia said with a hard t. She then proceeded to talk very fast in Romanian as Cristian just stood there nodding and smiling at her.

"Nadia…Nadia…O să

fie bine!" he said and looked at Brianna. "I tell her that it is going to be okay. My friend Nadia likes to worry." He smiled at Nadia. "She will be safe, now go to your meeting."

"He's right, Nadia," Brianna replied as she looked over and saw the old man sitting on the couch with his hat in his lap. "I'll be fine." She couldn't help but blush as the Holy Spirit winked at her. Everything was going to be okay.

Nadia picked up her phone and typed something. "I have sent you an email," she said to Brianna. "If anything happens…follow the instructions." She picked up her bag and

placed her hand on Cristian's arm. "Ai grija." She smiled at Brianna and left.

Cristian smiled at Brianna, "she said to me, be careful."

Brianna nodded. "So, you guys are just friends?"

He blushed and turned toward the kitchen. "For now, Evelyn Hanson…for now."

Brianna laughed. "So, it sounds like there's a story there."

"Nadia is…a…how do you say…a vault? Yes, she is a vault when it comes to love," he said, as he raided the mini fridge. "And love…is what I have for her. All I have for her."

"Awww, that's so sweet," Brianna replied. "You guys would make a cute couple. So, what makes her a vault?"

"She thinks because her job is…danger…she cannot be close to people…but I know her heart," he patted his heart. "She wants to love Cristian…but…stubborn wins for now." He smiled and offered Brianna a candy bar.

"No thanks," Brianna said. "I think I'm going to go shower and then take a really long nap." Cristian nodded and she grabbed her bag and headed to the bathroom.

JACKSONVILLE, FLORIDA

Carmen had been a complete mess for two days now. It was like walking in a dream. Nothing made sense to her brain. Her reason for existing was gone, and she had no idea what to do other than obsess over finding her baby. Her sweet Maria was out there somewhere, and her mother was not yet prepared to give up on finding her.

She had made fliers with a recent picture of Maria and one of the local churches had helped her print hundreds of them up and distribute them around town. Volunteers had plastered them on telephone poles, in store windows, on car windshields, and one group took them house to house in nearby neighborhoods. She had even been on the news with her story, begging people to help her find her daughter.

Sergeant Bernard had told her that the Jacksonville Sheriff's Office was doing everything they could to find Maria. They had placed her picture at the bus stations, the airport, and even distributed it to local taxi companies and on the Uber sight.

"Dear God," Carmen prayed, kneeling on the floor next to Maria's bed. "Please help me find my daughter, Maria. You know where she is, Heavenly Father…" She began to sob into Maria's blanket. "My baby! Oh God!!! WHY!!!"

Her older sister, Raquel, came into the room and sat on the bed next to her. She rubbed Carmen's back and prayed over her. Raquel had not left her side ever since she'd been notified of her missing niece. Both women stayed there for hours, praying and crying and holding each other.

Raquel eventually went to prepare something for Carmen to eat, for her sister had not had anything since her daughter had been taken. She knew Carmen would need her strength for the coming days. Days that, as of right now, showed no hope.

LYON, FRANCE

After taking a nice, hot shower, Brianna had climbed into the large, king-size bed that was as comfortable a bed as she'd ever been in. It had taken her all of about three seconds to be sound asleep. She had no idea how long she'd been asleep when a loud bang had awoken her. It was now dark outside, as she reached over to turn on the lamp.

What had that noise been? Just then, there was another loud crashing sound, as if a glass table had been thrown against the wall. Panic set in as she jumped out of bed. "Cristian", she thought. As she looked toward the closed door, she noticed the small pistol sitting on her dresser. She had completely forgotten that Nadia had given it to her.

"Evelyn!" She heard him yell, as if he were out of breath. "Evelyn! Get out!" Another loud crash.

Still wearing her gym shorts and an old t-shirt, she ran to the dresser and shoved all her belongings into her bag. She zipped it up, grabbed the pistol, and reached for the doorknob. Pausing for just a second, she said a quick prayer asking for God's protection. She slung the door open and saw a large man walk over to Cristian, who was lying on the floor in front of the sofa.

He reached into his jacket. Cristian looked at her and screamed for her to run. The large man pulled out an enormous handgun and aimed it at Cristian. Without even thinking, Brianna lifted her pistol and fired six times. Her first shot hit the kitchen wall on the other side of the man but caused him to jump back and turn away from Cristian. At which point, her next five shots hit the large man directly in the chest and caused him to fall backwards. However, as he fell, he managed to fire his gun several times, hitting Cristian in his thigh.

Cristian let out a loud groan as blood began to pour out. Quickly, he reached for a gym bag that lay on the floor next to him and produced a t-shirt. He wrapped it around his thigh, just above the wound, and pulled it tight. He groaned again and looked like he was about to pass out.

Brianna just stood there in shock, still aiming the gun in the direction she'd just fired it. "Is he dead?" She asked, slowly lowering the gun and looking at the large man lying awkwardly with his head pressed against the kitchen island.

"Five shots to chest will... have that effect," Cristian replied, attempting to stand. "Thanks for that, by the way." He let out a loud moan and fell back onto the sofa.

"Cristian!" Brianna yelled, as if just realizing he was in the room. "You're hit!"

"Oh, yes," he replied. "I appreciate you notice." He smiled at her. "We need to get out of here, do you have the envelopes, Nadia give you?"

"What can I do?" she asked, rushing over to him and seeing all the blood soaked into his pants.

He looked at the gun she was still clinging to with white knuckles. "You can put that down now, it is empty."

Brianna looked down at the pistol and tossed it quickly into a chair as if it were burning her hand. "The envelopes are in my bag," she replied, unzipping her bag. She handed Cristian the second one that Nadia had given her.

He opened it and pulled out a paper. "It appears that we need to get to Grenoble Alpes Isere Airport," he said. "There is a pilot here that we are to text, letting him know we need his services." He checked something on his phone. "We are thirty minutes away, so let me text him."

Brianna looked around the room for something that Cristian could use as a crutch or cane. The broken table leg was way too short. She noticed a tall lamp that had been knocked over and quickly removed the shade. "Here," she set it in front of him. "Until we can find a better crutch."

He smiled at her as he texted the pilot. "It still has the light in it…that is humorous."

"And the base, but unless you…"

"It is perfect!" He used it to stand and handed her the paper. "Where is your phone?" He asked and she pulled it out of her bag. "There is an emergency text on that paper to send Nadia. It will let her know that you are on your way to the airport…" he grabbed her arm. "Quickly, go change into something less…sleepwear. This lamp is going to draw enough attention. Hurry!" He said as she headed toward the bedroom. "They will probably be sending someone else to check on the gigant very soon!"

When Brianna returned, Cristian was removing something from the barrel of the dead man's gun. "What is that?" She asked.

"A silencer," he replied. "That is why his gun was quieter than yours."

"And it explains why it looked so big," she said. "I thought he'd pulled a shotgun out of his jacket."

Just then, there was a knock at the door. Brianna froze as Cristian hobbled over to the door. He peeked through the peephole and turned back to her. "It is hotel security; you will need to get rid of them."

"I can't lie," she said, in a panic.

"Then you had better think of something fast. I cannot convince them we are okay while holding a lamp and blood all over my pants."

Brianna said a quick prayer and walked over and opened the door a few inches. The man began speaking in French. "English?"

"Sorry, Madam," he replied. "Gunshots were reported on this floor, have you heard anything?"

"Yes, now that you mention it, I did hear something that sounded like gunshots…was it not someone's television?"

"We are not sure, madam," he replied. "So sorry to have bothered you."

"No problem, and thank you for keeping us safe," Brianna responded with a smile and closed the door. "We should give them a few minutes to leave the floor."

"We do not have a few minutes," Cristian said. "I just checked his phone, and they are sending someone else up. Perhaps more than one someone else. We must go."

Brianna grabbed her bag and slowly opened the door. She peeked down the hallway and saw that the two security officers were at the next door down. "Wait for the door to open," she said to Christian and nonchalantly stepped out into the hall. The elevators were about fifteen feet in the opposite

direction. She walked down and pressed the button, pretending to be on her phone. "There is a door to the left of the elevator in the lobby," her old friend whispered in her ear. She nodded at this information and thanked the Holy Spirit for being there. She saw one of the guards look her way. She glanced toward her door and Cristian was ready, his bag over his shoulder and lamp in hand. Ding! The elevator doors opened. She stepped inside and nodded to him.

As quickly as he could hobble the short distance, Cristian had almost made it to the elevator when… "Excuse me, sir!" One of the guards was heading their way. Brianna pressed the door close button at least five times before it began to close, just as Cristian cleared it. "Sir! Stop! Arrêter!" The doors closed.

"We are going to have to clear the lobby in record time," Cristian said. "If they stop me, you keep going!"

"I'm not leaving you, Cristian!"

"You must, Bri…Evelyn!" he replied. "Find a taxi and get to Grenoble…"

"I'm not leaving you!" The doors immediately opened, and she stepped out of the elevator and took a sharp left.

"Evelyn, darling!" He whispered loudly. "This way!" Using the lamp, Cristian hobbled as fast as he could across the lobby, receiving lots of stares.

"Oh, Sweetheart!" Brianna said, coming up behind Cristian with a wheelchair she had retrieved from the room the Holy Spirit had led her to. "Stop trying to be funny!" A woman smiled at them as Cristian took a seat. "He is always going for

the laugh." She headed for the door, both bags draped over the handles of the chair.

Just then, the stairway doors burst open. "STOP!!!" It was security, heading straight for them.

Brianna managed to get the chair perfectly into the rotating door and outside as Cristian let go of the lamp and caused it to jam the door. "RUN!!!" She sprinted down the sidewalk as fast as her short legs would take her. As they turned the corner at the end of the building, Brianna saw security coming out a second door.

"Quick!" Cristian yelled over his shoulder. "We must find taxi!"

"Uber?" a man, leaning against the passenger door of his car, asked.

"Yes, please!" Brianna aimed the chair toward him. "We need to get to…"

"Grenoble Airport!" Cristian finished for her. "Very fast!"

The man noticed the blood all over Cristian's pants and gasped. "Sir! You need hospital!"

"Airport!" Cristian placed a large wad of money into the man's hand. "Now!"

~ 70 ~

CHAPTER 8

SAN DIEGO, CALIFORNIA

Jonah was on his sixth or seventh cup of coffee, and it was only 7 a.m. He had answered the same questions from police detectives over and over for hours. No, he'd never seen the man; no, he nor his parents had any enemies; no, he had no gambling debts and on and on. His sister and mother sat in the living room; each having received just as much questioning. He walked in and handed Jaclyn her refilled coffee cup.

"Thank you, Jonah," she said, patting the couch for him to sit next to her as the officers continued to mill about. "Jonah, they said they don't think this was a random home invasion!" She whispered loudly. "This guy was European and possibly a professional hit man???"

"Yeah, Sis," Jonah replied. "Apparently, he's wanted in three countries. I'm guessing he was in the wrong neighborhood."

"Well, at least the wrong house!" She looked over at their basket case of a mother. "What if Mom had been here alone?" She whispered in Jonah's ear.

"He's dead now, Sis," Jonah said, gulping down his coffee and standing to go back in the kitchen. "I need more coffee." None of them had gotten much sleep last night. Jonah's cell phone rang as he entered the kitchen. He hoped it was Jerry calling about the bonus, he needed to vent about what had just happened. He didn't recognize the number, however. "Hello?"

"Is this Jonah Westbrook?" a woman asked.

"Yes, it is, may I ask who's calling?" Jonah replied.

"Mr. Westbrook, this is a courtesy call from Preby's Cardiovascular Institute, and I'm Nurse Richardson. I just wanted to let the family know that Mr. Westbrook, your father, is awake now. He's asking for his wife, but we can't seem to reach her."

"Oh, wow!" Jonah said, excitedly. "Okay, we had a break in last night and have been dealing with the police all morning. Please let him know that I will inform her to get right over there! And thank you!"

"I will let him know." She replied and hung up the phone.

Jonah went back into the living room and informed his mother and sister of the good news. He hurried them to the car and told them he would come up later once everyone had vacated the house. Back in the house, he informed one of the officers that he was going upstairs to shower. The officer told him they should be done in the next fifteen minutes or so.

A half hour later, Jonah came downstairs to a quiet house. He grabbed his cell phone and tried to call Jerry but got his answering service. "Hey, Jerry…it's Jonah again. You ignoring me or what? You'll never believe what happened to me last night, dude!... Anyway, give me a call as soon as you get this." He clicked off the call just as someone knocked on his door. He looked out the side window before opening it. It was a police officer. "Forget something?" He asked the large officer as he swung the door open.

"Sorry to bother you again, sir," the officer said, stepping into the house. "You ARE Jonah Westbrook, aren't you?" He did a quick glance around and faced Jonah.

"Yes, sir, I'm Jonah," he replied, feeling instantly uneasy about this guy. "How can I help…" Before Jonah could finish his sentence, the man drew his weapon and pointed it at Jonah. "WHOA, big boy!" Jonah jumped back and raised his hands. "I'm the victim here!"

"Turn around and walk into the kitchen," the officer said.

Jonah obeyed, keeping his hands raised. "Something tells me that you're not a police officer."

"Just shut up and do as you're told," the man said in a calm voice. "Now, turn around and face me," he said as Jonah reached the counter.

Jonah turned around and noticed the man was screwing something onto the end of his gun…a silencer. A chill ran up Jonah's spine. What was going on? Was this guy friends with the intruder. Was there some conspiracy to kill Jonah? There had to be a mistake. They had to have the wrong guy.

One thing Jonah knew for sure though…the fact that there was a silencer meant that Jonah was about to be a dead man. He'd seen enough movies to know that to be a fact. Just as he was about to look for a way out, the man lowered his eyes to check if the silencer was completely on…with one swift motion, Jonah reached over, grabbed the pot of hot coffee from the counter, swung his arm back around and hit the man square in the side of the head with the pot, causing it to shatter and soak the man with extremely hot coffee and glass.

The man backed away screaming and grabbed at his head. Jonah then grabbed the gun with one hand and began beating the man in the face with the other. The guy fell back

against the wall and hit his head on a small table that Jonah's mother kept the coffee cups displayed on. The cups hit the floor shattering in what seemed like a loud explosion of glass and cracking wood. The man was out cold.

Jonah stood up, panting and surveying the scene. He quickly kicked the gun across the kitchen and looked for his phone. He realized it was in his pocket and pulled it out. Again, Jonah called 911 and told the operator what had just happened. Within five minutes the place was crawling with police officers again. What was going on? Was this about Jonah? His parents? Or was it something much bigger?

LYON, FRANCE

As the Uber driver made his way through town, Brianna made sure that Cristian's leg was receiving enough pressure and not bleeding out. "I'm sorry you got shot, Cristian…it's all my fault."

"SHOT!!!???" the driver yelled, turning around in his seat and swerving the car a little. "Are you serious!?"

"Just drive," Cristian said to him. "You are in no danger, my friend…c'était une querelle d'amoureux."

The driver nodded with a smile, "Ah je comprends."

"So, you texted the pilot?" Brianna asked.

Cristian nodded. "Nadia as well. Hopefully she can meet us there."

"Where are we going?" Brianna asked.

"You are likely going home, where you will be safe."

"Cristian, I don't have a home."

"The states…" he replied, grimacing as he attempted to straighten up. "You are going back to America."

"But…" Brianna started to object, but Cristian held up his hand.

"It is no longer safe here," he responded. "Maybe, even time for you, to find different work."

Brianna looked out the window as it began to rain outside. She saw the city lights begin to thin away as more and more fields and trees began to make an appearance. "That's never been up to me," she muttered to herself.

After several minutes, the driver informed them that they were arriving at the airport. He pulled into a small parking lot and drove them up to the front of the main building. The sign on the building was in three different languages, but Brianna recognized the one that read, GRENOBLE ALPES ISÈRE AIRPORT.

"Thank you, my friend!" Cristian said to the driver as he opened his door. "For your silence," Cristian handed him another wad of cash.

"Merci, Monsieur," the driver said, smiling big at Brianna and winking at Cristian. He drove off as they stepped up onto the sidewalk.

"What exactly did you tell him?" Brianna asked.

"That I was shot during a lover's quarrel," Cristian replied, and she gave him a look. "Hey, it made him happy…the French love romantic story."

"Well, lean against that pole while I fetch you a wheelchair…Sweetheart." Just then a red and black Mini Cooper squealed into the parking lot and pulled right up to where they stood. Brianna jumped in front of Cristian, not knowing what to expect.

"OH MY…" Nadia jumped out of the car. "What happened to your leg, Cristian!? Are you, alright?"

Cristian nodded as she gave him a big hug. "Let's get Evelyn on this plane."

They met the pilot inside and he told them to meet him on the tarmac by Hangar 6 in fifteen minutes. Cristian gave Brianna a hug and they wished each other well. He took a seat in the waiting area as Nadia led Brianna outside using her Interpol credentials.

"Do you have your passport and identification, Evelyn?" Nadia asked her. Brianna held up the envelope. "Phillipe is going to take you to Mohammed V International Airport in Morocco." She handed Brianna a credit card in Evelyn's name. "I forgot to give this to you earlier. Use it to fly back to the states and hide away until I can contact you…do you understand the danger you are in?"

Brianna nodded. "I do now," she nodded back to Cristian.

"I will take care of him," Nadia said with a smile.

"Will you be, okay?" Brianna asked Nadia, placing her hand on her arm. "You aren't in danger, are you?"

"I will tell them that someone attacked you at the hotel and you have apparently disappeared. I will be fine."

Brianna smiled at her. "I will be praying for you, Nadia. Thank you for everything."

Nadia smiled back and the women hugged. "You be careful…and you BETTER pray for me." She wiped a tear and turned to go.

"Ms. Hanson?" Brianna heard someone say from behind her and it took her a second to remember that was her new last name. She turned to face the pilot, Phillipe. "We really should be going?" She nodded and wiped her own tears.

MURPHY, NORTH CAROLINA

Travis decided to take Jack up on his offer to "clean himself up." He'd decided the best way to forget all his troubles, was to go to his favorite place in the world. He'd checked into a room at Harrah's Cherokee Valley River Casino and Hotel and was presently sitting at the blackjack table trying to turn $3,000 into $30,000. He just knew he couldn't lose.

A scantily clad cocktail waitress came by and offered him a drink and he accepted a bottle of beer. "Keep 'em comin', Sweetheart!" he said a little too loud and started his firsthand. By the time she brought his next drink, he was down $700. He took the beer and downed half of it in one guzzle. "Hit me!... NO!!!" Another $500 gone. Just then, his cell phone rang. He looked down to see that it was Jack calling. He held up a finger and stepped away from the table. "Jack! What's up, man?"

"Let me ask you something, Travis," Jack started. "Do you think I'm a stupid man?"

"No, Jack!" Travis responded, taking another swig of his beer. "Why would you ask that?"

"Do you think I'm stupid enough to invest my time and money into something that I'm not going to keep tabs on?"

"Jack, what are you talking about? Do you need me to do something for you?" Travis asked, not sure what his boss was ranting about.

"Yeah, Travis, I need you to do something for me," Jack sounded quite upset. "I need you to look over by the slot machines to your right where my pal, Tony, is standing."

Travis looked over and sure enough…one of Jack's big goons was standing there in his black suit, arms folded in front of himself…staring right at Travis.

"Do you see him?"

"Yes…but why is he here?" Travis was really starting to freak out now.

"Why is HE there, Travis!? Why are YOU there???" Jack was clearly not happy. "I tell you to lay low and what…your first thought is to go to a casino and blow all your money?"

"Jack, this is how I relax…I only paid for one night!"

"Because even you are smart enough to know how stupid you are!" Jack replied. "It will only take you one night to blow the three grand I gave you!!!"

"No, Jack, I can make money, here!"

"How long have you been there?

"I don't know…about forty-five minutes."

"How much have you lost?"

"Jack, I've got a plan…"

"$1,200!" Jack said, cutting him off.

"How did you…" Travis looked back over at Tony, who was still watching him. "Anyway, what's it matter to you, Jack…you gave the mon…"

"What's it matter to me!?" Jack said. "I'll tell you what it matters to me you ignorant little…" Jack paused to gather himself. "Do you know who happens to be there in Murphy…staying at the same hotel you are presently standing?"

"Who, Jack?" Travis asked, but he already knew the answer.

"Micky Detuccio! That's who!" Jack said, and Travis cringed. "And do you know what Micky said he would do to you if he ever saw you again, Travis?"

"Break both my legs and cut off my thumbs," Travis replied, scanning the room.

"I'm invested in you, Kid…and I can't use you with two broken legs and no thumbs." Travis said. "Get out of there right now!"

"Yessir," Travis replied and ended the call. He nodded to Tony and headed up to his room to get his bag. He slid the key into his door and stepped inside.

"Hello, Travis…" it was Micky Detuccio, sitting in the chair next to the window, wearing a suit that probably cost more

than Travis owed him. There were two other men standing in the room as well. "Fancy seeing you here."

"Micky, listen…"

"No, Travis, you listen…have a seat." Micky pointed to the chair across from him.

"Micky, I'm paying you as fast as I can." He stopped talking when Micky held up his hand.

"And I appreciate the money your friend, Jack Watson, sends me, don't get me wrong," Micky responded. "It's the only reason you're not at the bottom of the Chattahoochee River wearin' a pair of concrete shoes." Micky stood and walked across the room. "You hid from me for two years, Travis…you never called, texted, or tried to contact me in any way at all. It hurt my feelings." He looked back at Travis. "Marco, tell Travis what happens to people who hurt my feelings."

"They scream," the large man closest to Travis responded. "A lot." He put his hand on Travis' shoulder.

Travis squirmed in his seat. "Micky…you know…I do jobs for Jack, you know…jobs I need my legs and thumbs for…so I can pay you…come on, Micky… Mr. Detuccio."

Micky turned and faced Travis. "About that…" He walked over and stood in front of Travis. "Exactly what kind of jobs are you performing for Mr. Watson that pays so much money?" He leaned down face to face with Travis and put his hands on the arms of the chair, causing Travis to lean back as far as he could. "A few things come to mind…and I sure hope I'm wrong about one of them."

"I'm not exactly at liberty to say, Micky…Mr. De…?"

Micky slapped him across the face and stepped back. "Answer me, punk! What exactly are you doing to make so much money for Jack Watson!?"

"Mr. Detuccio!...I..." Travis started to say, but Marco squeezed his shoulder really hard from behind.

"It would be wise to answer the question."

Micky leaned down in front of Travis again. "It wouldn't happen to have anything to do with trafficking children...would it?" He saw the flicker in Travis' eyes. "You little weasel."

"What!?" Travis choked out. "No Micky no! No child trafficking, I swear! That's sick!"

Micky slapped him again. "Don't lie to me, boy! I've suspected that's how Jack Watson makes his fortunes for some time now." He straightened up and walked across the room. "I am not a good man," he said, placing his hands on the kitchen counter. "I've done a lot of bad things in my thirty-nine years. I've stolen, I've cheated, I've smuggled drugs, I've broken the bones of half decent men, and I've even killed a few of them..." He turned to face Travis. "But I will neither tolerate nor take the dirty payoff for the trafficking of innocent children. They are all that's left in this world that hasn't been corrupted."

Travis shook his head violently. "No, Micky! No, it's not like that!"

"I don't believe you, Travis...and since you aren't offering me an alternate reason for your insanely large income...I'm afraid I'm going to have to assume I'm correct." He poured himself a small glass of Scotch and downed it in one

gulp. "Take this piece of trash somewhere in the industrial part of town, break every bone in his body, and feed him to the fish."

"No! Micky, listen!!!" Travis tried to stand up but the large hand on his shoulder kept him seated. "Micky, I can get the money another way!" Before Travis could react, a needle had punctured his left arm. "WHAT, NO!!! MICKY, PLEASE!!!"

CHAPTER 9

ATLANTA, GEORGIA

Brianna's nine-hour flight from Morocco to Atlanta was coming to an end. She texted Nadia to see if it was safe to go to her parents'. She didn't want to put them in any danger, but desperately wanted to see them. Nadia told her to use the credit card to lay low for now. She would let her know when it was safe. Her and Cristian were looking into who was behind the attack at the hotel. If it indeed was the Secretary-General, then his arm would reach across the pond and Brianna would not be safe there.

After getting off the plane, she found a restaurant and ordered something to eat. She hadn't eaten in days. When the food finally came, she said a quick prayer. When she opened her eyes, she noticed that her old friend was sitting across from her. She smiled and thanked him for keeping her safe. He nodded and set his hat on the table. He scanned the room and leaned in to tell her something.

"Call your mother."

"Are you sure?" she asked. "Is it safe?" He gave her a look that reminded her of who she was talking to, and she felt silly. "Sorry." She pulled out her phone and called her mother.

"Brianna, Sweetie!" her mother said, excitedly. "Your ears must've been burning! We were just talking about you!" Brianna could hear someone in the background gasp.

"Hi, Mom, who's with you?" Brianna asked.

"It's Carolyn from church," her mother said. "You haven't met her…she heads up the women's ministry."

"Oh, nice," Brianna was looking for a clue as to why the Holy Spirit had told her to call.

"So, it's good to hear from you, Bree! How are you doing? Where are you at these days? Oh, I got to see you speak in London! It's on YouTube! You were wonderful! Such a beautiful woman!"

"Like her mother!" Brianna heard Carolyn say.

"I'm good, Mom…I'm glad you got to see me speak, that's so cool." She didn't want to tell her mother she was in the states, or she would insist on getting together. She hoped that question wouldn't come back around. "How're you and Dad?"

"I'm good…your father stays busy what with having an A.C. business in Florida and all. He's not here right now but he'll be sad he missed you! Things are quiet here in Gateway."

"So, why were you guys talking about little ol' me?" Brianna asked.

"Well, Carolyn here was telling me about something that just happened recently in Jacksonville…you know how I don't watch the news. I had no clue. Well, anyway, a little girl was snatched right out of a restaurant on the northside…in broad daylight! Can you believe that? They apparently caught it on a bank's surveillance camera, but you can't even tell what kind of car the guy's driving, let alone what HE looks like.

Anyway, it turns out that Carolyn knows the woman whose daughter was taken. She used to be a server at a restaurant Carolyn frequented. Server? Do they call themselves servers or waitresses now? I can't keep up with that stuff, it's like are they stewardesses or flight attendants? It's all so confusing." Brianna heard Carolyn laughing in the background.

"Anyway, we got to talking about it and I reminded Carolyn about what you do, and we were wondering if maybe you could help this poor woman…Brianna, she's literally beside herself with worry!"

"Wow, I'm sure she is, Mom, but I…" Was this why she was supposed to call her mother? "Do you know her name?"

"Carolyn? What was that poor woman's name?"

"Carmen," Carolyn replied. "Carmen Sanchez. Can Brianna help her?"

"Mom…did she say Sanchez?" Brianna's heart skipped a beat.

SAN DIEGO, CALIFORNIA

"Well, he is definitely not one of ours," the officer said. "I don't think there's a cop on the force as jacked as that big boy."

"So, who is he?" Jonah asked, watching as they led the large man, in cuffs, to the rescue squad, where his burns and cuts could be treated.

"No idea," the officer shrugged. "No identification and he's not talking."

"Yeah, well get this…" another officer walked over. "His fingerprints have been burnt off."

"From the coffee I poured on him!?" Jonah asked, quite confused.

"No, this was done intentionally…so he couldn't be identified. This guy is probably a professional hit man. Silencer, strangle cord, he even had cyanide in a vile in his jacket…at least that's what the M.E. thinks it is."

"Sounds like you're lucky to be alive, Mr. Westbrook," the first officer said. "Lucky indeed."

"Thank you, gentlemen, I'll take it from here." An older Asian man in a cheap gray suit walked up and held out his hand to Jonah. The officers quickly walked away. "Detective Ken Chun." He shook Jonah's hand. "Let's take a walk, Mr. Westbrook." He led Jonah around to the side of his house. "Two attempts on your life in less than twelve hours, Mr. Westbrook…that's pretty intense." Jonah nodded, expecting the man to say more. Mr. Chun only stared at him. "Is there something you're not telling us, Mr. Westbrook?"

"Please, call me Jonah…and no. I've told your officers everything I know. I just got into town yesterday…my father had a heart attack."

"So, you live?"

"Henderson, Colorado…just outside of Denver."

"And do you have any enemies in Henderson, Colorado, Mr. Westbrook…I mean, Jonah?"

"No, I'm hardly ever there. My job takes me all over the world."

"And what exactly do you do?"

"I'm the structural engineer for Maitland Construction…" Jonah started to say when the detective glanced up at him.

"Maitland Construction?" Detective Chun asked and pulled out his cell phone.

Jonah nodded, "yes, why?"

"You've probably been too busy to watch the news, Jonah…what with fighting crime all night and morning." He swiped and clicked his phone for several seconds and then held it up to Jonah. "Looks like you were luckier than you thought." The headline read: PLANE CARRYING ENTIRE CREW FROM MAITLAND CONSTRUCTION CRASHES, NO SURVIVORS.

"What the…" Jonah took the man's phone and read the story from the Denver Chronicle. "This can't be…what!?" He read it again. "It says here that the plane crashed in Columbia, Missouri…that's impossible."

"Apparently not, Jonah…but why do you say that?" Detective Chun asked.

"Because the job we were doing was in Wyoming…north of Denver. Missouri is way east. Why would they have been over Missouri? The job was done…they should've flown straight home to Denver!"

"I have no idea, Mr. Westbrook, perhaps there's someone you could contact in Denver…a secretary or someone who wasn't at the job site?" Detective Chun stepped out of the sunlight and into the shade.

"That's just it…the people that hired us, insisted on all employees working onsite…you don't think…" Something wet splashed on Jonah's face and Detective Chun spun around and fell to the ground. Jonah jumped back and realized that it was blood all over his shirt and face. He looked down at the

detective who was lying in the ground with a bullet hole in the back of his head. Everything started to spin. Jonah didn't know what to do. What direction had the bullet come from? Where should he run? "HELP!!!" Jonah took cover behind some bushes as several officers came around the corner. As soon as they saw the fallen detective, they withdrew their weapons.

"What happened!?" an officer screamed at Jonah. "Who shot Chun!?"

"I don't know!?" Jonah replied. "He just dropped! I never even heard a shot!" Jonah did know, however, that the shot was meant for him. With two attempts on his life already…that was a no-brainer. He needed to get out of town and hide. He needed to disappear, and he knew just the guy to help him. "Listen!" he yelled to the closest officer. "Somebody is after me, I'm getting out of here!" He ran as fast as he could to his rental, the officer yelling for him to stop.

MURPHY, NORTH CAROLINA

"How about here?"

"No, just keep driving…this is too public…someone might see us."

"Yeah, there's a surveillance camera on that building."

Travis tried to open his eyes. His head was pounding, and his eyelids felt as if they weighed a thousand pounds. He was apparently lying on the hard floor of a cargo van. His hands were free, so they obviously expected him to be out longer. One of the perks of doing drugs and never really being sober…it took larger doses than normal people to affect you.

"So, what's the plan? How are we going to off this guy?"

Travis managed to perk up a little at that statement. He peeked out of his heavy eyelids and saw the two thugs from the hotel room. "Perfect," he thought.

"Find an abandoned building and make it look like a suicide I guess…~~whatta~~ ya say?"

"Sounds like a plan, but you're pulling the trigger this time."

Travis looked over at the side door and noticed that it was not locked. He needed to act fast but wasn't sure if he would be able to move with the drug still in his system. He didn't want to make them aware that he was awake and then not be able to move. He wiggled his toes. It felt like they were moving. He tried to move his leg just a little, so as not to draw attention. It seemed to move. His right hand was under his face. He moved a finger and scraped his cheek…there was pain…that was good. He seemed to be fine, but would his legs hold him up?

"Over there…that place looks perfect."

The van slowed…it was now or never…Travis reached up with all the strength he could muster, grabbed the door handle, slammed it down, and slid the door open.

"HEY! GRAB HIM, MARCO!" the driver yelled. "HE'S GETTING AWAY!!!"

In his mind, Travis was going to leap out of the van and take off running in the opposite direction. What really happened was more like he rolled out of the van and landed on his butt

and hands. His first attempt to get up ended with a face plant and he realized that his legs had absolutely no strength in them at all. Before he could adjust and maneuver his way up, he was tackled back to the ground face first again.

"Where do you think you're going, you big idiot!?"

"Please, just let me go!" Travis managed to say, with his mouth full of asphalt.

They picked him up and threw him into the back of the van. "Try that again and I'll break your legs before I kill you!" The van door slammed shut.

"Come on, guys!" Travis yelled. "Maybe we can work something out!" The doors opened and just as they were getting in the front seat, the passenger…Marco, grunted and fell against the door.

"Marco!" the other guy yelled. "Stop playing around…" And then he slumped over in his seat. Everything went quiet.

"Ummm, you guys, okay?" Travis asked. "What's going on?" Nothing. He raised himself up and that's when he saw the blood trickling from the side of the driver's head. "What in the world?" Just then, the door slid open and there stood the big guy from the casino lobby. "Thank God, Tony!"

The big man reached in and grabbed Travis under his arm and pulled him out of the van. "Could you be any stupider?" He led Travis to his SUV and pushed him in, slamming the door behind him. He went around and grabbed a large can of gasoline and began pouring it all over the van. Seconds later, they were driving away from the scene with the burning van behind them.

~ 90 ~

"I'm gonna get blamed for that, ain't I?" Travis said.

"I highly doubt it." Tony replied. "Now, just sit back and shut up. We have a long drive ahead of us."

"Thanks again, Tony…you saved my life." Travis leaned back in his seat and thought about that. His life…what a miserable excuse for a life. Hunting innocent children just to pay off a gambling debt…and how does he spend the little bit of money he gets…by gambling again. What a waste. Tony was right, he couldn't be any stupider. He closed his eyes hoping for peace and rest. All he got were visions of children screaming from fear of the future he'd given them. Their lives destroyed forever.

CHAPTER 10

ATLANTA, GEORGIA

After she got off the phone with her mother, Brianna checked herself into a nearby hotel under the name of Evelyn Hanson. She settled in and found a corner to sit and pray. She could not believe that her own mother had a connection with Maria Sanchez. That was definitely a God thing.

Now she needed to know what her role in this saga would be. She bowed her head and began talking to her very best friend in the world. She thanked Him, she praised Him, she worshiped Him, and she petitioned Him. Three hours later, when she open her eyes, He was standing near the doorway, hat in hand. He smiled at her and turned to go. "What do I do?"

"Trust my plan," He said as He placed His hat on His head and disappeared.

"I do…I just don't know it…" She thought about what it must feel like to have your own child vanish. To know that someone took them, and you will most likely never see them again. The pain would be worse than losing someone to death. "Jesus…" she whispered and held back a tear. "Comfort her, Holy Spirit…Comforter." Her cell phone buzzed from the nightstand. She walked over and saw that it was a number she didn't recognize. "Hello?"

"Yes…is this…Brianna?" the crying woman asked. Brianna's heart jumped.

"Yes, this is her," Brianna replied. "Who, may I…"

"My name is Carmen Sanchez…and my friend, Carolyn says…that you may be able to help me…please Ms. Brianna, I have nobody else to turn to."

Brianna could tell she had moved the phone away from her face and was sobbing. She couldn't believe that her mother had given this woman her number. It was a false hope. "Trust my plan," she heard the Holy Spirit say again. "Well, Mrs. Sanchez, I definitely believe that God has brought us together, but I'm not yet sure the reason."

"My baby…she is gone…God knows where she is, Ms. Brianna…I know He does…" She began crying again.

"Yes, I know He does, as well." Brianna was seriously at a loss for what to tell this woman. She did not want to give her a false hope, but she also didn't want to take away what little hope she had. "Can we meet?" She didn't know why she'd said it, but there it was. Sometimes when the Holy Spirit said to trust Him, you just had to jump out of the boat.

"Yes! Are you here, in Jacksonville!?" Her spirits seemed to lift.

"No, ma'am, but I can be by tomorrow," Brianna replied. "Just, don't tell anyone, including Mrs. Carolyn, that I'm coming. I will contact you when I get there."

"Yes, ma'am and thank you so much!" Carmen replied. "You have given me hope!"

Brianna clicked off the call and bowed her head. "Okay, God, I need you in this…Amen." She booked an early morning flight to Jacksonville and decided that it might be best to fast through this adventure. She'd learned long ago that fasting and praying were the best ways to get the attention of heaven…and

she felt very strongly that the coming storm would require a little bit of that heaven.

EL CENTRO, CALIFORNIA

Jonah made it as far east as El Centro, California before he decided to pull in for gas and call his friend, Paul Hutchins. Paul was Jonah's best friend from high school, and he was also a real estate guru, who had property all over the country. First, he texted his sister and told her that a work emergency had come up and he had to leave town. He went into the store and picked up some snacks for the road and then dialed Paul's number. If Paul couldn't help him, then he would just drive until he felt safe.

"Jonah?" Paul sounded surprised and excited. "Is this Jonah Westbrook calling me!?"

"The one and only," Jonah responded with a smile. "How are you doing, my old friend?"

"I'm great…living the dream up here in Santa Barbara…how are YOU!?"

"Well, right now that's a loaded question," Jonah replied with a slight chuckle. "Listen, I'll get to the point. The last time we spoke, you mentioned that you could hook me up with about any vacation spot I needed…that offer still available?"

"Absolutely, where are looking to go?" Paul asked.

"Bro, I just want to get somewhere unplugged and hide away from life for a week or two. So, somewhere off the beaten path."

"Okay, let me see what I have here…where are you, right now."

"Southern California, but I want to go east."

"Okay, I have property in Arizona, Texas, Missouri, West Virginia, Florida, heck I have several houses in the northeast, but they're all rented out right now."

"What do you have in Florida?" Jonah asked. It sounded like a million miles from San Diego.

"Let's see…off the beaten path in Florida…here we go…I just purchased it sight unseen about two months ago and haven't had a chance to check it out yet, but it's a double wide trailer in the middle of about twenty acres of woods in Hilliard. There's even a big pond for fishing. I can call and get the power turned on. Can't make any promises on the condition, but it's yours for free for as long as you need. Just let me know what kind of love and attention it needs."

"Sounds perfect…just shoot me the address." Jonah replied.

"You got it pal," Paul said. "Everything alright?"

"Yeah, I'm just burnt out…thanks for everything, Paul." A few minutes later, Paul texted him the address with a side note that the key was supposedly under one of the many flowerpots. Jonah pointed his car in the direction of Florida and headed out for the two-day drive.

JACKSONVILLE, FLORIDA

A very groggy Travis sat up in the backseat of the SUV and looked around. "Wow, I don't know what they injected in me...but I've never slept so hard. What part of Atlanta is this?"

"The Jacksonville, Florida part," Tony replied. "You're going to lay low here for a few weeks."

"Jacksonville? Wow, that WAS some powerful...No, dude!" Travis said, in a panic. "This is where I snatched that one kid!"

"Jack wants you here," Tony replied, pulling into the parking lot of a seedy motel. "I'm not going to be here to babysit you, so sit tight and don't go getting into trouble." He parked the SUV and turned around in his seat. "In fact, stay in your room." He tossed Travis a credit card. "Order in."

"There's not even a pool!" Travis said, looking out at the extremely trashy place. "This place is a dump."

"You had your chance, Travis," Tony got out and opened Travis' door. "Jack gave you enough money to take a nice vacation and you blew it." He grabbed Travis by his shirt and pinned him against the vehicle. "If you blow this...well, I'll be taking you for a long boat ride...one way." Tony went inside and paid for two weeks. Room 202. "If you aren't here when I come back, you'd better be dead." He reached in the truck and pulled out a plastic bag. "I got you some essentials... toothbrush, toothpaste...a change of clothes." He climbed into the SUV and drove away, leaving Travis in the parking lot staring after him.

Travis climbed the steps to his room and used his key to open the door to 202. It swung open and he just stood there

shaking his head. He walked over to the phone and called the front desk. "Hey, you got the number for a taxi?"

Thirty minutes later, Travis was walking into a plush hotel in downtown Jacksonville. He was greeted by marble floors that were so shiny he could see his reflection. Large ivory columns led the way to a big oak counter flanked on both sides by a massive staircase with blue and gold carpet leading the way to what he imagined was a five-star experience.

He handed Jack's credit card to the stunning brunette behind the counter and told her he wanted the works. Five minutes later a bellhop was leading him toward a shiny gold elevator where he would go to his twelfth-floor suite overlooking the St. John's River. It was total perfection.

He ordered a steak dinner to be brought up and served to him while he sat on the balcony and sipped red wine from a $1,400 bottle of Chateau Mouton Rothschild Pauillac. Travis didn't know how to pronounce it, but he was impressed by how well it had held its flavor…seeing how it was a 2010 bottle. He knew he'd probably get in trouble for all this later, but if Jack wanted him to lay low and not go anywhere…this was the price.

Carmen lay in bed next to her sister, Raquel. For the first time in days, she had hope. She knew sleep would escape her tonight…she was way too excited. She had known Brianna Bowers was a Godsend from the moment her old friend, Carolyn, had told her about her.

The detective had been honest with her from the start, telling Carmen that there was only a slim chance they would ever find Maria. Carmen had screamed, cried, punched and

screamed some more, but she'd appreciated the honesty. Her baby…her sweet, sweet baby. The thought of never seeing her little angel was overwhelming and God knew she couldn't handle that.

Didn't the Bible say something about God never put more on us than we could handle? She'd grieved, yes…but deep down she knew that God had a plan…and she would get her baby girl back. "Espera, niña." She smiled at the thought of meeting Brianna in the morning. This woman would help her…it was what she did. She rescued children from child traffickers. It would only be a matter of time. God had it all under control.

CHAPTER 11

Jonah stopped at a Best Western in San Antonio for the night. Being an avid lover of spy movies, he wondered how secretive he needed to be. Should he be using his credit cards? Should he just take out cash? Was someone following him or tracking his cell phone?

The question that really haunted him, however, was what was that underground bunker they'd spent all that time building actually for? Some kind of cult? Some secret government hideout? That had to be the reason behind his entire crew being killed. There would've been no reason for them to be flying over Missouri. So, when that woman called him about sending his bonus check…she was just wanting his address, to send a hit man. The detectives had said it felt like a professional job. He needed a plan. He needed to figure out who he could notify. This felt big…deep pockets big.

After eating a stale microwavable cheeseburger from a gas station, Jonah tried sleeping. His brain was too busy for sleep, however. After about an hour and a half of tossing and turning, he got up, put his stuff in the car, and headed out. Hilliard, Florida sounded like a nice, quiet place to lay low for a while. Glancing in his rear-view mirror, he noticed a van pull out of the hotel parking lot behind him. Paranoid…he was just being paranoid.

JACKSONVILLE, FLORIDA

Brianna's plane touched down in Jacksonville just a little after 6 a.m. She walked into the airport Starbucks and ordered a venti black coffee. She had not slept well for quite some time and would need a little assistance in staying awake. She booked a room close to the airport and ordered an Uber to the address Carmen had given her. She texted Carmen to let her know she was coming and again reminded her to tell no one.

On her way to Carmen's apartment, she prayed for wisdom. "Please guide my steps, Holy Spirit. I desperately need you in this." When she opened her eyes, he was there with her. He smiled at her and then looked out the window.

"A storm is coming," he said, taking off his hat and setting it on his lap.

Brianna looked out the window and noted the beautiful cloudless skies. "Metaphorically speaking?"

"Ma'am?" The Uber driver looked confused.

"Sorry, just praying."

"Our destination is just up the road."

Brianna thanked him, grabbed her bag, and exited the car. It was a nice-looking apartment complex, considering the area seemed somewhat industrial. Apartment 412 was a four story walk up, so she double checked the signs and made her way up. As soon as she reached the door and knocked, her phone rang. She looked down to see that it was Nadia. She was about to answer it, but Carmen swung the door open with a big smile on her face and she didn't want to be rude. She let it go to voicemail. She met the young woman's embrace with a "Good morning, Carmen! God bless you, girl!" Carmen's eyes had filled with tears as soon as she'd wrapped her arms around Brianna.

"Muchas gracias por ayudarme," Carmen said, crying uncontrollably into Brianna's shoulder. "Muchas gracias!" They stood there at her front door for several minutes, hugging each other and crying. Finally, Carmen let loose her grip on Brianna and stepped back wiping her eyes. "I'm sorry, please come in."

"You have nothing to be sorry about, Carmen." Brianna took her hand and squeezed it. "I'm the one who is sorry for what you're going through." She stepped inside and Carmen closed the door. They walked into the living room and Carmen had her sit on the sofa.

"Can I get you something? You have coffee, do you need more?" Carmen nodded to Brianna's cup.

"If it's no trouble," Brianna replied. "More coffee would be much appreciated." Just then her phone buzzed again, and Brianna saw that it was Nadia. She knew it would be important but again let it go to voicemail. She noticed that Nadia had already left her one message. She would need to cut this meeting short and call her back. "So, what are the police telling you?"

"Nothing promising," Carmen replied from the kitchen. "No leads on the car or the man. Nobody saw anything…isn't that crazy? It was the middle of the day."

"People are too focused on their own lives these days," Brianna replied. "Nobody notices anything that doesn't involve them."

~ 101 ~

"I blame the cell phones," Carmen said, coming in with a hot cup of coffee for Brianna. "So, distracting. Nobody is social anymore."

"Thank you for the coffee," Brianna said. "It smells delicious." She held the cup to her nose and enjoyed the aroma. "Did they ever find anymore video footage of the car, besides the bank?"

"They found some from a person's doorbell, but it just showed the car going by. They have no idea where he went once he got up to Main Street." Carmen stared down at her own cup of coffee. "You never think something like this will happen to you…Maria is my life." She began sobbing again.

"You poor thing," Brianna replied, getting up and sitting next to Carmen. She wrapped her arm around her. "Dear Heavenly Father, I come to you right now on behalf of my friend, Carmen Sanchez…in the name of Jesus Christ. Father, I pray that You would begin to guide our footsteps in this situation. We KNOW that You know exactly where Maria is at this very moment. First of all, I ask that You thwart the enemies' plans for Maria's life. That You would take what the enemy means for evil and turn it too good. Keep Maria safe and innocent, I ask, Father. I would also pray that You give the authorities favor as they attempt to find this precious daughter." Brianna could hear her phone buzzing again. "Give us favor as well, Father…lead us to Maria, I pray. In Jesus' name!"

They both said amen. She pulled away from Carmen. "You're a believer, correct?" Carmen nodded as she used a tissue to wipe her eyes. "Good, here's what I need you to do. First of all…and I know this is easy to say…stop worrying…until you have reason to doubt God…don't.

Secondly, your ONLY job at this point is to fast and pray. Drink lots of water and fast everything else…unless, of course you have a health issue." Carmen shook her head. "Good, starting immediately…storm the throne room of heaven with your pleads for God's help. Literally, this is your mission. Get as many of your friends as will join you to do so, but it is YOUR job as her mother right now. The Holy Spirit is saying, "faith over fear!" Do not let doubt creep in. Your prayers are the fuel for God's hands at this point. Do you understand me?"

Carmen nodded. "What will YOU be doing?"

"Honestly?" Brianna stood up and took a drink of her coffee. "Right now, I have no idea. I never know…until I do." She carried her empty coffee cup into the kitchen and rinsed it out. "I feel strongly that God is in the middle of this, Carmen." The woman had followed her into the kitchen. Brianna turned and faced her. "I want you to understand something, though." She took Carmen's hands in her own. "There is a possibility that this doesn't go our way."

Tears formed in Carmen's eyes, but she nodded. "That doesn't mean God is against us…it just means that His plans are different than ours." She squeezed Carmen's hands. "BUT…faith over fear." They hugged again. "Listen, I will be in touch. There's a very important phone call I need to make, and then I am going to be in deep prayer for Maria."

"Gracias, hermana! God be with you!" Carmen hugged her once more and walked her to the door.

"One more thing," Brianna said before she left. "Tell NO ONE that I'm here. If you need to contact me, this is VERY important. My name is Evelyn, not Brianna. Do you understand?"

~ 103 ~

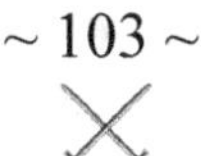

Carmen was very confused at this strange behavior but decided to just agree. This woman was her last hope at finding her daughter, if she wanted to be called Voldemort, it would be what Carmen called her. "I understand, Ms. Evelyn."

Travis awoke to a loud banging on his door. Who in the world would do that at a nice hotel like this? At first, he tried to ignore the knocking, but it wouldn't stop. "WHO IS IT!!!? PLEASE STOP KNOCKING!!!" he screamed from his place in the center of the king size bed. If they only knew how badly his head hurt. The knocking started back up. "You're very lucky I don't have a gun!" He rolled out of bed and stormed to the door, wearing the clothes he'd passed out in from yesterday.

He slung the door open. "WHA……" Before he could finish the word, Tony had punched him right in the face with his fist. Travis fell back into the room, blood pouring from his nose. Tony stepped inside and closed the door.

"Are you kidding me!?" Tony said to Travis. "I know you're a stupid man, Travis Scott, but I had no idea anybody was this stupid!" He kicked Travis in the side as he lay writhing on the floor. He walked over and closed the curtains. "Stand up!"

"I can explain," Travis mumbled, his head to the floor and butt up in the air. He was bleeding all over the white carpet.

"I said stand up!" Tony walked over and kicked him in the side again. "Now!"

"I'm sorry, Tony!" Travis said, grabbing onto a glass table and trying to stand. "I couldn't stay in that rat motel you left me at."

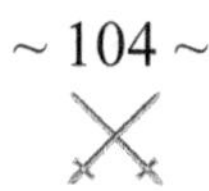

Tony grabbed him by the back of his neck and shoved him over onto the couch. "I have been informed by Jack that you are no longer worth your troubles." He lifted a large handgun from the waistband of his pants and put the barrel against Travis' head. "So, here's the deal…" He slapped Travis across the cheek. "The fact that about seven people saw me outside your room banging on the door, is the ONLY reason your brains aren't decorating that sofa!"

He turned and walked over to the counter and set his gun down. "There's a car down in the parking garage. A white Chevy Equinox." He picked up his gun, walked over and handed Travis a slip of paper. "You have six hours to deliver three kids to this address. This time they want boys."

"I thought I was laying low," Travis replied.

Tony slapped him again. "You don't know how to lay low, you piece of garbage! You wanna draw attention to yourself? This is how you'll do it!" Tony walked to the door. "If you're not at that address in six hours with three boys, I will empty this gun into your head." He opened the door and left. After several minutes of self-loathing, Travis got up and showered. He put on his same clothes and headed for his new car. Three boys…what kind of sick world was this?

When Brianna got back outside the apartment complex, she summoned an Uber with her app and then checked her three messages from Nadia.

"Brianna!" Nadia sounded winded and in a panic. "I've been compromised!" It sounded as if she was running. "Someone broke into my flat…tried to…tried to kill me. I think

he was Interpol. I am heading to meet up with Cristian. Call me soon! You are not safe!"

"Dear Jesus," Brianna muttered. "Thank you for keeping Nadia safe. Please help her to…"

The second message started: "Brianna! Please let me know you are okay!" It sounded like she was in traffic. "I'm not sure what we're going to do. I am almost at Cristian's home now. Please call me!"

Third message: Nadia was sobbing. "Brianna," she said in almost a whisper. "Cristian is dead." She was crying. Brianna covered her mouth in disbelief. "Brianna, I don't know where to go…I am being hunted. Cristian…my sweet friend is dead…it's all my fault for bringing him into this." A car door closed in the background. Brianna heard the car start up. "Please call me, Brianna."

Quickly, Brianna dialed Nadia's number. It rang several times. "Come on, girl!" Brianna said. "Answer your…"

"Brianna!" Nadia sounded relieved. "Thank God!" She began crying.

"Oh, Nadia!" Brianna replied. "I'm so sorry about Cristian!"

"It's all my fault, Brianna!" Nadia managed to say through her crying. "They apparently…they tortured him…for information."

"Father, please be with my friend, Nadia," Brianna prayed. "Give her comfort, peace, and wisdom during this difficult time." She listened while Nadia drove and cried. "Is there anything I can do, Nadia?"

"No," Nadia replied. "I am going to get my fake passport and identification that I have hidden. I will try and join you in the states. When I have more information, I will contact you."

"Please be careful, Nadia!" Brianna said. "I'll be praying for you!"

"Thank you, Brianna," Nadia said. "You are the only person I trust right now. Please continue to pray." She ended the call.

Brianna bawled like a child as she stood outside the apartment complex waiting for her ride. "Father, please surround Nadia with an army of your angels…I know you have them. Keep her safe." Her Uber driver pulled up and she wiped her eyes. She leaned back in the backseat and closed her eyes as he drove her to her hotel. Cristian…he'd taken a bullet protecting her. He'd helped her escape the country. He was such a good person…now he was in eternity. "God, forgive me for not sharing you with him."

CHAPTER 12

JACKSONVILLE, FLORIDA

Travis had left the hotel and driven north. The address that Tony had given him was on the north side, so he figured he'd keep close. He'd already gone through several neighborhoods and not a kid in sight. Stupid parents keeping their kids inside, letting them play video games instead of playing outside with their imaginations. What was the world coming to?

Just then, as he was passing a Family Dollar, he noticed a woman with several children getting out of a minivan. He quickly turned into the parking lot. He backed into a spot on the side of the store and walked inside. He scanned the store for cameras and only saw the one behind the counter. He kept his face away from it and walked to the back. He found the woman who had four kids. There was one in a stroller, two younger girls and a boy who looked about seven. He was over by himself looking at a display of rubber balls, but on the same isle as his mother.

Travis peeked around the corner, keeping an eye on the mother. He was waiting for her to be distracted. He pulled out his little rag and the small bottle of chloroform. He dabbed some onto the cloth and prepared himself to strike.

"Mommy, Lisa keeps poking me!" One of the little girls yelled out.

"Lisa, come over here with Mommy," the woman said. "Myka, stop tattling." She reached into her diaper bag to get something out and Travis had his moment.

With one swift motion, he grabbed the little boy from behind, covering his mouth with the cloth. He clamped the kicking kid to his side with his arm and made it out the front door in seconds. By the time he'd made it to the front of the store, the boy had gone limp. He'd left the back of the Equinox unlocked and all he had to do was lift it, toss the kid in, and go. It took less than thirty seconds to grab the child and be on the road. He pulled over into an empty parking lot about a mile away and tied the kid up, just in case he woke up too soon. One down.

A few minutes later he spotted a perfect place to find another victim. He found a good place to park and left the kid in the back. If everything went according to plan, he would be back out in a few minutes. God, he hated doing this.

Brianna started thinking about a few things she needed to buy like some more clothes, hair products, makeup, and so on. "Excuse me," she said to the driver. "Is there a Walmart or something close to my hotel?"

"There is a Walmart about two miles from your hotel," he replied. "Would you like me to take you there?"

"Yes, please," she answered. "If you'll wait for me, there's a nice tip in it for you."

"Yes ma'am," he replied. "No problem."

About ten minutes later they pulled into the Walmart parking lot. "Here," Brianna slipped him a twenty-dollar bill. "Go get you some lunch. I'll give you some more when I come back out." She climbed out of the car and headed in. In typical Walmart fashion, the place was packed with people. She

grabbed a cart and moved as fast as she could from section to section. As she was passing the toy section, she noticed that her friend had joined her. She smiled, knowing the God of the universe was by her side. It brought her so much peace. Immediately, she felt like she was about to be given a task. She looked over at him and he smiled at her and nodded toward a man that was standing next to a display of water guns. She sensed a feeling of hopelessness.

"Excuse me, sir," Brianna said, causing the man to startle. "I'm so sorry to bother you, but…are you okay?"

He nodded, appearing a little confused. "Why would you ask?" He looked her over, trying to figure out her angle, she guessed.

She smiled at him and chuckled. "You just seem lost, that's all." She noticed his attire. The poor man looked quite shabby. His clothes were all wrinkled and dirty. Was he homeless? His demeanor did not give off a homeless vibe. Why did the Holy Spirit point him out? Not her concern…she just needed to offer Jesus. "Is everything okay?"

"I'm fine…" Again, he looked her over. "Just looking," he said and started to walk away.

She caught his arm and he jumped. "Is there something I can pray for you about?"

"Listen, lady…Just leave me alone…okay?" He darted away.

"Jesus loves you!" she called after him and wondered if God wanted her to follow him. She said a quick prayer and headed for the health and beauty section.

Travis had walked around looking for the perfect target. After about fifteen minutes of studying the situation, he had a mark. The kid, maybe six, was with his extremely distracted dad. Probably a weekend dad that had better things to do than take his kid out and buy his love. Travis smiled. Daddy was on the phone and by the looks of it, with his girlfriend.

The kid kept wandering away to look at some new toy. After a few seconds the dad would call him back and tell him to stay close. Travis was moments away from making his move. He was only about forty feet from the exit he'd parked next to. The dad turned his back…it was now or never. Travis reached into his pocket and grabbed his rag.

"Excuse me, sir," some short, yet good looking woman had approached him. "I'm sorry to bother you, but…are you okay?" What was her deal? Was she security? Did she know what he was up to? Had she been watching him this whole time? He had let his guard down…and now he was busted! Jack was definitely going to kill him now.

"Why would you ask?" He needed to get away. She was looking him over. This lady was onto him. The creepy homeless looking man peeking around corners in the toy section. He had to get out of here without drawing more suspicions.

She smiled at him…weird. "Is everything okay?"

"I'm fine…just looking." He darted his eyes around. Was anybody else watching him? There was an old man in a suit and was that a fedora… glancing at him from across the aisle. He was busted. Time to make his escape and get out of town.

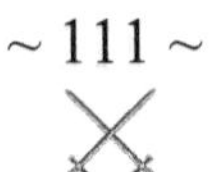

He glanced down at her one last time and attempted to move past her. She touched his elbow, and he swore he felt an electric jolt. It made him tense. He pulled away from her expecting a confrontation. Then he noticed her eyes…what was that in her eyes? Peace? Love? Definitely nothing he'd ever seen. "Is there something I can pray for you about?" WHAT!!!??? She wanted to pray for him. That's what this was??? She was just some crazy Christian trying to meet her quota?

"Listen lady, just leave me alone, okay?" He pulled away from her and headed for the exit. He fumbled with his keys trying to get in the car, dropping them twice. Why were his hands shaking so bad? He got the door open and climbed in. He dropped the keys on the floorboard and the frustration of it all made him breakdown. He just started crying. Real tears were flowing, and he wasn't even drunk.

Her eyes flashed in his mind. Her smile. The nerve of that stupid woman. Not only had she cost him a really good mark, but she'd messed with his psyche. Why was he crying? Those eyes. Such peace. Such love. What he wouldn't give for that kind of peace and love… The old gentleman beside him in the car reached over and took his hand. "Jesus loves you!" He heard her say as he'd walked away. "Jesus loves you!"

Brianna had finished her shopping and waited in the long line at the checkout. Nothing ever changed. No matter what city you were in, Walmart only ever had one register open. Of course, it gave her an opportunity to talk to this elderly black man about Jesus. He told her that he'd grown up in church but hadn't been in about twenty years. She told him that Jesus still

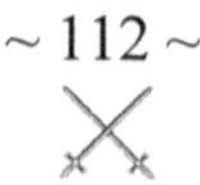

loved him and as long as he was alive, it wasn't too late to go back.

He nodded and made a few promises she hoped he'd keep. After she made it through the line, she headed outside and tried to remember what kind of car her Uber driver had been in. She was about to check her app when she heard a horn blow. She turned to see him waving at her from his car parked at the curb about thirty feet away. As she opened the door to get in, someone grabbed her by her elbow with a relatively firm grip, causing her to gasp. She turned to see the man she'd spoken to at the toy aisle. He looked terrified.

"Can we talk?" He let go of her arm and glanced around. "Please, it's important."

Brianna glanced toward the store and saw her old friend nodding to her. She set her stuff in the back seat of the car and looked at the driver. "Pick me up on that side of the store in ten minutes?" She pointed behind the car, and he nodded. "Thank you." She closed her door and proceeded to walk down the sidewalk with this man. "I'm Brianna, by the way."

He was quiet for a few seconds, and she started to wonder if maybe there was something wrong with his mind. "Travis." He kept looking around like he was maybe being followed.

"So, what can I do for you, Travis?" Brianna said, trying to sound nonchalant. She looked over at him and there were tears rolling down his cheeks. "What do you know about Jesus, Mr. Travis?"

He wiped his eyes and shrugged his shoulders. "I know I've done a lot of bad things, Ms. Brianna..." he replied

practically in a whisper. "I don't think there's any hope for a man like me with your Jesus."

She stopped walking, grabbed his arm, and turned him to face her right there in front of the T Mobile store. "Now you're just being silly, Mr. Travis. I happen to know Jesus personally and I know for a fact that He is WAY bigger than any sin you've committed."

He looked into her eyes for just a second and quickly glanced away. "I'm not so sure about that…you don't even know what I've done."

Brianna took Travis by the hand and squeezed it. "Dear Heavenly Father, I thank You for this opportunity to talk to Mr. Travis today. I pray right now that You would begin to break down the walls he has built up between You and him. That You would show him Your love for him, regardless of what he's done." Just then, an image flashed in Brianna's mind. Children being stuffed into crates. Mr. Travis being paid for delivering little girls to some very bad men. Her mind began to spin with hundreds of images of what was happening to these children.

Travis couldn't believe this. This woman was praying for him, and he could literally feel the weights being lifted off of him. The guilt, the shame, the feelings of inadequacy, the pain…all melting away. Jesus was real. There was forgiveness for his sin! Just then, she released his hand with a gasp and jumped back.

He opened his eyes to see her staring at him from about three feet away. She was panting like she'd been running. For just a second he wondered what had happened and then it hit him. "You know." Slowly she nodded, not breaking eye

contact. "I told you it was bad." After several seconds of her not replying, he asked. "So, is your Jesus still as big as you say?"

"How serious are you right now?" Brianna asked him. "Are you truly seeking forgiveness in an attempt to turn your life around or are you just looking for a way to battle your guilt?" She had bridged the distance between them in one step. All of a sudden, this short, little woman seemed to stand ten feet tall.

"I'm truly sorry for what I've done, Ms. Brianna," Travis replied. "In fact," he looked around, and leaned in to whisper in her ear, "There's a child in the back of my car right now." Her eyes got as big as saucers. "You have to understand, Ms. Brianna…I'm going to be killed when I don't deliver three little boys to a warehouse in downtown Jacksonville in about three hours. I'm not doing this because I want to…I don't have a choice anymore."

Brianna continued to stare a hole through his soul. "We always have a choice, Mr. Travis," she replied. "I'm sure, like most…you've just chosen the path with least resistance. Now, where are you parked?"

"Follow me," he replied and led her over to the side of the building that her Uber driver had already gone. "Are you going to report me?"

"Not yet," she replied. "I believe that God has placed you in my path for a reason." She peeked in the back of his Equinox and saw the little boy tied up. "My God…" She looked up at him. "Did you take him from here?"

"No," Travis replied and filled her in on how and where he'd taken the boy from.

~ 115 ~

"So, you were here to…when I approached you?" She was putting the pieces together. "You were about to grab another child."

He reached into his pocket and handed her the rag and bottle. "Seconds away…"

She took them and walked over and tossed them in a nearby trashcan. She walked back over to him. "So, you're serious about leaving this life?" He nodded. "And Jesus?"

"I want the peace and love that I saw in your eyes," he replied. "Even if it means I have to go to prison for the rest of my life. And what I told you was kind of a lie...well, sort of. I started off doing this because the man paying me was helping me to get out of some serious gambling debts...now, I just want out. It's sick."

She stared at him for several seconds, and then held out her hands. "Then take my hands and repeat after me, Mr. Travis...you're about to meet peace and love like you never imagined."

CHAPTER 13

JACKSONVILLE, FLORIDA

After praying the prayer of salvation, Brianna had Travis wipe down his prints in the car. They saw that there were surveillance cameras in the area and moved the car over to an abandoned parking lot next to Walmart. Brianna told Travis to make himself scarce and she opened the back of the car. She woke up the little boy in the back. He sat up all groggy and Brianna helped him out of the car. She hugged him and told him that everything was going to be okay. She led him over to Walmart and called 911 as they walked.

"911, what's your emergency?" the dispatcher asked.

"Yes, I seem to have found an abandoned child at the Walmart near the Jacksonville Airport."

"Ma'am is the child with you now?" the dispatcher asked.

"Yes, he's an adorable little blonde boy named Kyle Nichols…and he seems to have been separated from his mother."

"I'm sorry, ma'am, did you say Kyle Nichols?"

"Yes, I did," Brianna said in a sweet, motherly tone. "And he is being a perfect gentleman."

"Ma'am, I have officers in route now, where exactly, at the airport Walmart, are you at?" She sounded quite excited.

"We are outside near the garden center," Brianna replied. "Has Kyle's disappearance been reported, by chance?"

"Oh, yes ma'am, it seems that our little Kyle Nichols was reported missing about an hour ago. He was apparently abducted from a Family Dollar about seven miles away from where you are now."

"Oh…I see the police cars now," Brianna said. "Look, Kyle! Those policemen are going to help you get back with your mommy!"

"Ma'am," the dispatcher said. "The number you're calling from comes up without identification…can I get your name?"

"The police are pulling up now," Brianna said. "Thank you for your help!" She clicked off the call, not wanting to have either of her names involved in this. She led Kyle over toward the police cars as they pulled up. "I'm going to need your help getting out of this, Holy Spirit," she whispered under her breath.

There were about six police cars in all, that pulled up and blocked off that end of the Walmart parking lot. The officers climbed out of their cars and emerged on her and Kyle. "Hello, ma'am," the first officer that walked up said, smiling at Brianna. A female officer, put her arm around Kyle and led him over to a Rescue Squad that had pulled up behind where Brianna was standing. She hadn't even noticed it. "I'm Sergeant Moore with the Jacksonville Sheriff's Office. If you don't mind stepping over here and giving us a statement real quick. Can I ask where you found our little friend?"

"Yeah, he was in the back of a car over there behind that old…what is that…an old Payless?"

The sergeant motioned for one of his officers to go check it out. "Can I ask what you were doing over there?"

~ 118 ~

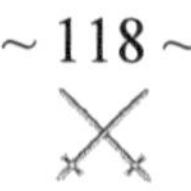

"What do you mean?" Brianna asked.

"I mean, it's over there away from everything else. I'm trying to figure out why a young lady like yourself was over there behind the building where this child just happened to be."

"I'm sorry, are you accusing me of something?" Brianna asked in as offended a voice as she could muster. "I'm the one who called this in, thank you very much!"

"OH, JESUS!!!" a woman screamed as she jumped out of a police car that had just pulled up. "KYLE, MY BABY!!!" She ran toward her son and embraced him right there in the back of the Rescue Squad. She was bawling and holding him tight. The whole scene had gained the attention of everyone involved.

"Ma'am, I just need you to…" Sergeant Moore started to say as he turned back to Brianna…who was nowhere to be seen. "HEY!" he called out. "Where did she go!? The lady that found the kid!? Did anybody see her leave!?" Everyone looked around, but nobody saw her.

Brianna made her way as fast as she could through Walmart, having ducked into the garden center and high tailed it into the store as fast as she could without attracting attention. She could not risk having her name or picture out there right now. She had no idea who was looking for her. Brianna found Travis standing in the grocery section and they slid out the front door where her Uber driver was waiting. She slipped him a fifty and told him to take her to her original destination.

"Did you see all the police?" Her driver asked.

"Yeah, I wonder what that was all about?"

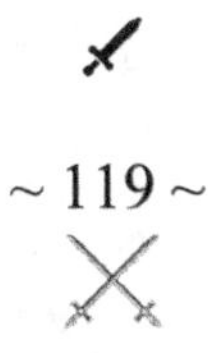

PENSACOLA, FLORIDA

As Jonah crossed over Escambia Bay in Pensacola, he decided to turn off his Spotify playlist that had been playing Imagine Dragons, Cold Play, and Twenty-One Pilots for the last eight hours. He tried to find something on the radio that might help him to stay awake. He decided to press on to Hilliard without stopping at another hotel. He had stopped in Houston and gone to one of the local branches of his bank and withdrawn enough cash to survive for several weeks on the run. It seemed like country music and rap/hip hop were his choices. Just as he was about to give up, he caught the middle of a news story.

"It's definitely a tragedy, this plane going down in Missouri and taking the lives of an entire company…I mean, no survivors. Our sources tell us that literally every employee of Maitland Construction was onboard that private plane. Apparently being taken from their home city of Denver, Colorado to a job site in Lexington, Kentucky, where they were going to be working on a project of building inner city homes."

"That's right, David," another reporter said. "But here's where it gets weird. Apparently, the families of this construction team are saying they had already finished their job at an undisclosed location and were supposed to be heading back to Colorado at the very time they were leaving Colorado. Now, from what I've gathered, Maitland Construction had been given a private contract months ago, to do a job, off record, for some rich tycoon. Probably a love nest or something for some elite. Anyway, their spouses and families were told that each employee had to sign an agreement not to disclose the site's whereabouts…to anyone."

"Well, then they all end up getting in a plane crash after they're supposedly done?" the first guy asked. "This has conspiracy written all over it, as I'm sure investigators will be all over it, as well. We need to take a commercial break, folks! We'll be right…"

Jonah clicked off his radio as his head began to spin. Conspiracy indeed. What in the world was going on? He needed to contact someone and tell his story before he, like his coworkers, was silenced. His phone chirped beside him with a text. It was his sister…"Jonah, what's going on?" Just as Jonah went to pull over to respond, his phone rang. "What's up, Sis?" He tried to sound nonchalant.

"Jonah, what in the world is going on?" His sister sounded panicked. "The police are here at the hospital. They're saying you think you're being hunted?"

"The less you know, Sis," Jonah was not getting her into this. "Please, just be careful and take care of Mom and Dad."

"What about your crew, Jonah!? They're all dead! Jonah, I'm worried about you!"

"Jaclyn, listen to me!" Jonah said, in as firm a tone as he could muster without sounding mad. "My crew is dead because they knew too much. I'm being hunted because I know what they knew…so you do not need to be talking to me right now! Do you understand?"

There was silence for several seconds. "Yes…yes, of course…it's just…"

"Jaclyn…I love you…I need to know that you're good. I need to know that Mom and Dad are good. I'm going into

hiding for a few weeks until I can figure out how to handle this. That's all you get to know. Don't contact me again, okay?"

"Okay, Jonah…I love you too. Please be careful!" She sounded as if she were on board with the plan, but also on the verge of a breakdown.

"Great," Jonah replied. "As soon as this is over, I will contact you." He clicked off the call and decided right then to stop at the next town he came to and buy a burner phone…wasn't that what they called them in the movies? That's when he saw it…about four cars back…it looked like the same white van that he'd seen at the hotel.

Panicked, he looked up to see that an exit was coming up for Defuniak Springs. He'd never heard of it, but he would need to get off there and try and lose this guy. No way could he lead him all the way to Hilliard. At the last possible second, he swerved to take the exit and saw that the van's blinker came on. Left would take him into Defuniak Springs and right would take him south toward Freeport and the Gulf of Mexico.

"I've never seen the gulf, let's try right," he said to himself. He turned right and sped up as fast as he could without attracting attention from law enforcement. The van also turned right. "Great, no way this is a coincidence." Just to be sure, though, he did a quick U-turn and headed north. When he stopped at the light, he noticed the van continued south.

"Okay, I'm just paranoid…thank God." He got over and proceeded back onto Interstate 10 heading east. "Better safe than sorry!" Jonah yelled out, reaching over to turn his music back on.

JACKSONVILLE, FLORIDA

Brianna paid for a room for Travis that was right down the hall from hers. She then led him to the gift shop and helped him get a t-shirt and a pair of cargo shorts that were both way overpriced. They walked out and found a secluded place to talk by the pool. She held out her phone for him to see a picture she'd pulled up. "Did you take this girl?" He looked at the screen and she saw his face register recognition. He looked away. "I'll take that as a yes."

"Chinese restaurant in Jacksonville," he said, his head now in his hands on the table.

"Look at me, Travis," Brianna said in a stern voice. He looked up at her with utter shame on his face. "There will be time for regretting your stupid decisions later...right now we have to find this girl!"

"WHAT!?" Travis replied with horror in his eyes. "That's impossible! I have no idea where they took those girls! They could be halfway to Tokyo for all I know!"

"Well, YOU may not know, but I guarantee you know someone who does."

"Brianna, I can't contact these people!" Travis replied. "They're going to be looking for me...to kill me!" He got up and paced by the pool. "There was this guy...my boss's boss...his name was Joshua!" He turned back to Brianna. "We were on a video call with him, and he was at this new place they'd just built to house the girls!"

"Perfect!" Brianna was getting excited now. "Where was it?"

"I have no idea," Travis answered and saw her disappointment. "They didn't trust me with that information…in fact, Joshua killed the entire construction crew right in front of me…on the video. He had them all gunned down while they posed for a picture." He sat back down and twitched nervously. "It was the most horrible thing I'd ever witnessed in my life. I can't cross these guys, Brianna. They'll be onto me…I'll be dead for sure."

"That's why we need to act fast, before they get suspicious. You still have time before you're supposed to be delivering those boys." Just then her phone started ringing and she saw that it was Nadia. She held up a finger for Travis to give her a second. "Nadia!"

"Brianna?" came the reply.

"Yeah, are you okay, you sound diff…" The caller hung up and Brianna's heart sunk. Not only was that not Nadia, but she had answered to the name Brianna and now they were onto her…and that also meant that Nadia was either captured or dead. Brianna stood up quickly and dropped her phone like it was on fire.

Travis looked up. "Everything okay?"

"I don't know what to do," Brianna said. Did they know where she was? Was she okay to keep using the credit card that Nadia had given her? Her phone…was she compromised?

"What's going on?" Travis asked.

"Um, some very important and powerful people want me dead…and I'm pretty sure they just found me."

~ 124 ~

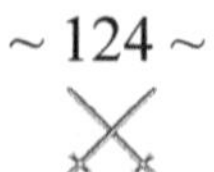

CHAPTER 14

LIVE OAK, FLORIDA

The fact that it had been almost 2 days since Jonah had slept, was starting to catch up with him. He'd caught himself nodding off several times already. Presently, he was driving down Interstate 10 with his front windows down and his radio blasting some One Republic. The sun was getting low in the sky behind him, and he was only an hour and a half from his destination. He had both hands on the steering wheel and was doing his best to keep focused on the road.

"I've been dreamin' bout the West Coast…I've been dreamin'!" He was singing along with the band, and quite well he might add, when he got that strange feeling that someone was watching him. He glanced over to the left and that's when he noticed the white van…right beside him…window down…was that a…he saw the muzzle flash before he heard the boom of the gun.

Jonah swerved into the emergency lane and stomped on the brake. His rental car slid to an abrupt stop, sliding slightly on the loose gravel. He quickly looked down at himself to make sure he hadn't been hit. He seemed okay but wasn't sure how he'd not been shot.

Looking up, he saw that the van had also pulled onto the emergency lane and was in the process of backing up toward him, quite fast. Jonah threw it in reverse and punched the gas, causing the tires to spin, and then the car lunged backwards. Cars and semi-trucks were speeding by as he and the van raced backwards in the emergency lane. Jonah was turned around in his seat, looking out the back window as he drove.

At the first opening that he saw in traffic, he made a quick turn across the two lanes of Interstate 10 and into the median, where he slammed on brakes, came to a stop, and slid it into drive. Turning the steering wheel hard, he pressed the gas and just missed the van's bumper as it crossed over right in front of him. Spinning dirt and grass high into the air, Jonah's car bounced across the median ditch and shot right into traffic heading in the opposite direction from where he'd been going.

He looked back and saw that the van was having difficulty getting onto the expressway. Just up ahead he knew there was an exit for Live Oak he'd recently passed. He punched it as hard as the little car would go and lost sight of the van.

Pulling off the interstate, he noticed a large truck stop to the right. It appeared to be one of those touristy stops where people could shop for clothes or choose from several restaurants. The parking lot was full of cars, making it the perfect place to go when someone was chasing you with a gun.

As he pulled in, he scanned the interstate exit, looking for the white van. After several seconds, he noticed it parked on the overpass. Were they just waiting to see what he was going to do? He didn't know the area so he couldn't just try and make a getaway. That's when he noticed a police car parked near the front door.

He pulled up behind it, but it didn't appear that anyone was inside. He glanced back up at the overpass and the van was driving away. He pulled over to the curb and checked the maps on his phone, realizing that if he took this road north, he would run into Interstate 75, which he could take south and get right back on Interstate 10.

~ 126 ~

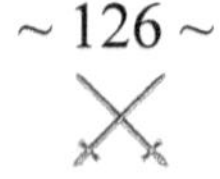

After a quick bathroom break and the purchase of a burner phone, Jonah texted a few important numbers to himself and tossed his old phone in a trash can. He pulled onto the road and high tailed it as fast as he could, checking his rear-view mirror for that van. He slid both of his windows up, no longer needing any help staying awake.

JACKSONVILLE, FLORIDA

Brianna had told Travis to go to his room and find a comfortable place to sit and pray. She was going to do the same thing and come get him when she had answers. Forgetting comfort, though, she knelt next to her bed and cried out to God. He already knew her situation, of course, but He liked it when His people included Him in their lives.

Brianna tried to live her life to include Him in everything she did. Of course, it didn't always work out that way, but it was always the goal. She prayed for Nadia, hoping with everything within her that she was still alive. She knelt there praying for over an hour until her knees began to hurt. Standing up, she started to sit on the bed when her phone rang. Nadia's phone again. Her heart lurched as she watched Nadia's name lit up.

"It's okay, answer it." He was there with her. Her old friend…a tear rolled down her cheek as the peace He offered with His presence poured over her. He sat down on the bed next to her and put an arm around her.

"Hello?" There was a long pause of deafening silence. "Hel…"

"Hello, Brianna," came the voice of what sounded like a German man. "My name is…"

"Is Nadia still alive!?" She'd just blurted it out, not caring about anything else right now.

"Yes, for now."

"Give me proof…I want to…"

"Brianna!" It was Nadia. "They're coming for….!" The phone went silent.

"Nadia!" Brianna screamed. "Are you okay!? Nadia!?"

"She's alive!" the man said, sounding quite annoyed at this point. "And she will stay that way as long as you do what I tell you!" Brianna could hear something going on in the background, like a struggle. "Can't you control a bound woman!?" The man shouted in a muffled voice. He'd apparently attempted to cover the phone with his hand. "Dear God! She's kicking your…."

"Brianna! They're going after your family! SAVE YOUR FAMILY, BRI…!!!" Nadia had yelled before the phone went dead.

Brianna jumped from the bed and gathered all her things. She left the room, ran down the hall, and banged on Travis' door.

"Jonah," the Holy Spirit whispered in her ear.

"Huh?" Brianna was clearly confused. Jonah? Her mind began replaying the story of Jonah from the Bible. Prophet called to deliver a message of repentance to a vile nation. Was she supposed to tell these people to repent? He didn't want to

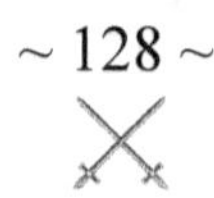

do what God asked so he fled the country. Was she supposed to have done something specific for God before she'd come back to the states?

He was thrown from a ship that was in the middle of the storm in order to save those on board. She was definitely in the middle of a storm. He was swallowed by a great fish and remained there until he came to terms with God's mission for his life. "What are you saying, Holy Spirit?" Silence.

She banged on the door again. Where was Travis? The sick feeling of Travis running away in fear slammed into her chest. What would she do without his ability to contact the people behind the scenes? Just then the door swung open and there he stood with a towel wrapped around his waist.

"Are you okay!?" he seemed clearly concerned.

"Get dressed and meet me in the lobby! They're going after my family! We have to get to Gateway!"

"They called you!?"

"Yes, just get ready…and hurry!"

"Brianna!" he called to her as she quickly made her way to the elevator.

"Hurry, Travis, my fam…"

"Brianna!!!" She turned and gave him a glaring look for not rushing. "We don't have a car."

HILLIARD, FLORIDA

Jonah found the address that Paul had given him, and it was as secluded as promised. He turned onto the long dirt driveway that led him into the woods. It was pitch dark outside and the tree cover didn't help. He drove through several deep ruts and wound his car around a few sharp curves until he finally came out of the thick forest of trees.

There was an open area in front of him with a double wide trailer to his right. It appeared that he was on the back side of the trailer, so he drove around to the front. There was a small carport attached to the side of the trailer. He parked in front of the front door, leaving his headlights on so he could search for the key. He walked around checking under the twenty or so dead potted plants.

Finally, of course, the last one he looked under had a key taped to the bottom. He walked over and opened the front door. He reached inside and clicked the light switch…nothing. Taking out his cell phone, he turned on the flashlight feature. Shining it up to the ceiling, he saw that there wasn't even a light fixture. He walked inside. There was absolutely no furniture in what appeared to be the living room and dining room.

He walked around the corner and let out a heavy sigh. The kitchen…or whatever you wanted to call it, was gutted. Not only was there no refrigerator or stove, but there were also no cabinets or sink or anything. Just a few pipes sticking out of the walls and what appeared to be a baby doll's head in the corner. "Perfect," Jonah muttered to himself.

Back in his car, he checked his cell phone and found that he had no service. He put his car in gear and headed back into town. He'd seen a Wendy's restaurant a few miles up the road.

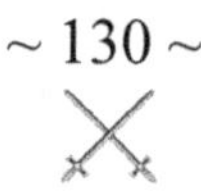

He'd go there and see if he could find a hotel. His lack of sleep was starting to hit.

Twenty minutes later, after learning that there were no working hotels in Hilliard, he headed for the next town over. The girl behind the counter had said it had a few small hotels and even a grocery store where he could pick up some supplies. He desperately needed a few personal hygiene items. A beer or twenty wouldn't hurt either. "Is this day ever going to end?" He sighed and laid his head back in his seat.

He had no idea the chain of events that were about to take place that would forever change the course of his life. He also had no idea that there was an older gentleman in a gray suit and a fedora sitting next to him. The only thing Jonah Westbrook was sure about was…he needed to pick up supplies…he needed to sleep…he needed to get to this town…what had she called it? Oh yeah…Gateway.

JACKSONVILLE, FLORIDA

Brianna had been pacing in the lobby while she waited for Travis. She had ordered an Uber but didn't feel like that was the way she wanted to arrive in Gateway to tell her family they needed to go into hiding. She looked around and didn't see her old friend but knew that didn't mean He wasn't right here with her. "Holy Spirit, I sure could use some help in getting to Gateway," she whispered under her breath.

"Did you find us a ride?" Travis asked as he descended the stairs. "Because I have skills that would allow us to commandeer any vehicle you want."

~ 131 ~

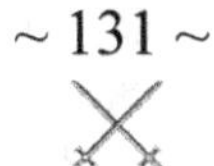

"Travis, you can't do those things anymore," Brianna said.

"Whoa!" Travis exclaimed and took a step back. "Popo alert!" He stepped behind Brianna to hide himself as a police officer walked in the front door.

"Travis, what are you…oh," she looked over and saw the officer heading for the front desk. He said something to the lady, and she nodded toward Brianna and Travis. "Uh oh…get ready to run, I don't have time for this." The officer turned around and looked right at Brianna and her heart soared. "Officer Ramsey!?" It was Matt Ramsey's dad.

Matt was one of the old Gateway gang…in fact, he was the drummer in Gabi's worship band. His dad used to be a police officer in Gateway, but he was presently in a Jacksonville Sheriff's Office uniform. "Oh, my goodness!" She saw the recognition register on his face as he approached.

"Brianna Bowers, as I live and breathe!" He gave her a big hug. He glanced at Travis…"Is it still Bowers?"

She nodded with a big smile. "This is my friend, Travis, and boy are you a sight for sore eyes. We need to…"

Officer Ramsey held up his hand and glanced between the two of them. "Hold on a second, I'm doing some mathematics…you're involved in that ministry that fights human trafficking, aren't you?" She nodded. "And that WAS you at the Walmart earlier, wasn't it?"

"Officer Ramsey, I can explain." She pulled him over away from the prying ears of the woman who'd apparently seen her on the news and called the cops. "Is my picture on the news or something?"

"A rendering the officer gave…and I knew she looked familiar. Brianna, what's going on?"

"Without getting you in too deep…we're on the run, Travis and I. Some very powerful people want us dead because of what we know about a child trafficking ring. I just found out that my family is in danger, and I need to get to Gateway as fast as possible."

"Have you called them?" Officer Ramsey asked.

"No, you've met my mother," Brianna said. "It will be so much easier telling her all this in person. Listen, we don't have a car, can you help us…and maybe not report that you found us?"

He let out a big sigh and got on his radio. "Dispatch this is Lieutenant Ramsey, I'm needing to give a piggy-back to Gateway…911. Over."

"10-4 Lieutenant Ramsey," an older sounding woman responded.

"Let's go!" He led them out to his squad car and Brianna got up front while Travis climbed reluctantly into the back. "Hold on!" He sped quickly out of the parking lot, causing Travis to hit his head on the door window.

"So, LIEUTENANT? I'm impressed!" Brianna said.

"Yeah, Jacksonville offered bigger opportunities," he replied. "We still live in Gateway, though…So, these powerful people…anybody I might know?"

"I don't know much about how far this reaches, but I'm pretty sure the head of Interpol is part of it."

"Oh wow! That IS big! He's involved in trafficking?"

Brianna nodded and looked back at Travis, who looked like he was going to be sick. "Travis, I believe you have a phone call to make."

"What!? Right now!?" His face appeared to turn green.

"Just be getting ready…pray about what you need to say." Grabbing her phone, she quickly canceled the Uber and left him a tip.

Officer Ramsey got out on the main road and floored it. "We'll be in Gateway in about five minutes!"

Brianna thought of how her parents would take this news. Having to go into hiding would probably be exciting for her father, but her mom…this was going to be interesting. "Going to need your help, Holy Spirit!"

"Jonah…" was His only reply.

CHAPTER 15

Jonah couldn't believe what he was seeing at this place. It looked like someone had tried to restore one of the old-fashioned one-story motels on the main strip in Gateway and given up about halfway through their renovations. The swimming pool was about a quarter full and whatever liquid was in it appeared to be brown…ish. Part of the roof was covered with a tarp that was held in place by cinder blocks.

It appeared that several people lived there but the owner said they had a few rooms available. It was a little scary, but Jonah needed sleep and apparently it was "the only hotel west of Jacksonville", according to the owner's wife. He got his key and checked out the room. Bed, bathroom, running water, window unit air conditioner…extremely strong musty smell. He turned the air on high and left for supplies. Beer…he needed lots of beer.

As Lieutenant Ramsey drove toward Gateway, Brianna was remembering her parents telling her they were going to move to Gateway. It was during the whole dragon incident thing. She'd been so excited to move back to where her best friend, Gabi, was. They'd even managed to get a brand-new house right next to Mark's family.

The house that had been on that property before had burnt down and a poor old woman had perished in the fire. That had happened right before their big summer camp trip where they'd been in a bad accident and lost some friends. The memories just came flooding in as Brianna thought back to all

the fun they had growing up in that neighborhood. Scotty had asked Gabi out on their first date at the cul-de-sac near where the Snyder's lived. Mark had asked Maria to the prom on his front porch when she'd come over to hang out with the gang. She'd had such a huge crush on him. They had all pitched in along with Mr. Bret and Pastor Brian and rebuilt the tree house at the Mumpower's place...in a different tree, of course.

They'd each raised money together through car washes and garage sales in order to save for college. Mark had proposed to Maria at a pool party at the Snyder's house. There wasn't a dry eye in the house when he told her that he wanted to slay dragons with her for the rest of their lives. Scotty had…

Travis' phone rang. "Oh no…it's Tony…oh no…"

"Who's Tony?" Lieutenant Ramsey asked.

"The guy who's after ME," Travis replied.

"So, there's somebody different after each of you?"

"Somewhat," Brianna answered. "They're all on the same team though…so to speak."

Travis had let it go to voicemail and saw that Tony had indeed left a message. His stomach tightened up as he hit the button to play the message and put his phone to his ear. "Hello, Travis…it's Tony. I wish you were doing what I told you to do and on your way to the meeting point with the three packages you were supposed to pick up and deliver in about twenty minutes…however…for some reason…you're in the back of a police car…by choice…heading out of town.

Not sure what's going on, Travis, but you'll be dead very soon and it won't matter." Travis jumped and looked

behind them…nobody was following. "They're onto me, Brianna…they know I'm in this car…I don't know how, but they know!"

"Nobody is following us," Lt. Ramsey said. "Who exactly is that?"

"These guys…" Travis was freaking out. "I work for them…or I did work for them, until a few hours ago."

"And what exactly did you do for them?" Lt. Ramsey was watching Travis squirm in the mirror. He looked at Brianna. "Talk to me, Brianna. Maybe I can help you guys."

"I'm sorry, Mr. Ramsey, but I've already lost one friend to this mess…I'm not pulling you in any further. You're doing enough just giving us a ride."

"How do they know where I am!?" Travis kept twitching and looking out the back window.

"Take off your shoes," Brianna said. She saw his confused look… "DO IT!!!"

He quickly obeyed, sliding his tennis shoes off. "Why am I doing this?"

"Because they're the only article of clothing we didn't replace…you probably have a tracker. Check between the laces and the tongue."

Travis slid his finger between the laces and froze. He pulled out a small square disc and held it up. "When did he…they were by the door…they know where I am."

"Throw it out the window!!!" Brianna yelled.

"But that doesn't explain how they know I'm in a police car!" Travis said as he tossed it out the window.

Lt. Ramsey slowed down to make a right turn. "They were probably watching you at the hotel and knew better than to follow a police car too close. They're probably about five minutes behind us." He sped up on the back country road and quickly made another right turn. He watched the rear-view mirror and saw that nobody was following them.

Within minutes they were in Brianna's parent's neighborhood and slowing down in front of their house. Brianna jumped out and ran up to the front door. She had her speech planned out as she rang the doorbell and waited. After a few seconds, she rang it again…nothing.

"Excuse me!?" A woman's voice made her jump. "They aren't home!"

Brianna walked over to the side of the porch and smiled. "Hello, Mrs. Gilmore." It was Mark's mom.

"BRIANNA!!!" She ran over and gave Brianna a huge hug and held her for several seconds. "It's sooo good to see you, sweetheart…oh my goodness, look at you…YOU are so beautiful!"

"Do you know where my parents are?" Brianna asked, with a big smile, attempting to ignore the compliment.

"If I know them, on a Thursday night, they went to The Pig Barbecue and then shopping at the Winn Dixie!" She laughed and smiled really big at Brianna. "They obviously don't know you're here, do they? Your mother would have told me for sure! Is that Officer Ramsey? How in the world did you get HIM to give you a ride…so awesome!"

"No ma'am, they don't..." she looked Mrs. Gilmore over and weighed whether to say something. She glanced at the squad car. "This is not a pleasure visit...I'm kind of on the run from some bad people...and they're threatening my family." Her eyes teared up and Mrs. Gilmore gave her a sympathy smile. "Please, go inside your house and keep watch of theirs...if you see anyone suspicious..."

"I'll call Gateway's finest, baby...go get your parents!" Mrs. Gilmore gave her a goodbye hug and pushed her toward the police car. She waved to Officer Ramsey, "I'll be praying for you, Brianna!"

Brianna jumped in the car. "They're at Winn Dixie!" Officer Ramsey quickly turned the car around and headed that way.

"Jonah," came the voice of the Holy Spirit in her ear again.

She closed her eyes and quietly asked her old friend what He was trying to tell her. It had to be important, since he'd said it so many times...and in the midst of a serious trial. She tried to remember every single detail about the book of Jonah that she could, but nothing significant was coming to her.

Within three minutes they were pulling into the Winn Dixie parking lot. "Okay, you guys stay in the car...I don't want to have to explain so many things at once. I will be back in a few minutes. Lieutenant, is there anywhere you can think of that I can safely hide my parents?"

"They're welcome to come stay at our house for a few days. I mean, we're only a few miles away, but nobody would..." Brianna gave him a big hug.

"Thank you," she cried into his shoulder. "That would be amazing." She reached for the handle and opened the door. "Please help me, Holy Spirit. I need Your guidance and protection." She headed inside the grocery store. She was so focused on the task at hand that she failed to hear the Holy Spirit trying to warn her about the car pulling into the parking lot at that very moment. They had seen the cop car go by as they were looking for the tracker in the ditch where Travis had thrown it.

She entered the store and looked around for any sign of her parents' whereabouts. Not seeing them, she decided to start on the left side and work right, knowing she couldn't miss them, as that was the opposite way they shopped. As she passed the middle of the store, she spotted them in isle 8 arguing over what kind of pasta to make for the Motes on Monday night. "Larry's favorite is spaghetti and Gae's is Lasagna!" She watched it register on both of their faces as she approached.

"Oh, my Jesus!!! BRIANNA!!!" her mother screamed. She burst into tears and grabbed her daughter into a massive bear hug. Her father wrapped his arms around both of them and silently cried.

"My baby is home," he whispered in her ear, and it made her smile.

"How did you know we were here!?" her mother asked. "How long have you been in town?"

"How long are you here for, Baby Girl?" her father added.

"Listen, guys, there's something I need to tell you," she backed away and held up her hands. "Listen to me!" They went silent and glanced at each other, having seen the seriousness on

~ 140 ~

her face. "You're not safe," she said and watched their reactions.

"What are you talking about Bree?" her mother asked. "What's going on?"

"Mom, some very bad people are after me and they have threatened to hurt you and Daddy if I don't turn myself over to them."

"Who, Baby?" her father asked, looking around. "I've got my gun." He patted his side to reveal that he was carrying his pistol.

"That's good, Daddy, but do you guys remember Officer Ramsey?"

"Of course, we do, he goes to our church, Sweetie," her mother replied. "We see him all the time...why do you ask?"

"Well, he's outside and he's agreed to let you guys stay with him for a few days until this whole thing blows over."

"Nonsense," her father said. "I can keep us safe."

"Daddy, please do this for me. I need to know you're good so I can focus on catching the bad guys."

"Since when are you chasing bad guys, Bree?" Her mother was starting to panic. "My baby, I knew this whole child trafficking thing was too dangerous."

That's when Brianna felt the familiar nudge from the Holy Spirit and a chill ran down her spine. She looked just behind her mother about ten feet back. A man was standing in front of the macaroni and cheese…and he was glancing over his shoulder at them. She looked just past him, and another man

was waiting at the end of the aisle. Turning slowly as her mother went on about how dangerous Brianna's world traveling job was, she noticed man number three at the other end of their aisle. There was no way out. "Daddy," she whispered, as her mother kept talking. Her father looked at her. "Is your gun ready to fire?" she asked, leaning in close to him.

He saw the look of concern on her face and looked past her to the man at the end of the aisle. "Is that him?"

She nodded. "There's two more behind you. Please don't do anything stupid, Daddy…if anything happens to you or mom…"

Just then, a burst of gunfire erupted from somewhere in the store. People began screaming, ducking, and running. It sounded like an automatic rifle or something and even the men watching Brianna were caught by surprise. She saw one of them withdraw a large pistol and take off running across the back of the store.

She noticed that all three of them were distracted and grabbed her mother's arm. "Let's go!" More bursts of gunfire from somewhere near the frozen food section. Her father had his gun out but stayed close to them as they, along with many others, made their way out of the store.

"Brianna!!!" It was Officer Ramsey, gun drawn, standing there guiding people to safety. "Backup is coming! What's the situation?"

Brianna shrugged. "I saw the guys that were after ME, but then somebody else started shooting…I have no idea what's going on!" That's when the Holy Spirit nudged her again and she looked past Officer Ramsey to see a dark blue car, with its

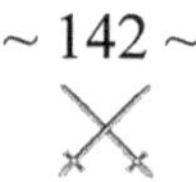

lights off, pull up beside the squad car and the window began to roll down. The barrel of a gun slid out. "OFFICER RAMSEY!!!" Brianna screamed and pointed at his car as an explosion of shots unloaded on the passenger side. "TRAVIS!!!!" Brianna took off running in that direction and Officer Ramsey grabbed her arm and slung her to the ground.

He began firing his weapon at the car with the gunmen. When Brianna looked up, it was squealing away. She saw two Gateway police officers take pursuit. She ran behind Officer Ramsey as he went to check on Travis. "Please be alive, please be alive!" Brianna said as she approached the car, and he opened the back door. The whole side of the car was full of holes, the windows were blown out, and even the window on the other side was busted out…Officer Ramsey held up his hand to stop Brianna. He shut the door and walked toward her.

"Trust me, you don't want to see that," Officer Ramsey said. "I'm so sorry, Brianna." Several other officers approached and looked inside. One of them made a call on his radio.

Brianna's world began to spin, and her legs gave out. Officer Ramsey tried to catch her before she dropped to the ground. Not Travis…what would she do now? He was literally her only link to finding the girl. She caught herself being insensitive for only being upset because of his usefulness and not for the fact that he'd just died. At least he'd given his heart to Jesus, she thought. He was in a better place. She heard a commotion behind her and glanced back to see several Gateway police officers storm the grocery store. People were being pushed back and encouraged to leave.

"Jonah," the Holy Spirit whispered in her ear again.

"Seriously, what are you trying to tell me, Holy Spirit?" He was silent again. Her parents came over and helped her up. Her mother pulled her close, Brianna could hear her praying.

Lt. Ramsey went over to help with the situation and Brianna and her parents walked over toward her parents' car. That's when she saw the three men that had been watching her. They were standing about three rows of cars away near a black SUV looking right at Brianna. Just then her cell phone rang. Without looking at the screen, she pulled it out of her purse and answered it. "Hello?" She kept her eyes on the men.

"Hello, Brianna Bowers," said the familiar German voice. She tensed up and glanced at her parents. They were watching the activity at Winn Dixie. "In about thirty seconds, my men are going to walk over and put a bullet into the heads of both of your parents. Then they are going to take you…and…let's just say, a pretty American woman like you, will sell for a nice price to one of my customers." He laughed what Brianna thought was the most evil laugh she'd ever heard. "Now, if you can just walk to them and surrender yourself right now, everybody else will get to go home safely. You have about ten seconds to decide."

"Okay," she replied without thought. "If you promise to leave my parents alone, I'll go with your men."

"Five seconds," he replied and hung up the call.

She kissed her father on the cheek, reached inside his hidden holster, and removed his 9mm. "Thanks for all the gun training, Daddy." Her father didn't even flinch as Brianna slid the pistol into her purse and headed across the parking lot. She looked back to see her parents were holding hands and praying.

Just as she was about fifteen feet away from the awaiting three men…

"Excuse me, Gentlemen!" It was Lt. Ramsey, walking toward them. Brianna stopped in her tracks. "If you don't have any business here, I'm going to ask you to leave!" He stopped as they looked at each other and then they each glanced at Brianna who stood smiling at them. "NOW!" They got in their SUV, staring hard at Brianna, and left the parking lot. "Brianna!" he yelled to her and motioned for her to follow him.

Brianna caught up to Lt. Ramsey as he headed to the front of the store. "So, what happened?" she asked.

"Two men opened fire on some guy over in frozen foods," he replied. "They escaped out the back before officers even got in the store."

"And the guy they were shooting at? Is he okay?"

"Yes," he said, pointing to a man sitting in the back of the rescue squad. "He's got some big story about these guys chasing him across the country…all the way from California. He even said they killed a detective in San Diego. Officers are checking his story out now. Does he look familiar to you, could he be someone involved in your story?"

Brianna's first thought when she saw the man was that he was one of the best-looking men she'd ever seen. She'd never been one to stare at someone in lust, but this guy was ruggedly handsome in a Hallmark movie kind of way, and his hair was…pull it together, Bree. She shook her head. "He doesn't look familiar…but it IS quite coincidental that all this went down at the same time," she replied. "What's his name?"

He checked his notepad. "Jonah…Jonah Westbrook."

CHAPTER 16

GATEWAY, FLORIDA

Lieutenant Ramsey had been asked to be in on the questioning of Jonah Westbrook, so Brianna was allowed to sit in the viewing room while he was being interrogated. He was taller than he'd originally looked, she noted, as they brought him in. He wore blue jeans, a light blue t-shirt that read "Whatever You Do, Don't Say Cali", and a pair of work boots that looked like they had a few years behind them. He was quite tan, lean in a muscular way, and his hair was light brown with a part on the left side. He smiled at the officers when they asked him to have a seat and Brianna had to say a prayer to keep her focus. "What are you doing to me, Holy Spirit?"

"Mr. Westbrook, I'm Captain Butler and this is Lieutenant Ramsey helping us out from the Jacksonville Sheriff's Office. This interview is being recorded, so please refrain from any head nods or shakes…a verbal response will be necessary. Do you understand?"

"Yes, sir," Jonah replied, leaning in toward the microphone.

"That isn't necessary, Mr. Westbrook."

"Please, call me Jonah," he replied, glancing at the two-way mirror. Brianna's heart rate quickened because she thought he was looking at her for just a second.

"Alright, Jonah," Captain Butler said. "Now, for the purpose of this recording, please tell us the events that led up to this evening's…situation."

"Starting?" Jonah asked for clarification.

"At the beginning…I believe you said this all began in California."

"Yes," Jonah nodded. "I was in California because my father had a heart attack. I currently live in Colorado."

Brianna imagined him living in a small log cabin in the middle of some Colorado forest, sitting by a roaring fire, drinking a mug of coffee and reading an adventurous novel with his German Shepherd sitting at his feet…or was that a wolf? "Girl!" she whispered to herself. "This man is either married or has a girlfriend, there is no way he is single."

"So, I was spending the night at my parent's house alone…my mother stayed at the hospital with my dad. At some point in the middle of the night I got up to use the restroom and heard a noise downstairs."

If he had a girlfriend or a wife, why was he staying at his parent's house by himself? Of course, if he was a Christian, he wouldn't be staying with a girlfriend, but this could definitely be a sign that he wasn't married. That and the fact that he wasn't wearing a ring.

"Is everything alright?" her old friend asked, as he pulled up a chair beside her and removed his fedora. Brianna blushed a bright red and looked away. "I thought you could use my company."

"I'll say…" she replied and turned her attention back to the interrogation.

"So, then all the cops had cleared out and I thought they were done with me when the doorbell rang…"

Just then, there was a knock on the interrogation door and an officer poked his head in. "I'm sorry, Cap, can you step out here really quick?"

Captain Butler stopped the recording and excused himself and asked Lieutenant Ramsey to join him. They both walked out of the room and left Jonah alone. Brianna wondered what could've been so important to interrupt an interrogation this important when an officer stepped back into the room.

"Mr. Westbrook, something big has come up in town and the captain and pretty much the entire police force are going to have to take care of it. Can you write down on this pad where you are staying? Here's your cell phone back…if you'll leave your number as well, someone will get in touch with you as soon as we can…perhaps in the morning."

"Is everything alright?" Jonah asked, noting the officer's excitement.

"Yeah, I'm not sure…there's been an explosion over at the local high school. Pretty bad, from what they say. Don't know if anybody was there, it being so late…but anyway, someone will get in touch with you in the morning." He held the door open for Jonah and they left.

Brianna got up and walked out of the viewing room. She saw the officer leading Jonah to the front door and followed them.

"Do not let him go out the front door," her old friend said from behind her.

"Excuse me!" Brianna called to the officer leading Jonah. He turned quickly as if she'd startled him. "I'm sorry, but is there a back way out of here?"

"I'm sorry?" the officer asked, as if irritated and confused.

"Do you have a back door?" she asked, slower.

"Ma'am, I'm going to need you to follow me this way."

"And I'm telling you it isn't safe for Mr. Westbrook to walk out that door," Brianna nodded. "Is there a way to get out the back?" She smiled at Jonah, once again surprised at how tall he was. "Mr. Westbrook?" she held out a hand. "I'm Brianna Bowers." He shook her hand and smiled at her.

"Not safe for me?" he asked with a slight smirk.

"I'm just going to need you to trust me, Mr. Westbrook…" Again, she turned to the officer. "Back door?"

"This is highly irregular, Ms. Bowers," he pointed down a side hallway and walked past her. "This exit is for emergencies only."

"And I can assure you, officer, this is the definition of an emergency." She motioned for Jonah to follow her.

"And who exactly are you?" Jonah asked as he followed her down the hall.

"I'll explain later Mr.…."

"Call me Jonah, please, and make this fast…I haven't slept in a couple of days and I'm absolutely exhausted."

"I'll explain later, Jonah," she replied. "Where did you park your car?"

"Around front, near the fire station."

~ 149 ~

"Well, that's not good." They stepped into the back alley, and she thanked the disgruntled officer. "Give me your keys and wait here," she said, holding out her hand.

"I'm sorry, I don't know you…" he put his hands on his hips and waited for some kind of explanation.

"My name is Brianna Bowers and I'm the acting head of The Human Trafficking Ministry out of Germany. I am presently being hunted by some very bad men from all over the world for information that I have on their child trafficking ring. My parents were threatened, which is what brought me home to Gateway.

I was at Winn Dixie attempting to convince them when all hell broke loose with you." She watched his face as he registered everything she said. "Somehow, I believe that the men that are after you for the information you have are connected to the men that are after me." His eyes got as big as saucers, as if something clicked. He reached into his pocket and pulled out his keys.

"Wait, why is it safe for you to go out front and not me?"

"I have no idea, but it just is." She grabbed his keys and turned to walk away. "I'll be right back, don't go anywhere."

Three minutes later, they were heading out of town. Brianna knew that Officer Ramsey was taking care of her parents, so that was one last thing to worry about. She couldn't decide whether to tell anyone about Travis' past. He had been attempting to turn his life around, so should she leave it at that? She would just drive one town over to Yulee and find a place to eat and discuss what Jonah knew.

~ 150 ~

She checked her mirror, and it didn't appear that anyone was following them. "So, what are you feeling like eating?" she asked and looked over. Jonah was sound asleep. "Okay, you did say you were exhausted." Her phone rang. She looked down and saw that it was Nadia's number again. Her heart dropped. "Hello?"

"So, you got lucky, this time, Ms. Brianna," the familiar German voice said.

"What have you done with Nadia?" Brianna asked. "Is she alright?

"She is alive for now…her future, however, lies in your hands," he responded. "If you…"

"Liar…" she couldn't believe she'd said it. "No matter what I do, you're still going to kill the both of us." Silence.

"Yes…you're probably right," he replied. "However, the manner in which you both die is still debatable. My men are waiting for you at some place called Gateway Barbecue…you have ten minutes to…"

"I'm no longer in Gateway," Brianna replied. "Let me talk to Nadia again, so I know she's okay…and I will tell you where they can meet me."

"I already told you that Nadia is alive…she is fine," he sounded irritated. "She spoke to you before."

"Call me back when she can talk, if she isn't alive then we have nothing to discuss anyway." Brianna said and clicked off the call. At least she knew they weren't following her. Jonah let out a snore and turned his head toward the window. Brianna pulled into a Wendy's and pulled around to the drive thru. She

ordered something for herself and Jonah and drove across the street to a Best Western parking lot…just in case they were watching the credit card that Nadia gave her, she didn't want to stay in one place too long. She parked behind the hotel, leaned her seat back, and started eating her burger and fries.

About two bites into her burger, she noticed a white van driving slowly through the parking lot. She locked eyes with the man in the passenger seat as they came to a stop about thirty feet to her left.

"Um, Jonah!?" she said, setting her burger down and starting the car. "Jonah!" The van attempted to block her, but she cut the wheel hard to the right and stepped on the gas. Jonah seemed to wake up from the instant g-force she'd produced from squealing around the parking lot.

"What is happening?" he asked in a groggy voice and looked around. "What are you doing!?"

"I think these guys are yours…I'm thinking there's a tracker on you or this car!" Brianna replied, as she made a hard right out onto the road. "There's no way those guys followed me from the police station!"

Jonah looked back just as the white van pulled out of the parking lot behind them. "That's them alright…and a tracker makes perfect sense. I've lost these guys several times and they always seem to find me again."

"So, that means we're going to have to ditch this car and find another one." She quickly did a U-turn and headed back the way she'd just come. "The Yulee police station is about three miles ahead!" She punched it as she saw the van make the U-turn behind her.

"Just in case you don't make it to the police station," Jonah said, looking around the car. "You wouldn't happen to have a gun, would you?"

Brianna gasped, "Yes! In my purse! I grabbed my dad's! Do you know how to use one!?"

Jonah pulled out the 9mm and checked to see if a bullet was in the chamber. "I know enough to be dangerous," he smiled at her, and she almost swerved off the road. "Whoa!"

"Sorry!" she replied, turning beet red. "The police station is just up ahead!" She quickly pulled into the parking lot and parked right in front of the building. They watched the van slow down and drive past.

Jonah got out of the car and started walking around looking and feeling under the wheelbases. He stopped at the driver side rear…"AHA!" He held up a small black device with a magnet attached.

"Throw it in the bushes!" Brianna yelled.

"No, I have a better idea," Jonah replied, walking across the parking lot. He walked right over to a police car and stuck it to the passenger door. Getting back in the car, he smiled at Brianna. "That should make things more interesting." She handed him his food and pulled out of the parking lot. "Awesome, I'm starving…where are we heading?"

"Somewhere to sit and talk, so we can figure out how our stories are connected," Brianna replied, looking in the rear-view mirror to make sure a white van wasn't following them.

CHAPTER 17

The room was really quite large...it was dark, musty, and cold...but quite large. The walls were made of stone and the floor was old wood planks that were splintering up as if the room had once held water for some time. The ceiling was about fourteen or fifteen feet high, and the room was probably twenty feet by fifteen feet. There was a long, thin embrasure in two of the corners showing Nadia a slight view of a distant lake with mountains beyond that. She had no idea where she was, but it definitely felt like she was nowhere near civilization.

She sat on a small, thin mattress on the floor with her back against the stone wall. The mattress was the only thing in the room besides her and an occasional mouse...well, there was an old tin bucket in one of the corners for, well, she didn't want to think about that. The large, wooden door was heavily barred on the opposite side. She knew this based on how long it took her captives to open it each time they brought her a meal, which wasn't very often...or appetizing.

Nadia could not believe her situation right now. She felt as if she were in a dream, or better yet, a nightmare. She could not stop the tears...the pain was unbelievable. Her best friend, Cristian, had been tortured and killed. She had found him in what was supposed to be a safe house. She would never be able to rid her mind of that image. Cristian...her sweet friend. His fingers broken...his eyelids removed...his body beaten and cut.

These people were monsters. She had tried to escape their grasp, but they had found her. Phillipe, her pilot, was supposed to be flying her to London. Everything had been in order. She'd gotten her fake passport and identification and everything else she'd needed. Just when she'd thought she would be able to get away…she'd received the call. It was her mother that had been screaming frantically into the phone. She could barely make out her words.

The men had come. Ana was taken. Papa was in the hospital for trying to stop them. Five minutes later another call had come. It was Ana…her little sister. She was screaming as if she were being tortured. Then… "Hello, Nadia…" the German voice of the man she'd known was behind this… Secretary-General Schmidt, had said, and she could feel his smile through the phone. "Ana is very excited about going back into the trade…can you hear her excitement?"

In the background her younger sister was screaming for someone to stop whatever they were doing. "I am going to text you an address and you are going to go there in twenty-four hours, or I can assure you that your little slut sister…how old is she? 10? 11? Will no longer even remember her own name, let alone the life she once had." He'd clicked off the call before she could speak.

Nadia's world had crumbled. Her reason for living had vanished with the news of her sister's abduction. She had failed to protect her family and she only wanted to die. She could barely remember anything that had happened after that. She wanted to kill these people, but she knew she was completely powerless. This was not one of those movies where the heroine escaped her captives and pulled out a few kung-fu moves on these child predators and shot up an entire village of evildoers with a six-shooter and a winning smile. This was reality…and the good guys rarely won.

~ 155 ~

Standing beside Nadia, with his claws buried deep in her mind, was a large, black, scaly creature. "That's right, Nadia…there is no hope. You have failed. Your sister is gone forever. Everything you've ever worked for was a waste of time. Yes…just let it all go…fall into my grip." He smiled down on her with his razor-sharp teeth and eyes of death.

YULEE, FLORIDA

"So, that's when I ran to my car and got out of San Diego as fast as I could," Jonah said, biting into his burger. "It probably had that tracker on it the entire time." He shook his head, feeling like such a dope.

"Wow, Jonah…he was shot in the head, right in front of you!?" Brianna was taken aback. "That's horrible!"

"Like I said…I didn't even realize it at first," he replied. "There was no sound of a gunshot or anything. It was like his head just exploded on its own. I was so confused for a few seconds."

"Still, I'm sorry you had to see that."

"Yeah, well, the realization that it was supposed to be my head exploding was much worse than seeing it happen." He wiped his chin with a napkin and looked over at Brianna. "So, what's our connection?"

"That guy that was shot and killed in the Winn Dixie parking lot, Travis, had told me about what I suspect was your hidden worksite already. He had seen it in a video call...and I'm pretty sure he witnessed them gunning down your entire crew… so, it has to be that compound that connects us all," Brianna

replied, noticing that Jonah had looked away when she'd mentioned his friends. "If I were a betting woman, I would say that it was going to be used for human trafficking and they want to tie up all the loose ends. That's what I do for a living…I search for kids that are involved in trafficking. So, you know exactly where this compound is at in Wyoming?"

Jonah nodded. "Yes, hold on…" he pulled out his phone and brought up maps. "Somewhere in here. Just north of Casper. I flew out of Casper-Natrona County International Airport when I left for California. You aren't planning to go there, are you?"

"I'm not sure what to do yet. I may get Officer Ramsey involved because I'm not totally sure about who we can trust." Brianna looked around, still paranoid that someone was watching them. She'd parked right in the middle of a Target parking lot, hoping to blend in.

"That's really cool, by the way," Jonah said, looking out the side window. "Helping kids like that. It's very…noble. I respect that." He glanced over at Brianna and smiled.

She quickly looked away. "Thanks," she replied. "It's extremely rewarding work."

"I'm sure…so, how did you get into that line of work?"

She laughed. "That's a very long story that I'm not sure you're ready to hear just yet." Just then, her phone rang. "I'm not sure who this is, but…excuse me for a second…Hello? This is Brianna."

"Brianna, it's Lieutenant Ramsey…are you okay?" It sounded like he was driving and in a hurry.

"For the most part, yes," she replied. "Why do you ask?"

"I was told that you and Jonah snuck out the back and made some kind of mysterious getaway from the police department. Sounded suspicious...and made me wonder if the high school explosion wasn't some kind of ruse to get us away from you guys."

"I'd thought the same thing, because I think someone was going to try and kill Jonah in the front of the station. We're presently being followed, or should I say we WERE being followed. I'm pretty sure we've lost them for now." She glanced over at Jonah. "Listen, I think we need to talk to you about what's going on."

"Are you sure? When it comes to you kids, I usually just let you do your thing…what with all the God stuff."

"Yeah, I'm sure," she replied with a chuckle. "I really feel like we need your input here."

"Okay, well I'm heading back to Jacksonville right now. I have to be there for a briefing on a few cases we're working on. Come on pal! Get out of the way!" He made some weird sound with his mouth and grunted. "Really!?" Brianna heard his siren come on. "Can you guys meet me at E&H Deli on Bay Street in about two hours? My treat."

"We just ate, but yes, we'll be there," she replied. "Thank you so much!" She clicked off the call and quickly pulled up the address on her phone.

"So, it looks like I have two more hours to nap," Jonah said, laying his seat back. "I'm really sorry Brianna, but I'm exhausted."

"It's fine," she replied. "Get your rest…Lord knows you'll probably need it." She pulled out onto the road and started praying as she drove back to Jacksonville. She prayed for Maria and all the children with her. She prayed for Carmen and that God would give her peace regardless of the outcome. She couldn't help but remember that the Holy Spirit had first prompted her to pray for Carmen and not Maria, which gave her a bad feeling about the outcome of this endeavor.

She also prayed for her parents and Lieutenant Ramsey…that God would protect them in all this mess. She glanced over at Jonah as he slept beside her, lightly snoring. She wondered about the state of his soul. "Help me to be a witness, Holy Spirit…I have a feeling this man is going to need you in his life very soon." Another glance led her mind to his chiseled jaw and handsome face. "Of course, if he was a Christian…"

"Focus, Brianna," came a still, small voice from the backseat.

She looked in her rear-view mirror and saw her old friend smiling at her. "Yes, sir…"

"I wait for the Lord, my whole being waits, and in his word, I put my hope."

"Beautiful…isn't that a Psalm?" she asked. He gave her a slight nod and smiled. She glanced back at Jonah and sighed. "I'm sorry, Mr. Westbrook, but you will have to wait and see if we're meant to be." She chuckled to herself and focused on the drive, continually glancing back to make sure they weren't being followed.

After several minutes, her old friend broke the silence in the car again. "Schwert der Dunkelheit."

"Wait," Brianna replied. "That's that sword of darkness thing again. What are you telling me?" She glanced back and he was gone. She quickly pulled over and googled it in English. There were a few books of that title…and a whole lot of swords with the name Sword of Darkness. They varied from swords used in movies and cartoons to video games and even board games. "What are you trying to tell me, Holy Spirit?" Brianna mumbled to herself.

She tried googling it in German and, of course she couldn't read what it said, but some of the pictures were the same. Mostly of the swords. For well over an hour, she researched into the whole sword of darkness thing, looking for clues. She studied pictures, the link to Dungeons and Dragons, the comic book stories. Nothing really jumped out at her though.

Just then, her phone buzzed with a text from Officer Ramsey. "Heading to the restaurant."

She looked at her GPS and replied, "be there in twenty-five minutes." She got back on the road and made a mental note to investigate this sword of darkness thing a little more later. Fifteen minutes later, Brianna was maneuvering through downtown Jacksonville.

Apparently, everyone was getting off work for the day because traffic was quite thick. She finally made it to Bay Street and saw the restaurant to her right. She had no idea where to park but then she saw Officer Ramsey standing on the sidewalk in front of the restaurant. He was looking for them. "Jonah!" Brianna said, nudging him to wake up. "Jonah, we're here! I'm rolling your window down!" She slid it down as she pulled up to where Officer Ramsey was standing.

"Where are we?" Jonah asked, a little groggy.

"Jacksonville...we're meeting..."

Officer Ramsey walked up to the window. "You can park in the lot right over there..." he started to point.

"BRIANNA!!!!" Jonah screamed and pointed to the white van directly in front of them as the back door slung open and a man with an automatic rifle opened fire on them. Jonah threw himself in front of Brianna as the windshield exploded in on them. They could hear people screaming all around them. Brianna slammed on the gas on instinct and slammed into the back of the van, causing the man with the gun to fall onto their hood.

He dropped his gun as he attempted to stop his fall. Jonah raised up off of Brianna and she slid the car into reverse and punched the gas. The man on the hood reached his hand up and grabbed at the dashboard...Brianna's attention for a split second went to the tattoo on his upper right arm. It was a black sword with a skull on the end of the hilt. She had just seen that exact sword on her google search.

Jonah leaned his seat back and lifted his leg quickly, kicking the man right in the face as hard as he could, causing him to lose his grip and slide off the hood.

Brianna had driven up onto the curb and sidewalk when she'd thrown it into reverse. She scanned the area for Officer Ramsey and saw him lying in a pool of blood about five feet from where he'd been standing. "NO!" she screamed.

"GO, GO, GO!!!" Jonah yelled, pointing to the guy who'd just fallen off the car. He was picking up his gun and aiming it toward them.

Brianna put the car back into drive and in a fit of absolute anger, aimed the car directly at him and punched it. He attempted to jump out of the way, but she managed to hit his legs as they were in mid-jump. She slammed into the back of the van again, causing her airbag to deploy and her car to shut off.

Jonah quickly jumped out of the car and began punching the man as he tried to get up. He grabbed the rifle out of his hand and swung it like a baseball bat, hitting the man right in the side of the head and knocking him out. He looked up just as the driver of the van rounded the corner, holding a handgun. Jonah lifted the assault rifle and shot the man multiple times in the chest before he could even take in the scenario.

Brianna grabbed their things out of the car. "Come on, Jonah!" They both jumped in the van and took off. "Father, I pray that Lieutenant Ramsey is okay, please heal him in Jesus' name!" She said as she dodged quickly through traffic.

"There were people helping him," Jonah said. "Hopefully he's okay."

"Jonah! You're bleeding!" Brianna yelled, seeing blood running down his arm. "Are you shot!?"

He looked down at his right shoulder, where apparently a bullet had passed through. "OUCH!!!" he yelled as he touched the spot. "I've been shot!"

"Quick, grab a shirt out of my bag and put it over it!" Brianna said, sliding her bag over to him. "You need to apply pressure!"

"Yeah, I'm losing blood," he replied, grabbing a shirt out of her bag and wincing as he placed it over the wound.

"You saved my life, Jonah…that bullet was meant for me," she said, tearing up. "Why would you do that!?"

"Why wouldn't I do that?" he replied. "Although, I'm not going to lie…I'm kind of a wimp when it comes to pain."

"All guys are, aren't they?" Brianna said with a chuckle. "We need to find a place to lay low." They found themselves in an industrial area along the river. Brianna saw what looked like an abandoned warehouse and pulled into the parking lot. She pulled around the building and parked in the back. They were totally out of sight. She got out of the van and walked around to his side. She checked his wound and he winced again. "Yeah, it looks like the bullet went straight through…thank you, Jesus."

"So, I take it you're some kind of Christian?" Jonah asked.

She smiled at that. "Yeah, guilty! I'm definitely some kind of Christian."

CHAPTER 18

CODY, WYOMING

The truck had finally come to a stop. Maria attempted to stretch her legs in the small cage they had her in, but she could barely move. Her entire body ached from being in this position for hours. She had needed to pee for so long before she'd finally relieved herself. It was embarrassing, but apparently it was what everyone had been doing. In fact, her shirt was still wet from the person in the cage above her. The entire trailer, stacked to the top with cages of children, smelled like a bathroom. A very hot bathroom where nobody had ever flushed.

She missed her mother terribly and had cried herself to sleep several times already wishing this nightmare would end. She'd kept hoping that her mother would wake her up for school at any minute. Where was she at? Why were these men doing this? She knew better than to ask them. Her friend, Stacey, had asked, and they had taken her into a back room at the warehouse they'd been at. She'd heard Stacey screaming for hours. When she'd come out, her clothes had been torn and she'd had bruises on her face. She'd refused to talk to Maria or anyone else.

Stacey had thrown up several times and not long after that she had fallen asleep. The men had covered her with a white sheet and carried her out the back of the building. Maybe they'd let her go home since she was hurt. Maria had prayed that's what they'd done. Stacey had been nice to her.

The door slid open, and a very bright light shone into the trailer. Maria heard several of the children gasp and begin to cry. Some of the older kids tried to make them be quiet but it didn't help. It only made them cry louder.

"God, it stinks in there!" a man yelled. "Let's get this over with!" He jumped up into the back of the trailer and slid a cloth over his face. He slapped a few of the cages as he walked down the middle isle. "I think we have a few corpses!" Maria wasn't sure what that meant, but based on the bad words he was saying, he wasn't very happy about it. "I told you we shouldn't have left them in here this long…what a waste!"

A little boy of about five was screaming at this point and the man reached up and slapped his cage. "SHUT UP!!!" It only scared the poor boy and made him scream louder. The man opened his cage, reached in and grabbed the boy by the shirt and pulled him out of his cage. He dropped him to the floor and kicked him up against the other cages. "I SAID SHUT UP!!!" The boy tried to stifle his crying but continued to whimper. "Get up here and get this kid out of here!" the man yelled to someone outside the trailer. "Come on! Let's get these rats out of their cages!"

"We're not rats!" a little girl under Maria yelled in defiance. "We're people and you're a terrible person!" She began to cry.

The man laughed. "Oh, little girl…you'll find out soon enough exactly how terrible I am." He slapped her cage. "And if I hear you speak again, I'll cut out your tongue! That goes for all of you!" He left the trailer screaming demands to his workers and about seven men climbed in and began releasing the kids from their cages and leading them out of the trailer. Maria was yet to see where they were or what was outside. As the men got closer to her cage, she saw an old man standing outside the

trailer helping the children climb down. She thought he looked quite out of place in his gray suit and hat.

MUNICH, GERMANY

Nadia jumped awake at the sound of her cell door's locks being opened on the other side. She stood up, preparing herself for whatever they would do. She knew this was no normal visitation or food delivery because it was night time. This was either going to be another call to Brianna or them letting her know that Brianna was dead, and they no longer needed her.

The door swung open and two armed guards entered the room and stood on either side of Nadia. A young, petite Asian woman, wearing a tiny black dress and heels, entered behind them carrying a green shopping bag. "Good evening, Nadia Skutnik," she said with a slight smirk, looking Nadia over. "You look as though you could use a shower."

"Yeah, well, the conditions at this establishment have been anything but five star," Nadia replied, her senses on overdrive. She was prepared for anything. The woman handed her the bag.

"Well, if you'll follow me, I'll see if I can remedy that."

Nadia peered into the bag and saw fresh clothes, everything from underwear to what appeared to be a pair of jeans, a t-shirt, socks, and shoes. "Am I going somewhere?"

"This way, please," the woman stepped aside and one of the guards nudged Nadia toward the door. She warily led the way into the hallway beyond. The woman was the last one out the door and she stepped in front of Nadia giving her a slight smile as she passed. "Please follow me."

Nadia stayed close behind her as they made their way up a set of winding stairs that led them about four floors higher into the building they were in. One of the guards moved ahead and punched in a pass code as they came to a large metal door at the top of the stairs. The door opened on its own. They stepped into what looked like the hallway of a hospital. The other guard nudged Nadia to the right. After walking past several closed doors with numbers just like a hospital, they came to a stop outside a door with a sign that read FEMALE SHOWER over it.

"You have twenty minutes," the woman said to Nadia with a smile. "Try and enjoy your five stars."

"Thank you," Nadia stepped inside the large room that was a bathroom with individual stalls that were showers. Each stall had a curtain for privacy. She quickly stripped off her clothes and placed them in a laundry bin that sat against the back wall. After a quick trip to the loo, she reached into the shower and turned on the water. She said a quick prayer that there would be hot water…and there it was. "Thank you, God."

She couldn't believe she'd said it, but quickly blamed Brianna for her weakness. The water felt amazing to her sore muscles. She closed her eyes and enjoyed the moment of peace. A moment that would probably be followed by anything but peace. She was ready for whatever they had for her. She was ready for death…Brianna's face flashed in her mind. Her smile, her eyes. That was the face of someone ready for death. Ready for whatever death had to offer. Nadia found herself longing for THAT peace.

"Ten minutes!" One of the guards yelled from the door.

She grabbed the shampoo and quickly began washing her hair. "Okay, God of Brianna, I need to know how to get what she has."

Ten minutes later, Nadia emerged from the bathroom feeling as fresh as a newborn. She smiled at the woman and thanked her. "So, what now?"

"Now," the woman said, nodding to one of the guards. "We're going on a little trip." The guard grabbed Nadia's arms and quickly placed her in cuffs. He nudged her down the hall toward God only knew what.

JACKSONVILLE, FLORIDA

"I'm not going to lie," Jonah said, with a smirk. "It was quite hilarious how you lost all reason and tried to run that guy over."

"What!?" Brianna replied from the driver's seat. The sun had gone down, and they were just laying low for a while, trying to rest. Neither of them seemed to be able to fall asleep after that incredible adrenaline rush. "I didn't have any other option! He was about to shoot us!"

Jonah laughed, wincing at the pain that moving caused in his shoulder. "Still…my daddy always said to watch out for short girls…they got fire in their bones."

This made her smile. "That's not a lie." She thought about Officer Ramsey lying on the ground in a pool of blood and wanted to call him. Jonah had told her to take the battery out of her phone, though, because that was probably how they'd found them. She clicked on the van's radio in hopes of hearing about it on the news.

"So," Jonah said, in a more serious tone. "How does your boyfriend feel about you being an international woman of mystery?"

Her heart jumped at the question, and she had to close her eyes and whisper a prayer for wisdom. "No boyfriend," she replied. "Who has time for that?" She looked over at him and saw that he was looking out the passenger window. "What about you?"

"No boyfriend here," he replied in as serious a tone as he could muster. He looked over at her and smiled.

She laughed and slapped his good arm. "You know what I meant."

"Yeah, I don't have time for a girlfriend either. I'm pretty much married to my work."

"What exactly is it that you do in construction?"

"Structural Engineering," he replied. "Basically, I make sure that buildings don't fall."

"Sounds important," Brianna replied. "So, you enjoy it?"

Jonah shrugged. "It's not exactly what I wanted to do when I grew up, but it pays the bills."

She nodded. "Yeah, I know how that works. Traipsing around the globe searching for missing children wasn't my first choice either…but I wouldn't trade it for all the money in the world."

"Well, I might trade MY job for all the money in the world," Jonah replied. "This shoulder really hurts."

"We should go to a pharmacy and get you something for the pain. Whoa, hold on!" Brianna turned up the radio.

"A shootout in downtown Jacksonville today!" Sounds of gunfire were played in the background. "All the details have not yet been released from today's shootout on Adams Street. All we have right now is that a van stopped in the middle of the street during the five o' clock rush and a man opened fire on the car behind them.

Police Lieutenant Matthew Ramsey was injured in the crossfire and is presently in critical condition at Shands Hospital. The two men from the van were killed by the man who'd been in the car originally being fired at. Apparently, he jumped out of his vehicle and beat the gunman with his own gun and then shot and killed the driver. Police are still searching for the man and the female that was with him. They were last seen driving away in the white Dodge van after their car had been shot up. Photos of the man and woman can be found on Fox News 30's website at…"

"Wow, they made me sound like an action hero!" Jonah laughed.

"The police are searching for us, and they have our pictures!" Brianna said.

"Fifty people probably recorded the whole thing, so yeah…"

"We need to get out of town!" Brianna started up the van.

~ 170 ~

"We need to find another vehicle!" Jonah said. "Don't you have friends and family in Gateway?"

Brianna nodded and pointed the van in that direction.

"Stay on the back roads if you can," Jonah said.

She handed him her phone. "Put the battery in so I can quickly call my dad and then we'll take it right back out. He has a car that we can probably use."

Jonah slid the battery in and powered up her phone. It immediately alerted her of several messages. "Well, aren't you Ms. Popularity?"

"People probably recognizing my picture on the news," Brianna replied. "Are there voice messages?"

"Uh, yeah," Jonah replied in disbelief. "Try fifty-seven."

"Read me the ones where the caller is identified." She looked both ways before crossing traffic.

"There's a bunch here from your mom," Jonah said. "Several from a woman named Carmen."

"That's the mother who's kid I'm searching for. Who else?"

"There's a Donna, a Gabi, a WOW, this one appears to be an international number."

"Play it!" Brianna said, looking over and swerving the van off the road a little. "Sorry, just put it on speaker and play it!"

He did, holding the phone closer to her. "So, Brianna Bowers," the familiar German voice said. "Apparently you have joined forces with someone else that my people are hunting…a Mr. Jonah Westbrook. This is good, since they have apparently lost all contact with Mr. Westbrook. If you will please inform Mr. Westbrook that his sister…Jaclyn, I believe is her name…is being held by my men at the place where he helped to build…in Wyoming."

Jonah's eyes got as big as saucers and his hand holding the phone began to shake. "I'm really hoping that the two of you get this message, because you have until midnight on Tuesday to get here. Just the two of you, no tricks. Nadia and Jaclyn's futures are depending on you." He ended the call.

"Jonah…I'm so sorry!" Brianna started. "Oh, Jesus," she whispered.

"No freaking way!!!" He dug out his new phone and called his sister. It went straight to voicemail. He reluctantly dialed his mother's number.

"Hello?" his mother's voice sounded frail and weak.

"Mom! Where's Jaclyn!?"

"Jonah!? Oh my God, Jonah! Where have you been!? I thought I'd lost both of my children!!!" She was frantic. It sounded like she was walking…probably somewhere dad couldn't hear her. "Jonah, these men came…they grabbed Jaclyn and threw her in their van right in broad daylight! The police have been searching for her for about twenty-four hours now! The neighbor's saw them, Jonah! And they just took her and some other woman...I haven't been told who yet!!! What's going on!!!"

Jonah had closed his eyes as his mother spoke. He was picturing the whole thing. Jaclyn must be terrified. What was going on!? Who did these people think they were? "Mom, listen to me," he said in as calm a voice as he could muster. "Everything is going to be fine. I know where Jaclyn is and I'm about to go get her."

"WHERE!? Where is she, Jonah!? Tell me so I can tell the police!!!" She yelled into the phone. "Are you alone!? Don't put yourself in danger unnecessarily, Jonah!"

"I won't…listen, you have to stay calm for Dad's sake, so please calm down…everything will be fine. Okay, I have to go, Mom…I love you!" He clicked off the call and punched the dash. "They have my sister!"

CHAPTER 19

GATEWAY, FLORIDA

Brianna's dad was waiting for them when they pulled into the yard. He gave her a massive hug when she stepped out of the van. "I love you, Sweetheart," he whispered in her ear.

"I love you, Daddy," she replied and stepped back to look at him. "Are you sure you want to do this?" she asked, glancing toward the detached garage at the back of the house.

He smiled and nodded. "I've never been more sure of anything." He walked over and shook Jonah's hand.

"Mr. Bowers," Jonah said with a grim look on his face.

Brianna's dad handed Jonah a large black duffel bag. "Supplies…just some things to help you keep my daughter alive. I already know you know your way around a firearm…that video is all over YouTube." He led them over to the garage. "There's also some clothes, snacks, and other survival junk in there." Bending down, he unlocked a large padlock and removed it from the door. He slid the garage door up and stepped back.

"Holy…moly," Jonah said in total reverence at the sight of the amazing cherry red beast before him. "Is that a…

"1969 Ford Mustang Boss 429," Brianna finished for him. She noticed the stunned look on his face. "My dad and I have been restoring Bruce since I was eleven."

"Bruce…The Boss, I get it. I would've never pinned you a car chick, though," Jonah replied with total respect. "I'm impressed. These babies are extremely rare…and fast."

"I'm more of a daddy's girl than a car chick," she chuckled. "And yes, Bruce is quite fast."

Her dad handed her a credit card. "For gas, hotels, whatever else you need."

She hugged her dad again. "Thank you, Daddy. I'll take good care of him."

He shrugged. "If not, we'll restore him again." He kissed her on the cheek. "Just come back alive…take care of my girl, Jonah!" He handed Brianna the keys. "I've got to get back to your mother before she notices me gone. I love you!"

"I love you too, Daddy…this whole thing is in God's hands."

"It always is, Bree!" He waved over his shoulder and climbed into his pickup truck.

"Wow, Brianna!" Jonah said. "Your dad is like the coolest guy I've ever met."

She smiled at that. "Close the garage down when I back out."

Ten minutes later, they dropped the van off at the Winn Dixie in Gateway and headed out of town. Brianna asked Jonah to drive while she looked into the whole Sword of Darkness thing. "Let's just get out of Florida. Since neither one of us has had much sleep lately, we can maybe get a hotel in Macon, Georgia…it's less than four hours away." She was looking at the map on her phone. "The whole trip is…"

"32 hours, if we go this way," he pointed on her phone. "And take 24 from Nashville. I already mapped it."

"Well, don't let me get in your way," she replied with a smile. "Just let me know if you get tired. "We should be in Macon before midnight."

"Yes ma'am," he said, pulling out onto US 1 again and heading North. "This baby handles nice."

ROME, ITALY

It was an outside venue in the heart of Rome, Italy with literally over 100,000 people in attendance. At least 2,500 people were there just to protest the event. There was a serious amount of intensity in the air. Police and military had been called in for standby just in case there were any problems. Mark had alerted the teams to be praying nonstop for what God was about to do in Rome. He knew that the enemy was not happy and was pulling out all the stops.

Gabi was presently sitting in one of the staff tents with the rest of the worship team going over the battle plan. They had been working on some new songs and were contemplating whether to use them tonight. As Andy and Matt argued over what key to transition into after the third song, Gabi checked her phone to see if Brianna had returned her call.

She had been worried sick about her friend after her mom had told her about the shootout in downtown Jacksonville involving Brianna and some mystery man. Two people had been killed in that shootout and Matt's dad was injured. Just as she was about to step outside and try to call again, a sweet, still small voice whispered in her ear. "Pray for her." Gabi stopped in her tracks and closed her eyes.

"Dear heavenly Father, I lift up Brianna Bowers to you right now!" she prayed silently. "You know exactly where she is and what she needs, Father. Please be with her and give her your favor! Keep her safe and make her prosperous in her endeavors. In the name of Your precious Son, Jesus Christ, I pray…Amen."

She opened her eyes and the first thing she noticed was that the room had gone totally quiet. She looked over at the others and they were facing her with their eyes closed and their hands lifted in prayer toward her. She smiled and teared up. What an amazing team of worshipers God had assembled in these misfits. Their love for each other was definitely a reflection of God's love for all of them.

Just then, someone came up behind her and placed their hand on her shoulder. The gentle squeeze let her know that it was her beloved husband, Scotty. He leaned in and whispered in her ear. "Is this for Brianna?"

She nodded her head. "Not sure if they know it or not, but yes."

"Mark and I were stopped dead in our tracks by the Holy Spirit," Scotty whispered. "That girl is at war."

"She knows what to do," Gabi said with a smile, remembering her friend wearing the full armor of God and standing over ten feet tall. "This is definitely not her first rodeo."

"Gabi and the gang are praying for me," Brianna said as a rush of warmth flowed over her like oil.

"I'm sorry, what?" Jonah asked.

"Oh, sorry," Brianna replied. "My friends are praying for me."

"What, did they text you that they were?"

She smiled a cheesy smile at him. "No, I can feel their prayers. I know that probably sounds weird, but…"

"Yeah, just a little bit," Jonah replied with a chuckle. "You really take this Christian thing serious, don't you?"

"Of course," Brianna said matter-of-factly. "God is my everything."

He nodded. "I mean, as long as you practice what you preach, I guess that's cool."

"It's not about me, though," she replied.

"Huh?" He was clearly confused.

"Whether or not I practice what I preach doesn't change anything about how amazing God is. True Christians know it isn't about them. It's about Jesus. My life is supposed to be about pointing people toward Him…not me."

"I'm just saying," Jonah continued. "A lot of Christians say one thing and do another."

"True…but that doesn't matter…it isn't about them," she responded, sitting up and turning in her seat to face him. "So many times, people stop going to church or they make

judgment calls about God based on something that a person does. They miss out on the real thing by focusing on the wrong thing. If every Christian in the world is a fraud and a fake, that doesn't change the truths of God's word. It doesn't change who HE is!"

"Oh, I see what you're saying," Jonah said. "People can't see the forest for the trees."

"In a sense," Brianna replied. "If I tell you about Jesus, I don't want you to put your focus on me…because I'm going to eventually do something stupid and disappoint you…God never will."

Jonah nodded, clearly deep in thought. "So, does that mean you're going to be telling me about Jesus?"

"Not if you don't want me to," Brianna replied.

"Because I've had some bad experiences that concerned God…or at least bad examples of Him, like you said. I just need time to process what you just said about it not being about them."

"I get it, trust me. I've been a Christian for a very long time, and I've dealt with some stuff."

"And oh, what are your thoughts on those freaks that made the news several years ago with the dragon?" he asked with a laugh. "Those whack jobs were insane…that was so fake! CG much!?"

"Yeah, do you remember where that happened?" Brianna asked with a smirk.

"Wasn't it in Florida?" he asked, trying to remember? "I was a teenager, so I don't remember many details. I just

remember that it was the saddest attempt at converting people over to Jesus that I'd ever seen." He looked over and she was smiling at him. "What? You have to admit that it was pretty pathetic."

She held up her phone and showed him a news headline. "Gateway Teens Battle A Dragon In The Name Of Jesus!" There was a picture of the dragon fighting some really tall teenagers that were dressed in full Roman armor with swords, shields, and helmets.

"Gateway, yeah that was…wait!" it clicked in his brain. "GATEWAY!!!??? YOUR GATEWAY!!!???"

She smiled and nodded as she watched his brain connect the dots.

"Were you there!?" Jonah asked, watching her reactions now. "Those bystanders had to have been drugged because…" he stopped talking when Brianna put her hand on his arm.

"Jonah, I was one of those teens…it was real," she said, patting his arm. "I'm dead serious."

Jonah got really quiet for a few moments. He put both hands on the wheel and looked straight ahead.

"Are you okay?" Brianna asked. "Are you processing?"

Jonah slowed the car down and pulled over onto the grass shoulder. He put it in park and turned to look at her. Brianna looked around to make sure no cars were coming because they were still partially on the road. "You're telling me that YOU were one of those teens that were fighting that, that…dragon? Come on, Brianna, you have to be punking me!"

"Jonah, you don't have to believe me if you don't want to, but it really happened. I know you're going to say that dragons aren't real, but we were dealing with the spirit realm, not the physical realm. That dragon was a demon! That's all!"

"Oh, that's ALL!!??" He turned his head and looked out the window. "I'm sorry, Brianna, but I can't do this anymore. When we get to Macon, I'll give you directions to the compound, but I'm out. I'll rent a car, and head back to San Diego…I'll get the police involved in order to get my sister back."

"Jonah, we can't get the police involved," Brianna said. "This is bigger than the police. This is international crime…heck, some of the police are probably involved…I can guarantee you that politicians are!"

"Sorry, but I can't do this with someone as delusional as you are," he replied. "No offense, but…"

She burst out laughing. "Oh my gosh, did you just say no offense at calling me delusional? That's hilarious!"

He put the car in drive and pulled back onto the road. "Demons and dragons are not normal."

Brianna turned in her seat and looked out the window. She thought back to how many people over the years had tried to debunk what had happened that night. So many news stories had been run to show them as a bunch of crazies that had spiked the Kool aid to make everyone think they'd seen what they saw.

How many documentaries had been made proving it all to be a hoax? How many people had protested in Gateway for years to show their disdain for the group? She had literally heard every angle and was perfectly fine with people calling her

crazy…but she needed Jonah's help. She closed her eyes and prayed.

"Holy Spirit," she said silently. "I need You to intervene here. I need Jonah to see the truth…YOUR TRUTH! I don't care if he thinks I'm bonkers, but I need him to see Your truth…" Within moments she drifted off to sleep with her head leaning on the glass. It had been a very long and draining day.

CHAPTER 20

CODY, WYOMING

Maria and about thirty other girls ranging in age from four to twelve, were led into a large bathroom area lined with open toilets on one side and open showers on the other. They had all ridden an elevator, ten at a time, to get there. It had felt like they were going up, but from what Maria could remember, the building was only one story.

They were instructed to strip off all of their clothing and put them in a large bin. Maria didn't want to do that because she was afraid, she would never see her Hermione shirt again…it was her very favorite shirt. A man shoved her to the floor when he saw her not doing what she'd been told. She quickly removed her clothing and tossed them in the bin.

Each girl was handed a bar of soap and a washcloth and told how and what to clean. They were also told that if they didn't do it properly then one of the men would help them. Maria made sure to do everything exactly as she'd been told. The men screamed at them to hurry and some of the younger girls were crying.

"There are towels over on this bench for those of you that are done," one of the men called out. "After you have dried off, someone will inspect you. STOP CRYING!!!" He walked over and smacked a young white girl in the back of the head causing her to fall forward and slip on the floor. An older black girl helped her up. "Did I ask you to help her!?" He grabbed her by her hair. "Did I!?"

"She's just a little girl!" the older girl replied. "Leave her alone!" He smacked her across the face and knocked her to the ground.

"Justin!" one of the other men yelled. "Are you sure you want to damage the goods!? Boss man ain't gonna be so happy when he first sees these girls and they're all beat up!"

"Get up and finish cleanin' up!!" Justin told the older girl. He looked down at the younger girl who was covering herself and shivering. "And clean her up properly too…before I do something we all regret!"

Maria dried off and sat on the bench as instructed. Once everyone was done, they had to stand up as the men inspected them. Maria hated this part. They kept touching her. She was cold. She wanted her mother to walk through that door and set these people straight. When the men were finished, they handed each of the girls a white slip to put on. No underwear, no socks, no shoes…just a thin slip that barely covered anything.

"I'm cold!" one of the younger girls said through chattering teeth.

"There will be blankets in your rooms!" the guy, Justin, said. "Now, follow me in a single file line!" He led them back out into the hall and to the right. As they approached a door, he would call out the names of two girls to go into that room. "There's a toilet and a sink. Get some sleep. Tomorrow will be a very busy day." Then he would push them inside and lock the door. When he called out Maria's name, he paired her with the older girl that had helped the little girl…her name was Bridgette. "There's a toilet and a sink. Get some sleep. Tomorrow will be a very busy day."

"Busy doing what?" Bridgette asked him. He shoved her into the room quite hard, yet she managed not to fall down.

"You'll find out soon enough, pretty girl!" he replied with a toothy grin and burst out laughing as he locked their door. "Yes, you will!!!"

MACON, GEORGIA

Jonah had not spoken to Brianna very much after their discussion last night. They had checked into the hotel and gone their separate ways. She had continued to pray not only that he would continue on with her, but that the Holy Spirit would open his eyes to the truth. She had called to make sure he was awake at 7am and to see if he was going to meet her for breakfast.

"Yes, and we need to talk. I'll be down in twenty minutes," he'd said and hung up.

That had given her a very bad feeling about how this morning was going to turn out. "I really need your help, Holy Spirit."

Presently, she was sitting at a table in the hotel dining room, drinking a cup of black coffee and eating a cheddar bagel with garden vegetable cream cheese. She silently prayed for Jonah as she waited for him to arrive. She had no idea what she would do if he abandoned her at this point. Yet, she had no idea what she was planning to do if he stayed.

The only plan they had right now was to show up at this compound and surrender to these evil people with only a hope and a prayer. Yes, God had gotten her out of bigger jams, but right now she was starting to feel like the ground beneath her was crumbling. This felt like it was the end. She was a dead woman walking. "Get it together, girl," she whispered to herself and shook her head. "Faith is the confidence in what we hope for and the assurance about what we do not see."

She looked up just as Jonah rounded the corner and headed to the breakfast bar. He really was a good-looking man. She had to divert her eyes, but the damage had been done. His hair was still wet from showering, and it appeared that he'd finger combed it. He wore an old t-shirt and jeans and had a couple days' worth of stubble. He grabbed his food, poured himself a cup of black coffee and headed toward her table. Why was her heart beating so fast? Seriously!

"Good morning!" he said a little more cheerfully than she'd expected.

"Good morning, Jonah!" she replied. "How did you sleep?"

"Literally the best night of sleep of my life," he responded. "I slept like a log. Wow! I never would've taken you for a black coffee drinker!"

She smiled. "Yeah, I'm usually a two cream and three sugar girl, but I apparently didn't get the good night's sleep that you did."

"Gotcha!" he replied and took a bite of his scrambled eggs.

"So, we need to talk?" She decided to go ahead and rip off the band aid.

He nodded as he finished chewing. "As much as I want to go into this place, guns blazing, and kill all the bad guys like

I'm in some Bruce Willis movie…let's be real. We're literally stepping right into our own caskets here. Not to mention, we aren't going to save anyone. My sister and this woman you're trying to help, will either be killed…or worse."

Brianna nodded. "So, what are you thinking?" She was just glad he wasn't calling a cab to rescue him from the crazy lady.

"I know they said to come alone, but can't we just somehow get the cops involved here? The F.B.I. or something…I know you think this goes deep but there has to be somebody we can talk to."

"I agree, but I don't know who to trust. Lieutenant Ramsey is literally the only policeman I KNOW I can trust. If we alert the wrong person, all our efforts will be in vain. Trust me, I've thought of all this…hence, no sleep."

"So, what?" Jonah asked with a shrug. "We just resign ourselves and our loved ones to the gallows?"

"I've been in some pretty hairy situations in my life, Jonah." She knew she was treading on shaky ground here. One wrong word and he would be out of here. "I've found that just trusting God is usually the best plan. Especially when you can't find a better option…which is where we are."

"Well, forgive me, but I've never stared down a dragon before…" he replied with a smirk. "Stepping off a cliff and hoping some all-powerful being will catch me is a little out of my mindset." He took a bite of a slice of bacon and never broke eye contact.

Brianna smiled at the jab and finished off her bagel. "There's nothing more peaceful than knowing that an all-

powerful being has your back, though. He really expects us to do that. It says in Proverbs to trust in the Lord with all your heart and lean not on your own understanding; in all your ways submit to him, and he will make your paths straight."

"Listen," Jonah said as he took a sip of coffee. "Before I drifted off to blissful sleeping paradise last night, I googled you. You are a very respected woman…internationally. Literally thousands of testimonies from parents, children, government officials, law enforcement, coworkers, and people from all over the globe.

You've helped save a lot of children and even some women, Brianna Bowers. I had to admit that you're an impressive woman. Another thing I noticed was how you always deferred any praise you were given…to either God or your 'friend' who helped you…who I genuinely believe is also God."

She smiled at his observation and this clear demonstration of how the Holy Spirit was bringing Jonah around. "You are correct."

"So, as much as I hate to admit it…I'm also willing to trust your God…for a while anyway. Although, truth be told, it's you I'm in fact trusting."

"Thank you, Jonah," she replied. "I'll take what I can get, and I'm honored that you would trust me…basically with not only your life, but your sister's also."

"After learning about your 'dragon adventures,' I was almost out of here," he replied. "And I'm ashamed to say that there's only one reason that I even decided to google you in hopes of finding a reason to stay."

"And what is that?" she asked, not sure where this was going but thanking God nonetheless that he was still in the game.

"I honestly think you are THE most beautiful woman I've ever seen in my life."

She almost spit her coffee out when he said that. "Ummm…thank you?"

"I'm just being open right now…I know that sounds cheesy and shallow, and I'm seriously not trying to hit on you." He blushed and looked away. "Heck, I don't even consider myself to be in the market for looking for a woman right now."

Brianna was literally screaming inside her head. She had no idea that he thought that about her. This was seriously the first man that she'd had to control her thoughts around in a very long time. She had long ago resigned herself to being married to her ministry and growing old all alone. Her brain was going a thousand miles a second right now, but she had to maintain her cool. "Well, thank you very much for the compliment, Jonah…you're quite the eye candy yourself." She blushed as she heard herself saying it. "For now, we should just concentrate on the task at hand."

"Agreed!" Jonah said, glad to change the subject. "So, I'm thinking Kansas City should be our goal for the day. It's about a thirteen-and-a-half-hour drive."

"Sounds good," Brianna said, getting up and gathering her dishes. "Let me grab my bags and I'll get us checked out. Meet back down here in fifteen?"

"Perfect." Jonah dumped his plate and headed for his room. Instead of taking the elevator, he decided to make the

three-story trek via the stairs. He needed the exercise and the distraction. About ten steps up, his head began to spin. He grabbed a hold of the rail in order to maintain his balance. All of a sudden, the stairs beneath him opened up and he began to fall.

At this point, he thought he was losing his mind, because nothing he saw was making sense. Even though he was falling at an insane rate of speed, he was able to register the fact that he was no longer inside a hotel, but what appeared to be deep in the earth. As he spun downward, he noticed that it was getting hotter and hotter. He kept catching a glimpse of fire. Something was burning and he was falling toward it. Was this hell? What was going on?

"God help me!" he tried to call out, but no sound came from his mouth. "JESUS!" Everything stopped. He was lying on the side of a cliff in what looked like the belly of a volcano. He peered over the edge and saw what appeared to be lava lapping up the edge of the cliff. He felt like Frodo looking down into Mordor. He stood up and looked around. Where was he? The lava and fire were the only light in the entire cavern…and it was a huge cavern.

"HELLLOOO!!!!" He called out, and this time a sound came out. "What is happening? Am I dead?" He looked all around for some kind of sign as to where he was. He looked down and noticed that the lava was rising and beginning to pour up onto the lip of the cliff. He jumped back just as his shirt burst into flames.

Quickly, he patted the fire out with his hand and backed as far away from the cliff as he could. It was so hot in here. The wall behind him was solid and the lava was beginning to splash

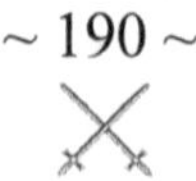

over and move closer. "Somebody help me!!! Anybody!!!" He tried to find a way to climb up but couldn't find anything. He was beginning to panic when a large hand grabbed him by the shoulder and spun him around.

He looked right into the shark-like eyes of a very large, black, scaly demonic looking creature. It gripped its hand around Jonah's neck and lifted him off the ground. He turned toward the cliff and tossed Jonah like a rag doll. Jonah tried to grab onto anything he could as he flew through the air screaming. Just before he landed in the boiling lava, he jumped out of his bed screaming at the top of his lungs. "NOOO!!!" Clearly dazed and confused, he looked around his hotel room as Brianna ran over to him and knelt down.

"Jonah! It's okay, it's okay…you're here with me!" She pulled him into a hug and stroked his hair. His heart was beating a million miles a minute. He started crying as he clung to her. He was literally sobbing. "It's okay, everything is fine...Ssshhh!" She rocked him back and forth and continued to pat his head.

"What happened?" he panted. "How did I get back in my room?" He managed to ask, looking around frantically.

"Jonah, someone found you passed out in the stairwell hours ago. You were lying there burning up. Your skin was very hot to the touch. I had some guys help me get you to your bed and I've had a cold cloth and ice on you trying to cool you down. I was just about to call 911 when you woke up. It's just now that you appear to be cooling down, has anything like this ever happened before?"

He shook his head no and attempted to stand up. Brianna helped him to his feet, and he made his way to the bathroom.

"Wow, is it really eleven already?" He closed the bathroom door.

"Are you good for traveling or should we stay another night?" She asked through the bathroom door.

"No, we have to go…we only have until Tuesday! Just give me a few minutes to wash my face and stop freaking out."

Brianna called down to the front desk and let them know they would be a few minutes late in checking out. She set all their bags by the door and sat next to the window and prayed. "I'm not sure what's going on, God, but we are definitely going to need your help here. Jonah is trusting me and I'm trusting you. Also, please heal whatever is wrong with Jonah and help me to guide him to a closer relationship with you."

The bathroom door opened, and a refreshed looking Jonah stepped out. His face was still slightly wet from where he had splashed water on it. "So, I have to ask...did you put something in my food or drink earlier?" he asked, as he walked over and sat down on the bed. Brianna gave him a confused look.

"No, why would you ask that?" she asked, walking over and standing near him.

He lowered his head and thought for a second.

"Jonah? Are you alright?"

"I don't know...but I do think I should tell you what happened..."

CHAPTER 21

CODY, WYOMING

Maria and Bridgette had not really spoken much the night before when they'd been made roommates. Other than Bridgette telling her which bed she wanted and to mind her own business, that was pretty much it. Bridgette was older and bigger, so Maria decided to just stay out of her way. Maria had laid down on her very uncomfortable bed and pretty much just cried herself to sleep. She missed her mother so much. Would she ever see her again? She silently prayed for God to send someone to rescue her from this place.

The next morning, they were awakened by a loud alarm that went off out in the hallway. Their lights came on and their doors unlocked. "GET UP!" a man yelled from out in the hall. "YOU HAVE FIVE SECONDS TO BE STANDING OUTSIDE YOUR DOOR!!!"

Maria had to pee so badly that her bladder hurt, and she could barely stand, but she ran out into the hall anyway. All the girls were coming out with their hair disheveled and their eyes puffy. A few of the younger ones were crying and rubbing their eyes.

"STOP CRYING!!!" the man, wearing what looked like a guard uniform, yelled. "Your mommies are not coming to save you! You need to get used to the idea that you will NEVER see your families again!!!" He slapped one crying little girl that looked to be around six. She fell to the ground and started screaming. He lifted her up by the hair and drug her down the hall. She screamed even louder as he tossed her by the door at the end of the hall. He pressed a button and the door opened.

"You're going to regret this little tantrum, Missy! He threw her out the door and yelled for someone named Frank to come take the first volunteer. Before the door closed, Maria saw the older man with the hat standing there watching what was happening just on the other side of the door.

The guard slammed the door closed and turned back to the rest of them. "Anyone else want to volunteer for today's auction!?" He walked to the center of the hall and looked at each girl. "Personally, I'd rather get you all dolled up and ready for the party tomorrow night. Now, we have a lot to do today! Anybody gives me any slack…I'll sell you to the lowest bidder that we have!" He laughed so hard that he was spitting.

Maria looked up at Bridgette and saw her quickly wipe a tear away. She didn't know what was going on or understand anything this man was saying, but if it made Bridgette cry…then it must be bad.

(SOMEWHERE BETWEEN PADUCAH, KENTUCKY AND ST. LOUIS, MISSOURI)

Jonah had told Brianna what had happened while he was out, but he'd still refused to accept Christ into his life. He thought it was just some hallucination or something…caused by fatigue. Brianna knew it had been a spiritual experience quite like the valley of the shadow of death she and her friends had gone to when they were younger. They had battled the dragon and death while in there, but thankfully Jesus had been there to fight for them…although their friend Billy Mumpower had died.

"I'm really feeling a sense of urgency," Jonah said, bringing her out of her thoughts. "Like we need to hurry up and get to Cody."

"Okay," Brianna replied. "We'll do whatever we have to do."

"I think, for now, that we should rotate driving and sleeping. It's less than a day if we don't stop to sleep."

"Then let's do it!" Brianna replied. "I'm not tired just yet, so if you are, I can drive."

"I'm good for now," Jonah replied. "Would you mind reading me some scripture?"

"Would I mind reading you some scripture?" she asked, extremely confused at his request. "There is nothing I would rather do right now. Anything in particular?"

"The only thing I can remember from Sunday School is that for God so loved the world one…what was it? John 3:16?"

"Yes, it was," Brianna said proudly. She pulled up the book of John on her Bible app and began in chapter one.

By the time Brianna finished with the book of John, they were close to St. Louis, Missouri and in need of gas. Jonah pulled off of Interstate 64 and pulled into a large truck stop. Brianna unbuckled and was about to open her door when he put his hand on her wrist. She stopped and looked over at him.

"I don't want to go to hell," he said, his eyes glazed over as if remembering every detail. "I'm just not wanting to jump into something I'm not fully ready to commit to just yet."

~ 195 ~

"I understand," Brianna gripped his arm. "Just don't wait too long, Jonah."

He nodded and seemed to be reliving the experience in his mind.

Brianna remembered Mark telling them about his experience with hell as well, and Jonah's sounded like it was on point.

"I've always prided myself in how strong I am…I was typically stronger than all my peers…but that demon, he threw me like a rag doll. Brianna, I've never been so scared. I didn't know I could possibly BE that scared."

"Well, you're safe now!" she replied, squeezing his hand. "Jesus already paid that price for you, you know?"

"Thank you," Jonah said with an intense sincerity. "Thank you for being such an unwavering Christian…not one of those…"

"You're welcome," Brianna replied. "Now, you pump, and I'll go pee."

Several hours later, it was 2am and Brianna was driving somewhere near North Platte, Nebraska. Jonah had opted to sleep in the backseat and was presently sprawled out underneath an Indian blanket they'd bought at the truck stop. He was lightly snoring over the praise and worship music Brianna had playing.

She was talking to her old friend, who just so happened to be sitting in the seat beside her with his hat in his lap. He looked out his window in deep thought. "So, are we going to be, okay?" she asked, loving the chance to have small talk with her best friend.

He looked over at her and smiled. "Define, okay?"

"Are we going to survive?"

"From my point of view, you are," he teased. "But my point of view is much broader than yours. If you die in this body, you still 'survive.'"

"Well, technically, yes, but I want to know if we die," Brianna asked.

"That will depend on the choices that you make, Brianna," he replied. "One bad decision and you could die in the next few moments."

"But still, you know the outcome…"

"I know everything, but that doesn't mean I'm a fortune teller. You still have a free will. If you turn this car around and go back to Gateway, you will not die in Cody, Wyoming."

"And if I keep going?" Brianna asked, hoping for some kind of nugget.

"Then you will be exactly where I have called you to be," he replied, slipping his hat atop his head. "Continue to listen for MY voice, Brianna, and never deny me…I am always with you…even in death." And with that, he was gone.

"Well, that was quite bitter-sweet," she said to no one in particular. Just then, her cell phone began vibrating. The screen read WASHINGTON D.C. She answered it with the push of a button where it was mounted on the dash. "Hello? This is Brianna," she said, clicking it onto speaker.

"Hello, Brianna," a nice, serious sounding male voice responded. "My name is Agent Donnie Wright…that's with a

~ 197 ~

W. I am with the F.B.I., and I can assure you that I am one of the good guys."

"I'm sorry, Agent Wright, but I don't know you, and…"

"Lieutenant Ramsey from the Jacksonville Sheriff's Office has contacted me this evening and informed me that you could possibly be needing some help," he replied.

"That's impossible, Agent Wright, Lieutenant Ramsey is in intensive care and unable to contact anyone at this time."

"Feel free to contact him, Ms. Bowers," the agent replied. "I'll wait."

Brianna quickly pulled her car to the side of the road and shot a quick text to Officer Ramsey. "Are u awake and fine? FBI has contacted me. Can you confirm???"

Within seconds a reply came. "YES!!! All is well here. A little sore but alive PTL. Sorry I did not alert you, but yes, Agent Wright is legit. I can personally vouch. He's a good guy. And thank God you guys are good."

"Praise Jesus you are fine!!!" Brianna replied. "Thanks for confirmation."

"Okay, Agent Wright, you have made the cut." She heard Jonah stirring in the backseat. Her conversation was pretty loud.

"Perfect, so what is the situation?"

"What all did Officer Ramsey tell you?" Brianna asked, wondering how up to speed this man was. She knew that Ramsey had little to no knowledge of what was really going on, but his insight was usually on target.

"Well, he explained to me that you worked for a ministry that helps find trafficked children. And, that he thought you might be in some trouble with the people who are trafficking those children…since he was caught in the line of fire and all."

At this point, Jonah sat up in his seat and stretched. His yawn was quite contagious as Brianna watched him in the mirror. "Okay, well, I'm pretty sure that the head of Interpol is involved, which is basically the reason I'm a little freaked out about who to trust."

"Are you talking about Secretary-General Gunther Schmidt?" Agent Wright asked. "And do you have any proof whatsoever for that allegation?"

"Only that my friend, Agent Nadia Skutnik, of Interpol, was suspicious of him…and now she is being held hostage in an attempt to lure me in. Also, I can't be one hundred percent positive, but the German man who keeps calling me, sounds a lot like him…but, like I said, not positive."

"So, you are going to this yet to be disclosed location in an attempt to rescue an Interpol agent with this man…Jonah Westbrook…what is his involvement?" He had Jonah's full attention now, as he leaned forward with his arms on the back of the front seats.

"First of all, the location is not undisclosed. We know where we are going, thanks to Jonah, who unknowingly helped them build the facility."

"Facility?"

"Yes, according to Jonah, it is an underground bunker that some billionaire had them build…and then Jonah's entire crew was murdered."

"Are you referring to the plane crash in Missouri, involving the entire Maitland Construction crew? Are you saying that was murder?"

"I'm saying that was a cover-up!" Jonah called out.

"Is that Mr. Westbrook?" Agent Wright asked.

"Yessir," Brianna replied. "You're on speaker."

"Mr. Westbrook, what is your knowledge of this so-called cover-up?"

"First of all, we were done with the project," Jonah began. "All the guys had been on this job for months and not been allowed to leave. Nothing would've kept them from going home to their families."

"Okay?" Agent Wright replied.

"So, the job was in Cody, Wyoming, they all lived in Colorado… the plane crashed in Missouri…why was it over Missouri? It was going away from Colorado. I'd spoken to my supervisor the night before and he said the guys were ready to get home, but they were told to hold off for some big bonus. My guess is, that bonus was a mass execution."

You have to admit, Mr. Westbrook," Agent Wright said. "That's a huge leap. Maybe they were being flown somewhere else to receive their bonus. Maybe they'd been given a huge contract to start another job."

"No way, we never jump straight into another job without some R&R," Jonah replied. "Not one of those guys would've done that, including the bosses. Don't you find it strange how when we took that job, we were required to sign a disclaimer that we would not disclose the location to anyone. They didn't even want us communicating with the outside world. Luckily one of my buddies had snuck a cell phone in or I wouldn't have known about my father's heart attack. Oh, and they insisted on every single employee, even the secretary, be onsite. Our Denver office was literally vacant for two months."

"It's not exactly unheard of to have to sign disclaimers on job sites, Mr. Westbrook," Agent Wright replied. "Especially when you're doing a job for a billionaire eccentric like, Joshua Coff."

"Wait, how did you know that's who we were working for?" Jonah asked, leaning forward in his seat.

"I've been doing my homework, Mr. Westbrook," the agent replied. "I looked you up as soon as Lieutenant Ramsey contacted me."

"So, you know about what happened in San Diego?" Jonah asked.

"If you're talking about the occurrence at your parent's house, and Detective Ken Chun being shot in the head, then yes, I know about what happened."

"Then you're pretty much caught up to speed with me," Jonah responded and leaned back in his seat. "Except for the fact that these crazies have now kidnapped my sister and plan to kill her if we don't show up at the facility by midnight Tuesday."

"Also," Brianna added. "The man that was shot and killed in Officer Ramsey's squad car, Travis...something...he said that while on a video call with Mr. Coff...he was forced to watch a mass execution of a bunch of construction workers being gunned down."

There was a short pause and then Agent Wright came back. "Travis Scott was a very bad man, Brianna...not sure how credible he is."

"I understand that" Brianna replied. "But he was helping me to find a specific little girl."

Another long pause... "Mr. Westbrook...where exactly IS this facility?"

"I can't tell you that, sir," Jonah replied. "We were told to show up alone or they would kill my sister."

"Mr. Westbrook, I can pretty much assure you that not only are they going to kill your sister, but you and Brianna as well...if you show up without my help. Now, why don't you at least meet with one of my teams...let's say...you're heading to Cody...my tracking has you in North Platte, Nebraska right now...how about Casper, Wyoming in about five and a half hours?"

"Okay," Brianna said. "We'll call this number when we get there."

"Perfect," Agent Wright said. "I'll have a team there."

CHAPTER 22

SYDNEY, AUSTRALIA

During the entire flight, Gabi had felt the urgency to pray for her friend, Brianna. Something big was about to go down and Brianna was in grave danger. Gabi's heart was literally breaking for her friend. She desperately wanted to call her, but the Holy Spirit had said no. Gabi loved the concept of trusting God, but sometimes it was just so difficult.

They were at the hotel now and Scotty was sound asleep. It was several hours before they needed to be at the venue for tonight's rally. Her body was exhausted, but her spirit needed to pray. She was about to kneel down by the sofa when there was a light rap on the door. Opening it, she was greeted by Mark's wife, Maria McGee, smiling from ear to ear. Maria had just now joined them from the states, having always wanted to visit Australia. This was Gabi's first time seeing her old friend in several weeks. They hugged and Gabi invited her in. "I was just about to…"

"Pray for Brianna?" Maria asked. She noticed her friend's shock and smiled. "The entire flight I've done nothing but lift that girl up in prayer. Do you know what's going on?"

Gabi shook her head. "With her job, there's no telling. I'm just so worried, Maria. I've felt the need to pray for her before, but NEVER this strong. She is facing something HUGE!"

"Well," Maria said, taking Gabi's hands. "Let's show it what a HUGE God looks like!" They both knelt down in front of the sofa and entered the throne room of God with their petition.

~ 203 ~

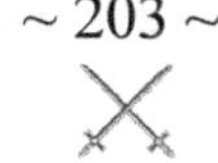

CODY, WYOMING

Yesterday had been a horribly busy day. The children were primped and fashioned in every possible manner, and pictures were taken for the auction. Boys were dressed in several fashionable scenarios, including girls' clothes and makeup.

Girls were made to dress and pose in unthinkable manners. The entire day was spent posing for pictures with loud music blaring and people yelling at one another. Several of the older children attempted to rebel against those in charge…they were carted away and the ones who returned were more than willing to do what they were told. No one was sure what happened to the ones that did not return, though.

There had been little to no food for the children the entire day. Even the young ones were too afraid to complain. All the children had been escorted to their rooms extra early and told to go to bed immediately. The following day would be even more eventful…and if they were lucky enough, they would be given a forever home.

Maria did not like the sound of that at all. She had a forever home…with her mother, whom she missed very much. She had no intention of ever calling someone else her mother, so they might as well get that idea out of their heads. Even though she was quite upset about what the next day held, she was even more exhausted, and fell fast asleep as soon as her head hit the pillow.

The loud alarm went off again after what felt like only a few minutes but in reality, it was nine long hours. The doors to each room swung open and again the girls were informed to line up in the hall. Once they were in place, a woman wearing a gray skirt suit with her hair up in a tight bun, walked out in front of the girls.

"Today, you will be taught manners. You will learn how to behave as young women…or whatever it is that your new family wants you to become. You will learn extreme obedience…or you will suffer my wrath. Extreme obedience is doing exactly what you are told, when you are told, and smiling while you do it…whether it is pleasant or not. I can assure you that if you follow the rules, you will learn to love your new lives. First, though, you have to understand that your old lives are in the past. You will NEVER see your old families again."

Several of the girls looked around to see what the older girls would do. Maria looked up at Bridgette, her roommate. Bridgette had been one of the girls that had rebelled the day before. Maria had noticed that she walked differently after she came back. She'd also noticed that she agreed with everything that was said. Right now, Bridgette was nodding at everything this lady was saying. Maria would not nod. Maria would go along with this craziness for now…but she knew that Jesus was going to save her in the end…and she would see her mother again.

The girls were told that there would be visitors on sight tonight. Most of the people would be viewing the auction through video, but there would be many people in attendance. Many very wealthy people that were going to be paying a lot of money for these children. They were to remain on their best behavior…or else.

CASPER, WYOMING

Brianna and Jonah had swapped spots just after the phone call with the F.B.I. Jonah was now driving and Brianna was sound asleep in the back seat. He pulled off at the exit where they were supposed to be meeting with the agents. "Hey, Sleeping Beauty!" he called to her. "Time to stop snoring and wake up! We're almost there!"

She opened her eyes in a fog and had to remind herself where she was. "Oh my gosh, did I really snore?" she asked, as she sat up and looked at herself in the rear-view mirror.

"I kept thinking I had a flat," Jonah replied with a laugh.

She shoved his shoulder. "You did NOT!" She ran her fingers through her hair and sighed. "I look terrible."

Jonah peeked back at her. "Oh my God! Yeah, that's bad!" He laughed way too loud.

"Jonah!" she replied a little more whiny than she'd planned. "Be nice!"

"I mean, no way!" he replied. "You're stunning!!! As always!"

"There, was that so hard!?"

"I already called them and we're meeting at the Waffle House," he said. "There's supposed to be like six agents and they're buying us breakfast." He pointed up ahead where the Waffle House sat just on the right.

Okay, perfect," Brianna replied. "Breakfast sounds good, but we need to talk about something. I need you to give Jesus some serious consideration before we get into this

situation too deep." She saw his confused look in the mirror. "I'm serious! If something happens to you, I would love to know you're ready to go to heaven." Just as they approached the turn, her phone rang. "It's him!" Brianna said, looking down at the screen. Jonah clicked the speaker button to take the call. "Hello, Agent Wright," Brianna answered. "We're just pulling into the parking lot!"

"GET OUT OF THERE!!!" Agent Wright screamed into the phone. "There was an ambush!!! I'm pretty sure all my agents are dead!!!"

Jonah slammed on the brakes, but he'd already pulled into the parking lot. A quick scan revealed the Waffle House to potentially be empty. In fact, other than a few scattered cars, there was no sign of life. "It doesn't look like…" Just then, a large black man wearing black military attire, and carrying an extremely large automatic weapon, came walking around from behind the building.

"JONAH!" Brianna screamed, as the man lifted the weapon toward them. "GO!!!"

Jonah punched the gas and squealed the tires as he spun through the front parking lot, hopped the curb and hit the road with all 475 horses roaring to life.

"Guys!?" Agent Wright called out. "What's going on!?"

"YES!!!!" Jonah screamed, as he made an immediate right and punching it down a side road in an attempt to lose the bad guys.

"Brianna!" Agent Wright yelled. "Do you have another phone!?"

"Yes! Jonah has a burner!"

"Throw your phone out the window and call me back on that one! NOW!!!"

She immediately dialed his number with the burner and tossed her phone out the window as if it were about to explode. "DONE!" she said, when he answered.

"They've been tracking you the whole time with it, but when we contacted you, they felt threatened!" Agent Wright said. "My guys walked right into a trap!"

"NO WAY!!!" Jonah yelled, looking in the rear-view mirror. "You better dig out that pistol, Bree…they're coming up behind us! I can only go so fast in this traffic!"

"Who knew this many people lived in Wyoming?" Brianna asked, still blushing from Jonah calling her Bree. Her parents were the only ones that had ever called her that. When Jonah said it, it sounded intimate… "Focus, Bree," she thought to herself, and looked back to see two large black SUV's catching up to them. "Is there any way you can get us some help, Agent…"

"Already ahead of you!" Agent Wright replied. "I'm in contact with Casper P.D.! What road are you on and what are you driving!?"

"It looks like Beverly Street!" Jonah yelled. "But I'm going to need to get off of it soon…they're catching up!"

"Candy apple red 1969 Ford Mustang Boss 429!" Brianna yelled. "They can't miss it!"

"The police are aware of where you are…and WOW! Nice car!!!" Agent Wright said. "I think they're behind the suspects!"

"Oh my gosh!" Brianna exclaimed. "He's hanging out the window of the SUV!" She put her hand over her mouth as the large man aimed a big gun at the police cars behind them and opened fire. "He's shooting at the police!"

"Use this opportunity to lose them, Jonah!" Agent Wright said. "Or they'll be shooting at you next!"

Jonah scanned the distance and saw a gas station parking lot ahead on the left. If he could get across traffic, he could cut through to the road behind it. He checked his mirror and saw that one SUV had the guy hanging out the side, but the other one was fast approaching them. Looking ahead the upcoming light was red, so he had a few seconds.

He needed to use the other side of the road before the turn lane released its traffic. The problem was…the gas station was about a quarter mile away. Without another thought, Jonah crossed the grass median, shot into oncoming traffic, and punched the gas. He felt nothing but raw power beneath him as the Mustang surged forward and hit 70 mph in less than two seconds. He quickly hit the brakes and squealed into the gas station parking lot.

"WHOA!!!" Brianna yelled, as the car's thrust pushed her back in her seat. "I think I'll buckle up now!"

"You think!?" Jonah said, as he dodged a pickup truck and made his way onto the next road. "This baby is fire!!!" He punched the gas again and darted down the back road as fast as he could. Checking the mirror, he saw that he had not been

followed…yet. He saw another road coming up on the right and quickly made the turn. Without thinking, he made another right and found himself heading straight for the second SUV. "NOOO!!!" He slammed on the brakes, turned the wheel hard, and punched it…the engine sputtered and died. "What the….NO! WE'RE OUT OF GAS!!!!"

"NO WAY!!!" Brianna yelled.

"I knew I'd forgotten something…HAND ME A GUN!!!" Jonah yelled, as two big guys climbed out of the SUV with automatic weapons.

"Get out and run!" Brianna said, pushing the passenger seat forward and opening the door. "NOW!!!" She stepped out of the car and opened fire on the two men. She hit the one on her side of the car right in the chest and he flew backwards and hit the ground. She saw Jonah take off running down an alley and shot in the direction of the other man. She dove behind the car just as he unloaded his weapon on the passenger side of her beautiful Mustang.

As soon as he stopped shooting, she raised up over the hood and shot him right between the eyes. He dropped like a sack of potatoes. Even though it broke her heart to send someone to hell like that, her father would be very proud right now. All those trips to the shooting range had paid off. Two other doors opened on the SUV just as Brianna took off down the alley hoping to find Jonah.

CODY, WYOMING

Joshua walked over to the edge of the cliff and looked down over his five thousand acres. His compound was just

below the tree line, and completely out of sight from the air. There would be no prying eyes over the goings on in this place. Of course, he had so many politicians, judges, and law enforcement officers in his pocket, that worrying about such things as being caught was absolutely hilarious. He smiled as he took it all in. This was his kingdom. His world. Heck, it was his universe. He was totally untouchable.

Of course, there was the small problem of that meddling woman and the rogue construction worker. What luck that they just so happened to find each other. He hadn't even known about her until then. She'd been with that loser, Travis, when he'd had him killed. Too bad she hadn't stayed in the police car with him. Two birds…one stone. Sometimes tying up loose ends wasn't as easy as it should be. That would all be over soon enough though.

His men were presently in Casper intercepting them from the Feds…thanks to his special connections. In just a few short hours, Brianna Bowers and Jonah Westbrook would be arriving here like lambs for the slaughter. He had something special in store for them. Jonah would get to watch his sister be killed in front of his eyes…slowly. Brianna would get a special show of her own. She liked to "save the children" so much. He would have a couple of men demonstrate what little boys and girls were good for. The thought of that made him smile.

"Excuse me, Joshua," his beautiful Asian assistant said, bowing as he turned to acknowledge her.

"Yes, Chi?"

"Some of the guests have begun to arrive, sir," she replied.

~ 211 ~

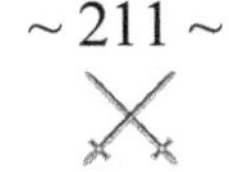

"Have they now?" He looked past her, down by the trail head that led back down to the compound. Several men from his private security team were standing, heavily armed. He turned back to his view of his immense kingdom. "Make sure they are comfortable, won't you?"

"Of course, sir," Chi responded and bowed again. She turned to go.

"Chi?" he said, not bothering to turn around.

"Yes, Joshua?"

"Has there been any word from our friends in Casper?"

"Not yet, I'm afraid."

"Let me know the very minute you hear from them."

"Yes, Joshua," she bowed a final time and walked away.

Joshua watched below as several cars went by slowly just out of sight beneath the trees. Billionaires, politicians, Hollywood elites, judges, and disgusting pigs from around the world would be joining him tonight in person or on Zoom to bid for the ownership of hundreds of children and adults alike from all over America. "Yes," he said. "You're about to be richer than even you thought possible, Joshua. Richer than even HE promised."

CHAPTER 23

CODY, WYOMING

Nadia had been escorted to a long black limo and driven to a private airport. They'd boarded a Cessna where she'd been cuffed to her seat at the back of the plane. The only person that she recognized, other than those who'd brought her, was the Secretary-General of Interpol, Gunther Schmidt.

He had looked at her disappointingly as he'd passed her on the way to the front of the plane. Not a single word had been spoken to her by anyone until just before they'd landed at their final destination, almost 24 hours later. There had been three landings for refueling along the way and Nadia had not been able to find out where they were, at any of them. She had no idea where she was.

"We had high hopes for you at Interpol, Nadia," Secretary-General Schmidt said, in his thick German accent. He'd walked back and sat in the seat across the aisle from her. "It is a shame that things have to end this way."

"Where are we?" Nadia asked, sensing another descent in altitude. "Where are you taking me? And where is my sister!?"

He smiled at her. "Your sister is already too far gone to save, Nadia. You should forget about her." He watched her face to see the torment in her eyes. "We are taking YOU on a fishing trip, Nadia," he said with a boisterous laugh. When he saw her confused look, he continued. "I am the fisherman…your friend Brianna Bowers is the fish…and YOU!" He poked her in the side of the neck. "Are the bait."

"Wait," things were beginning to click in her mind. "Are we in America? You're NEVER going to catch her, you know!" Nadia smiled at him. "Her God will protect her!"

He knelt down in the aisle, so they were face to face. "For you, it does not matter where we are. Because, you see, Nadia…regardless of the result of a fishing trip, it is never pleasant…for the bait." He laughed another annoyingly boisterous laugh and walked back to the front of the plane. Just before sitting down, he turned back to face her. "And as for Brianna's God…he will watch me fillet the skin from her bones!"

Moments after they landed, Nadia was escorted off the plane. She squinted in the morning sun and noticed the rolling hills and mountains in the distance. Given the desert-like appearance and arid feel, if this WAS America, she would have to guess northwest…maybe Montana.

They led her toward a caravan of large, black SUV's. Once inside, she noticed the three enormous men that were with her. Two in the front and one seated beside her. A black hood was placed over her head. "This isn't necessary, you know! You guys are not THAT unpleasant to look at!"

"Oh, for God's sake, Damien!" the driver yelled. "What is the point of the hood!? She'll be dead this time tomorrow!"

"She is with Interpol," Damien replied, in a thick German accent. "Did you notice she was watching and looking at everything? The hood stays on…I don't trust this one."

A few moments later, she felt the vehicle surge forward, leading her to God only knew where…God…Brianna's God. She couldn't stop thinking about Him. Was He as real as

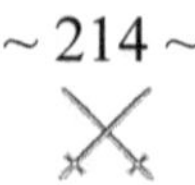

Brianna believed Him to be? The peace in Brianna's eyes, the passion in her words, the warmth in her smile, would say yes…her God is real. Nadia could use what Brianna had right now. "Jesus."

"What did you say?" Damien asked. She remained silent. "You would be wise to remain quiet."

After about forty-five minutes of driving in complete silence, the vehicle lurched to a sudden stop. She could hear what sounded like the driver's window sliding down and then the beeping sound of numbers being entered into a keypad. They were at a gate. Moments later, they pushed forward again, and within seconds it seemed like the whole world went dark. "Are we in a tunnel?" she asked, not expecting a response, but her head was immediately shoved against the window. "I told you to shut up!"

"Damien!" Someone in the front seat called out. "The boss won't like it if you damage the goods," Nadia could almost hear him smiling. "He has big plans for this one."

They came to a stop, and she heard their three doors open and then close. "I'll just stay here," she said to herself. Immediately, her door swung open, and someone grabbed her arm and pulled her out of the truck. She sensed a concrete floor and assumed they were in some kind of parking garage.

She was shoved forward by someone behind her, but the other person kept a firm grip on her arm. They stopped for a moment, and she heard an elevator door open. They entered and within seconds were moving…down. "Ahhh, an underground lair," she thought to herself. "This just keeps getting better." The elevator stopped after several seconds, and she was led forward. They stopped immediately and her hood was removed.

~ 215 ~

She looked down and allowed her eyes to adjust to the fluorescent lighting.

She was in a very long, four-foot-wide hallway, lined with doors set apart about every seven feet. She was shoved forward again and began following the man in front of her. They were almost at the end of the hall when he stopped and turned to face her. He produced a key and released her from her cuffs. He then proceeded to unlock the door and open it. The man behind her shoved her inside and slammed the door.

The room was small, maybe eight by eight. There were two beds, one on each side of the room with a dresser between them. A small sink was in the corner at the foot of the bed to her left, where a twenty-something blonde was sitting with her back against the wall and her knees pulled up to her face. She was looking at Nadia and appeared to have been crying. "Hello…" Nadia said, with a slight nod. "I am Nadia."

The young woman wiped her eyes with the back of her arm. "Hi, Nadia," she replied in an American accent. "I'm Jaclyn."

CASPER, WYOMING

As Brianna ran through the alley, lined mostly with garbage cans, dumpsters, and old pallets, she looked back and forth, hoping to see where Jonah had gone. As she neared the end, she saw him as he stepped out from the back door of a restaurant and waved her in. She quickly ran to him, and he closed the door behind her and locked it. He led her into the small kitchen of an Asian restaurant.

"This is Mrs. Tang," Jonah said, pointing to an older woman dressed in a beautiful red dress, a robin's egg blue apron and a red hair net. "She says she has a place we can hide until the coast is clear."

The woman led them down a narrow hallway to a thin door. She opened it and exposed a tiny broom closet. Brianna and Jonah just stared at it for a second. The woman reached in and slid a large shelf full of cleaning supplies and towels over with ease. They noticed that it was on rollers and hiding a small room behind it. She pushed them in and rolled the shelf back into place. She flipped on a light for them and then turned off the light in the broom closet.

"So, what happened out there, Dirty Harry?" Jonah asked. "You just shooed me away like a knight in shining armor! You know, the guy is supposed to be the hero, right?"

"Jonah, I killed two men!" she replied in a whisper and saw the shock on his face.

"Wait, are you serious?" Jonah asked.

Brianna nodded and teared up. "Those men are dead and in hell right now…and I did that."

Jonah pulled her into a hug and stroked her hair. "Bree, you had to do it…they were going to kill us both…wow, that's really awesome that you did that."

She pulled away and sat down on a nearby box. "My dad taught me to shoot. He always said I was a natural…but I never really thought I would have to shoot another person."

"You didn't even hesitate!" he whispered loudly. "Get out and run!" he reenacted with a smile. "The next thing I know,

I'm hearing what sounds like a scene from Saving Private Ryan behind me."

"I killed them."

"You had to."

"Jonah, listen to me…you need Jesus." She stood from her box and took a step toward him. She saw the skeptical look on his face. "I'm serious! This is life and death stuff we're dealing with. We could both easily be dead right now! Where would you be!?"

"Calm down, Bree!" he said. "I'm good. I'm not going to die."

"Everybody is going to die!" Brianna hit back. "Please! I need to know you're taken care of!"

Just then they heard shouting from inside the restaurant. Brianna clicked off the lights. Jonah put his hand on her shoulder. "You still have the gun?" he whispered.

"Yes," she replied. "But there's only six shots left. The clips are in my bag in the car."

There was a loud crash and more shouting that seemed to be getting closer. "I'LL KILL EVERYBODY IN THIS PLACE, OLD LADY!!! NOW, WHERE ARE THEY!?"

Brianna flipped the light back on and opened the door. "We have to get out there, I won't be able to live with myself if something happens to these people."

Jonah slid the shelf out of the way, and they stepped into the closet and then out into the hallway. "We're back here!" he

yelled. He walked in front of Brianna. "Take the shot if you get it," he whispered over his shoulder.

"Jonah," Brianna called from way behind him.

He turned to see that an extremely large man had already pinned Brianna to the wall and taken her gun away. Before he could turn back around, someone hit Jonah right in the face with the butt of a rifle. Everything went black.

"NOOO!!!" Brianna screamed as she saw Jonah drop to the floor with blood all over his face. "That was not necessary!"

"Put him in the back of the truck!" one of the large men said in a thick European accent. "And you!" he said, pulling Brianna backwards by her hair. "Would be very wise to not give me any trouble."

"What about the others?" the man who hit Jonah, asked.

"Kill everyone who saw us, Marco…you know this!"

"WHAT!?" Brianna yelled. "These people haven't done anything!!! Just let them go!!!" As they pushed her out of the backdoor, she heard the gunshots. "JESUS!!!"

SYDNEY, AUSTRALIA

Gabi had just stepped off the elevator into the hotel lobby and started heading toward the front door. Mark was supposed to have ordered a van for them to get to tonight's venue. She looked around as she walked and didn't see any of the others around. She was usually met by Matt or Andy in order to go over the playlist for the night. Sometimes the guys

liked to mix it up. Matt said it made it more interesting for people who watched them on YouTube at every event they did.

The further she walked, though, the more people seemed to be in the lobby. She stopped in place and surveyed the area. Tons of people were milling about, yet she didn't recognize a soul. She shrugged and continued on toward the door, though noticing that it didn't seem to be any closer than it was when she'd exited the elevator.

"Excuse me!" a tall, ruggedly handsome man grabbed her by the elbow, and she spun around. "Have you seen this woman?" He held up a picture of a pretty, young, blonde woman. "I can't find her anywhere." Gabi noticed he had an American accent…something she hadn't heard much outside of her group since arriving in Australia.

"No, sorry," Gabi replied. "How long has she been missing?"

"Never mind…" he grabbed someone else and showed them the picture.

She turned away from him and bumped right into her husband's chest. "Oh, thank goodness, Scotty!"

"Where have you been!?" he asked in an irritated voice. "We've all been waiting for you!"

"Sorry," she replied, grabbing his arm as he led her through the crowd. "I desperately needed a nap!" The crowd in the lobby was getting thicker by the second. She attempted to hold on to Scotty's arm, but he pulled ahead of her and slipped from her grip. "Scotty!" She couldn't even see him now. People were pushing around her from every direction. She couldn't move. "Oh, my goodness! What is going on!?"

The entire lobby fell silent. Everybody stopped in their tracks…and turned toward the front door. People began to move out of the way, walking toward the windows and the walls. There was something going on outside. Gabi saw Mark with his arm around Maria, who was crying. Matt, Andy, Eddie, and Yvette were standing there with shocked looks on their faces.

Something was going on just outside of Gabi's view. People began to step aside as men in suits came into view. They were carrying something…coffins…and they were coming into the lobby. Gabi was completely confused. Why were they bringing coffins into a hotel lobby? Was this some kind of Australian thing? They entered the lobby and she noticed that several people were mourning. They sat the coffins down on small carts and one of the men walked around and proceeded to open one of the coffins.

"No way!" Gabi actually said out loud.

A young girl next to her looked at Gabi with tears in her eyes. "Can you believe it? After all the good she did."

"I'm sorry," Gabi leaned down to the girl. "Who is it?"

The girl began slowly approaching the caskets as the first one was opened. Gabi walked behind her to get a better view. It felt disrespectful, but necessary. She stopped where she was when she heard a man begin to wail. It was the man who'd shown her the picture. He had fallen on the floor in front of the first casket and was crying out in horror. That's when Gabi noticed that it was the woman from the picture, in the casket. How could that be? Hadn't she just gone missing? Had Gabi misunderstood?

~ 221 ~

Then the entire room went quiet again as the man who had opened the first casket stopped in front of the second one. He looked over his shoulder and actually made eye contact with Gabi. "Well, that was eerie," she thought. That's when Scotty walked up and put his arm around her. He led her toward the casket. "Scotty, what are you doing?" she whispered in his ear. He just pulled her up to where she was standing in front of him as the man opened the casket. A loud, ominous moan flowed through the room as people saw who it was.

Gabi leaned forward for a better view and gasped....

"BRIANNA!!!!" she screamed as she shot up in bed. The room was dark with the curtains drawn. She was breathing so hard she was practically panting. Her clothes were soaked with sweat. Out of the corner of her eye, something moved. She jumped and looked over just in time to see a large, black, scaly creature vanish into the wall. The phone next to the bed rang, causing her to yell out loud. She reached over and picked it up. "Hello?"

"Gabi?" It was Brianna's mom, and she was crying. Her heart stopped beating for a split second. "Please be praying for my Brianna...I've got a really bad feeling...Gabi...Gabi?"

"So do I, Mrs. Bowers..." Gabi replied, eyeing the spot where the demon had just exited the room. "So do I."

CHAPTER 24

CODY, WYOMING

Joshua walked down the long-carpeted corridor, surrounded by his usual well-armed entourage. The white marble walls were brilliantly bright in the LED lit halls. He could practically see his reflection and found himself admiring his muscular physique as he approached each corner. Chi approached him as he entered the main lobby where all the offices branched off from.

She pointed to the screen of her iPad, alerting him to the arrival of several dignitaries and world powers. Unfazed by this news, he entered the lobby without breaking stride. The carpeted floors ended where the beautiful mahogany began. The lobby walls were made of pearl white stone and held some of the most expensive artwork in the world. Each of the offices were made of glass walls and doors and each contained a glass topped desk, a black leather chair, and a single laptop.

The entire operation was designed to remain as simple as possible…just in case there was a raid on the compound…and someone actually made it this far in. All the brains of their computer operation, such as customer files, were hidden deep inside the compound in an extremely secure room. Joshua had spared no expense on the security of his clients.

Joshua passed by the office area and motioned for each of his guards to take up their known positions. His world was a well-oiled machine. He walked to the end of the corridor and opened a large oak door. As he entered the enormous conference room, everyone inside went silent. He stopped just inside the door and smiled as his eyes roamed the room.

Politicians from several countries, judges, religious leaders, C.E.O.'s, lawyers, businessmen, Hollywood elites, and the heads of several law enforcement agencies from all over the world…including the Secretary-General of Interpol, Gunther Schmidt. He was Joshua's latest addition to the organization…and would definitely come in handy. Joshua glanced toward the medium sized cage in the back corner and realized that Gunther had already made himself useful. He nodded his head in approval to the man and took his seat at the head of the table. "Gentlemen…and ladies."

Several people acknowledged him with welcomes as he looked over his notes. "Joshua, before we begin," the senior vice president of a popular children's amusement park said, "I would just like to say, your new facility is top of the line!" This elicited an applause from around the room.

"Thank you, James," Joshua replied. He smiled at the room again and straightened his tie. "Let me just say, we have taken special measures to assure that the rat…that caused us to abandon the last facility…has been taken care of. In fact, some of you might even get a chance to have a go with her later." That caused several of them to sit up in their seats.

"Do tell…" a Federal judge from California blurted out.

"Keep it in your pants, Frank…" a senator from Massachusetts said with a snort. "The fun begins later." Several others laughed at this, and others nodded in agreement.

"We have a long evening ahead of us, people!" Joshua said without looking up. "I would like to ask my good friend, Jack Watson, the Southeastern United States Coordinator of…." He looked up and met Jack's eye. "Confiscation." Joshua

and Jack shared a smile as Jack approached the head of the table.

"All rise!" Jack said as he stood next to Joshua. Everyone in the room, except Joshua, stood to their feet. There were approximately twenty people around the table and another twenty-five lining the walls of the conference room. All eyes were on Jack. "Lock arms in unity!" Jack called out and everyone locked arms at the elbows with the person beside them. "Eyes closed!"

At that point, Joshua rose from his seat and scanned the room. "Oh, great God of Teuflisch, destroyer of our enemies. We rise in your presence. You are patient with us oh magnificent God. We have come before you tonight with a sacrifice. May your ways be eternal. May your path be ever open. May all who stand against you be brought low. May your thirst for the blood of your enemies be ever quenched. May those who come against your followers feel the sting of your blade. Use us oh God, your chosen ones…for we are…"

Everyone in the room said together…. "The Sword of Darkness."

They all opened their eyes and dropped their arms as one.

"Prepare the child for tonight's ceremony," Joshua said, and two men lifted the cage that Nadia's little sister, Ana, was being held in. She was taken from the room as each man smiled at the thought of what was to become of the little tramp. Perhaps one of them would own her…

Dustin's heart skipped a beat as the gate opened to allow his limousine to enter the compound. He sat up straight in his seat and wiped his palms on his expensive designer jeans. He'd never been this nervous in his life and considering the nineteen-year-old heart throb's past, that was saying a lot.

Dustin Knight: up and coming pop star sensation, and according to a survey in Teen Magazine, the "hottest musical talent in over a decade." He was blonde, tanned, muscular, and sported a smile that teenage girls melted over. His voice was considered the most unique and original voice in pop history. It was practically its own instrument.

He was compared to a cross between Steve Perry and Justin Timberlake. He was told to prepare himself for greatness…which was why his manager had insisted on his being here tonight. "This…is how you go from a ten to a thousand, my dear boy!"

Dustin, however, had heard rumors. He'd been told by people that he didn't associate with much anymore and that this would be his downfall. "Be careful, Dustin!" his old band mate from Shreveport had emailed him. "You're dancing with the devil now!" "They're after your soul now, Dustin!" a previous Youth Pastor had messaged him on Facebook.

His own mother had even called him and said she had a bad feeling about the direction he was heading. "Posers, wannabes, and buzz kills," his manager, Seth Stevens had said. "They fear what they don't understand OR deserve! This is YOUR ride, Son…they can either get on or get out of the way!"

Dustin looked across the limo to where Seth now sat with a woman on each side of him. He was drinking a cocktail and enjoying their company in a manner that Dustin wished he

didn't have to watch. "So, what exactly am I going to have to do in this initiation, Seth!?" he yelled over the blaring music.

Seth smiled that million-dollar smile that had landed him contracts with the biggest names in music. "Relax, kid…what you are about to experience is what separates the posers from the greats!" He shared a laugh with his lady friends.

"My friends tell me I'm making a deal with the devil!" Dustin replied.

Seth leaned forward in his seat, almost spilling his drink. He came within inches of Dustin's face. "You ARE, my boy! You ARE!" He gave Dustin a serious look and smiled. "But it's the devil who makes the best deals!" This caused the ladies to cackle in laughter and Seth smiled really big and sat back. "Just do as you're informed to do tonight and by this time tomorrow…you'll be bigger than Michael Jackson!"

Dustin looked out his window as the car came to a stop next to this massive compound. His mind was spinning, his heart was pounding, and his spirit was screaming for him to run. A large bald man opened his door, and he stepped out. Two extremely beautiful women appeared out of nowhere, took him by the arm, and led him into the building.

This was all happening so fast. He squeezed his eyes shut and tried to muster the strength to go on. As he walked down the marble-walled halls, he heard someone whistling to his left. The song was from his youth. He loved that old song…what was it? He looked over as the old gentleman, whistling, began to close the door. He smiled at Dustin and tipped his hat. What was that song and why was he suddenly thinking about Sunday school at Grandma's church?

~ 227 ~

"May I please check to see if he's, okay?" Brianna asked anyone who would listen. They had pretty much ignored her for the entire ride. Jonah had not stirred once from the back of the SUV. She desperately wanted to see if he was alright. He had taken quite a nasty hit to the face. "Please, just let me check for a pulse!" She turned in her seat and the large man beside her gave her a death stare that made her skin crawl.

"For his sake," the man leaned close to her and said through gritted teeth. "You'd better pray he's dead."

"Yeah, Sweetheart!" the guy in the passenger seat said, in a thick southern accent. "What they have planned for you two is WAY worse than death!" They all laughed.

Brianna closed her eyes and began to silently pray. She prayed for Jonah to be alright. She prayed that the Holy Spirit would keep them safe and help them to rescue hundreds of children from these mad men. She prayed for Maria…and remembered that the Spirit had told her to pray for Maria's mother…not Maria. She did pray for Maria's mother…but found it very difficult not to pray for the girl as well. "Your will be done in Maria's life, Father…but let your Spirit hold her close."

"We're here!" The driver announced in his European accent as the SUV came to a stop in front of a large iron gate. He punched in some numbers on a keypad and the gate slid open. "Is the princess ready for the night of her life?" He asked, looking at Brianna in the rear-view mirror. His eyes were smiling. "You took on the wrong organization, Darling." The others laughed and nodded. "Probably the most powerful organization in the world…you never stood a chance."

"Soon enough," Brianna replied with all the courage she could muster. "You'll experience the most powerful organization in the universe." That really made them laugh.

They wound their way through some beautiful landscapes on the road beyond the gate. There were hills covered in grass, bushes, trees, and flowers Brianna had never seen with a backdrop of desert and mountains that reached to the sky. It was absolutely stunning. In any other circumstance, she would be speechless…right now, she prayed in the spirit like she'd never prayed before.

There was a sense of dread and despair in the air, and she couldn't let it grip her heart. The SUV pulled into what appeared to be a dark tunnel but ended up being the entrance to an underground parking garage. They made their way over to an elevator and the truck came to a stop.

"End of the line, Darling!" the man in the passenger seat said, looking at her over his shoulder. "I sure hope Joshua gives me a shot at you before he cages you up for the barbecue!" He smiled an evil smile that made Brianna look away. The other two men laughed as they opened their doors.

"Cover us with your protection, Holy Spirit," she said aloud as the driver opened her door.

He brought his face close to hers and she could smell his aftershave. "Even your God cannot help you now."

Joshua finished the meeting and immediately felt an urgency to go to his quiet place. With everyone pressing in on him and wanting a moment of his time, he quickly excused

himself and exited the room. His security detail attempted to catch up to him and he turned and told them to leave him be.

After taking a few steps away from them, he turned back. "Position men outside my office...I am NOT to be disturbed!" He turned back and headed for his office at the end of the corridor. Opening the large oak door, he entered his office and paused. His heart was pounding as he desperately needed to enter his sanctum. Walking to his large glass desk, he opened his laptop and pressed a few buttons that killed the security feed to his office.

His cameras were off. Feeling the urgent pulling of his master, he stood and walked over to the large, oak bookshelf that lined the back wall of his office. Three shelves from the top, dead center...his prized possession...hand crafted centuries ago. Made of a pure silver blade and solid gold handle...some said it had been the sword of Goliath...some said the sword of Herod, who'd ordered the execution of hundreds of children in order to kill the false king born to take his place...

But Joshua smiled as he ran his fingers over the handle. No matter who had held it in the past...no matter who had wielded its power before...it was his to master now... The Sword of Darkness. Forged as the weapon to destroy God himself.

He lifted the handle and the bookshelf shifted. He pulled it back toward him and it opened like a large door. Walking through, he entered his holy sanctum as the shelf closed behind him. Smiling, he walked over to a side door and withdrew his robe. Solid black with red lining. It always made him happy to hold it. So heavy...so much power. The wearer had to be chosen...not just anyone was allowed. Sliding his arms into it,

he could feel his chest growing...making room for...them. He closed his eyes and smiled as he felt them stirring within. Raw power...he was like a god.

After several minutes, he opened his eyes and walked over to the altar. He lit the six candles and bowed down. The urgency was stirring within him like never before. Had he done something wrong? Were all his plans about to change? Were...he felt the presence as it entered the room. Squeezing his eyes tightly shut, he burst with excitement, knowing he was in the presence of the one true God.

He felt a stirring surround him. He was near. He could hear his master breathing...grunting...or whatever that sound was that he made with his nostrils. The footsteps beyond the altar.

"OPEN YOUR EYES!" the deep voice said, echoing off the walls around him.

"Master, you've always instructed me to keep them closed...to never look upon you! Is this a test, my Lord!?"

"OPEN YOUR EYES!!"

Looking toward the ground, Joshua opened his eyes, terrified, to lift his face. Even the spirits within him were shaking. "They are open, my God!"

An enormous, black, leathery hand slowly slid under his chin and raised his head up. Joshua could not believe his eyes. The sight before him was magnificent. He could never describe what he was seeing. "God of Teuflisch! You are truly glorious!" A tear rolled down his cheek. His master stood before him a giant...a monster to human eyes. Solid black with eyes of blazing fire. The horns upon his glorious head were larger than

a man and curled around with the tips pointing to the sky. "I am not worthy."

"SHE IS HERE! THE WOMAN!"

"Brianna, sir?"

"YES...SHE IS IN MY HOUSE AND HER VERY PRESENCE IS A DISTURBANCE OF MY EXISTENCE!"

"Should I have her killed immediately, my Lord!?"

There was a long, awkward pause and..."NO! THAT WAS MY FIRST THOUGHT AS WELL! JUST BE DONE WITH HER! BUT...I WANT HER TO SUFFER! SHE HAS COME AGAINST ALL THAT WE HAVE BUILT!"

Joshua smiled. He loved making people suffer...especially if it brought glory to his master. "How, my God? What should I do?"

"SHE HAS COME FOR THE GIRL NAMED MARIA SANCHEZ! HER FOOLISH MOTHER IS EVEN PRAYING FOR HER DELIVERANCE NOW!" He laughed and looked down at Joshua. "YOU KNOW WHAT TO DO!"

"Yes, my Lord!" Joshua said, as the tears flowed down his face. "Yes, I do."

CHAPTER 25

SYDNEY, AUSTRALIA

Gabi was still shaking from the dream she'd had earlier. She was at the conference venue now and was having a difficult time focusing on the tasks at hand. She had sent three of her interns to a back room doing nothing but praying for Brianna. Poor kids didn't even know her, but it made Gabi feel better knowing that Brianna was being covered in prayer as she got ready for the event.

After the dream, she'd tried calling Brianna but it had gone to voicemail immediately. That definitely did not help the sick feeling that she had in the pit of her stomach. "God, please protect my best friend...keep her safe from her enemies."

Mark and Maria had come to her room after Scotty had told them about the dream and the phone call. Mark had told her that he also had an uneasy feeling that Brianna was under attack. They had prayed together for about a half hour. Gabi continued to fast and pray after they'd left.

Now, she was trying to put together the playlist for the evening and was having extreme difficulty. She knew that the crowd wanted to see and hear her, because of her part in the dragon story, but she would much rather skip out tonight and pray for her friend.

"I press on toward the goal to win the prize for which God has called me heavenward in Christ Jesus." She heard the Holy Spirit whisper in her ear. She closed her eyes and thanked Him for His word. "Can any one of you by worrying add a single hour to your life?"

"Okay, God, I get it!" she conceded. "I leave the situation in your hands. Not only are you more capable than me...YOU'RE literally right there with her as we speak!" With that she felt a peace and continued getting ready for tonight's service...for now.

CODY, WYOMING

Dustin had been in the main hall mingling with all the elites...most of which he'd never heard of, but several actors and singers that were more than legendary were there as well. He had been talking with one of the biggest names in music history when a tall, thin man approached him and stood to his right while he finished his conversation. Dustin turned to him and gave him a quizzical look.

Leaning in close, the man whispered in a British accent. "Excuse me, sir, but your presence is required upstairs."

Dustin turned to excuse himself but the woman he'd been speaking with had already walked away. He watched as she was surrounded by several admiring fans. He turned back to the thin man. "Lead the way."

"This way, sir," the man said, turning toward the large set of stairs at the far end of the massive room.

"So, what is this about?" Dustin asked.

"I believe your manager, Seth, has arranged this, sir," the man replied.

"So, this is the initiation?" Dustin asked as he followed the man quickly up the stairs. When they reached the top, the man took a sharp turn to the right and walked at a quick pace toward the end of a long marble corridor. Their heels clicked as they walked. Dustin noticed the expensive artwork on the walls and wondered if they were originals. The man stopped just outside a doorway. He turned and faced Dustin. Dustin stopped short… "Anything I need to know before I go in?"

"There are several things you need to know before you go in!" A voice from behind them said, causing Dustin to jump and spin around. "You may go, Bennet." The thin man bowed and walked away in the direction they'd just come from.

"I didn't even hear you walking," Dustin said, covering his heart.

"Sorry for startling you, Dustin," the man extended his hand and gave Dustin quite the firm grip. "I'm Joshua."

"Wait! Joshua Coff?" Dustin asked, star struck.

"The one and only," Joshua said with a billion-dollar smile.

"Oh, WOW!" Dustin refused to let go of his hand. "You're a very powerful man! They call you the star maker...such big names as…"

Joshua held up his hands. "Such names as Dustin Knight???" Dustin felt the blood rush to his head.

"Does my initiation have something to do with you!?"

"NOT an initiation, Son...it's a welcoming." He put his large hand on Dustin's shoulder. "I need to know how much you want the life."

"The life?"

"I'm prepared to make you the biggest name in music history, Dustin, bigger than even Elvis and Michael." Joshua said. "But I need to know that you want it."

"Oh, Mr. Coff, I want it more than anything."

"That's what I was hoping to hear," he said with a broad smile. "Now, you're going to go through that door and you're going to be given a gift. That gift is yours for the next two hours. Do whatever you like with it."

"I'm so confused, but okay."

"Everything will be explained when you get inside." Joshua gave him a slight nudge. "Don't disappoint me, Dustin."

"I won't, sir."

"Excellent...because that would not be a good thing."

Dustin recognized a threat when he heard one, but the smile that Joshua flashed at him as he said it, made it feel like a joke. He chose to take it as a joke rather than a threat to his future. "Yes sir…" Dustin opened the door and stepped inside.

The room was larger than Dustin had expected. It was set up like a hotel room. The walls were light blue, and the lighting was quite dull as if it were supposed to be mood lighting. There was a queen-sized bed in the far-left corner and a sofa directly to the left of the door.

A bathroom was to the right. The door was slightly open, and he could see the sink inside. Next to the bed was a dresser with several lit candles on the top. Everything in the room looked perfectly normal except for the little girl sitting on the edge of the bed.

"Well, hello," Dustin said with a smile, looking around for some kind of explanation.

She smiled a shy smile and nodded her head.

"I'm Dustin," he said, trying to assess the situation and determine why there was a young girl in the room with him.

"I'm Maria," she replied so softly that he could barely hear her.

"Um," he stepped over and took a seat on the sofa. "Do you know why you're here, Maria?"

She nodded. "I'm your gift. I'm supposed to do anything you want me to...and then they're going to let me see my Mommy again."

It was at that moment that Dustin realized what was going on. His heart began to pound in his chest. He'd only had a small bit of the clam chowder they'd served earlier but he felt as if he were about to...he rushed to the bathroom and threw up.

"Are you sick, Dustin?" Maria asked from the other room. "Can I do anything for you?"

Dustin wiped his mouth with a hand towel and splashed water on his face. He stepped back out into the room and looked up. There were cameras mounted in all four corners of the room. He looked over at Maria still sitting on the bed, her legs rocking back and forth. She looked so excited to do what she had to do in order to see her mommy. "How old are you, Maria?"

"I'm eight," she replied. "I'm in the third grade at Sheffield Elementary in Jacksonville, Florida. My Mommy is on her way to get me."

Dustin squeezed his eyes shut and rubbed his temples. "Jesus loves the little children…" That was the song that old man with the hat had been whistling! He'd sung that song a thousand times at his grandmother's church. Why was that the thing on his mind right now!?

"So, what is it that you want to do?" Maria asked. "They said you would probably want me to take my clothes off, but I told them that was just silly…you don't, do you?"

Dustin opened his eyes and looked at that sweet little girl in the frilly pink dress, looking like she was dressed to go to church. His eyes teared up as he thought about what was expected of him. Was this really how the big stars became the big stars??? He looked up at the cameras.

"Mr. Dustin, do you want me to…"

"NO!" He said it so loud that it made her jump. "I'm sorry, Baby…no… you keep your clothes on…Mr. Dustin just wants to talk." He sat down on the sofa again, his hands shaking…knowing that he was most likely throwing away the career he'd always dreamed about…but not like this. "Tell me about your Mommy."

Jonah awoke with a start. He looked around the small, dimly lit room and immediately realized that opening his eyes was a bad idea. The entire right side of his face felt as though all the bones were crushed. He had the headache of his life.

Everything started coming back to him as he pressed his head back into the pillow. He and Brianna had been on the run from some very bad people…and they'd been caught. Brianna? Where was SHE!? Was she okay!?

He jumped out of the bed and walked over to the door...he was locked in. There was a small bathroom that he went in to look at his face. His eye was black, and his cheek was blue and red. He couldn't see out of his right eye. What had he been hit with? A refrigerator!?

He walked back out into the room and kicked the door with everything he had. Solid steel. Sitting back down on the bed, he thought back over the last few days. It wasn't that long ago he'd been working on...this was the place. He was in one of the rooms! He looked around. He'd helped build this place!

"Great, now I know I'm doomed," he said aloud. "This place is built like Fort Knox." He hung his head and wondered if Brianna was alright. He'd known for days that they were heading to their graves when they started this mission, but the thought of something bad happening to her...such a good woman. Sweet, kind, beautiful...so beautiful.

Her beauty haunted his dreams...but they were so different. He was a beer drinking, swear word saying construction worker who'd been burnt by Christians in the past, and she was...what was she? "Perfect." She had faith...in God. A faith he'd never seen, and he'd been to church a lot. The thing about her faith was that it wasn't judgmental, it was...contagious. He wanted it but knew he didn't deserve it. "God...help me to see you like she sees you."

Nadia and Jaclyn had gotten to know each other in the past few hours. Nadia had learned that Jaclyn was here because her brother knew too much. They had apparently drugged her...she said she'd woken up in this room and had no idea how she'd gotten here. She had told Nadia that her brother had

recently had several attempts on his life and had escaped and was on the run from these people.

Nadia had told Jaclyn about her little sister, Ana, being in the same situation because of Nadia's knowledge of this child trafficking operation. She seemed quite optimistic that he would be able to get the authorities involved...although he was being hunted by them as well, for fleeing the scene of a detective's murder. Nadia didn't have the heart to tell her that even if he did get the authorities involved, they would both most likely be dead by the end of the day.

Other than bringing them their lunch earlier, nobody had been by to visit today. No threats, no promises, no deals to be made. As odd as it seemed, Nadia thought that to be a bad thing. It either meant that Brianna was dead or captured. Which was why she had excused herself from Jaclyn to go into the bathroom and think.

She was a sweet lady, but goodness she did like to chat. Nadia supposed it was her nerves, but either way...she needed to concoct a plan of escape. Of course, to make things even more difficult, she would need to find her little sister first.

Perhaps Brianna's God was the ONLY way of escape here because she couldn't come up with anything but play it by ear. "Okay, Brianna's God...I'm literally putting ALL of my trust in You. I don't know how all this works, but please help me and Ana and Brianna and Jaclyn and her brother get out of this alive...especially Ana and Jaclyn..."

"Nadia!" Jaclyn called through the bathroom door. "I hear someone coming!"

Nadia opened the door just as the door to the room opened and two guards walked in. They had the women turn around and put their hands behind their backs. Their wrists were quickly zip tied and they were led out into the hall.

"Where are you taking us?" Nadia demanded. "We have the right to know!"

"You have no rights here, now shut up and walk," the guard behind Nadia replied in a thick German accent, shoving her forward.

They led them to an elevator and made them face the back of the elevator as they rode it down. When it came to a stop, the guards took them by the arm and pulled them into what looked like a large warehouse area that was obviously way below ground level.

The walls were made of rock, like a cave. It was well lit with stage lighting lining the walls. Nadia had to squint in order to look in certain directions. There were forklifts being driven and crates being moved down to one end of the giant room. Men were yelling at each other in different languages, and it seemed like they were in a rush for something. It was all so confusing...why had they been brought down here?

Then they rounded a corner and both women gasped... there were hundreds of cages, stacked on top of each other...each one with a child inside...some older, some very young...all being deathly quiet.

"What in God's name!?" Jaclyn said with fear in her voice. "What in God's name!?"

One of the guards slapped her in the face and told her to shut up. They cut their ties and were shoved forward. "Get in!"

It was then that Nadia noticed the two slightly larger cages right in front of them. They were forced inside them, and the cages were immediately locked.

"NO!!!" Jaclyn screamed as the guards walked away. "What are you going to do with us!!! COME BACK!!!"

Nadia's faith in God was already being shaken...for this was not good at all. Looking around at all the children and knowing their fate...she had to wonder if God had abandoned them all...long ago.

CHAPTER 26

Brianna sat on the edge of her small bed with her hands clasped together on her lap. She was trying her hardest to concentrate on her prayers. She could not deny the overwhelming darkness that was attempting to pull her under. It was as if fear himself were sitting beside her and whispering in her ear. With every sentence she prayed, her mind would begin to drift.

She had to admit...it didn't look good for her or Jonah or Maria or Nadia or Jonah's sister or any of the children involved in this. It honestly felt as if they'd already lost. She tried to remind herself of how Daniel must've felt in the lion's den. How Shadrach, Meshach, and Abednego must've felt as they stared at that fiery furnace. How Stephen must've felt as he knelt down on the ground just before being stoned to death.

But who was she, Brianna Bowers, to be comparing herself with these great people of the Bible. She was a nobody. Tears began to slide down her cheeks. "God, I'm sorry I've failed you," she cried. "So many people are about to die because of my failure."

Suddenly, she heard movement in the hallway outside her room. Her heart jumped with fear as her door was opened and two guards entered. One walked over to her dresser and began setting up a laptop. The other one stood, holding the door open for someone else. A tall, good looking man with jet black hair and eyes greener than any she'd ever seen, entered the room. He smiled at Brianna as the second guard closed the door, remaining in the room.

"Good evening, Brianna Bowers," he said in a thick European accent. "My name is Joshua Coff," he said and paused as if expecting her to respond or recognize his name.

She felt as if she'd heard that name before but couldn't be sure. The one thing she could definitely attest to was the darkness that seemed to follow him into the room. She almost felt like she was going to be sick." Am I supposed to say it's a pleasure to meet you?" she asked, as she stood up from the bed.

He smiled a million-dollar smile and tilted his head to the side as if studying her. "I suppose not...but I must say Ms. Bowers, you're not as impressive as I would've thought."

"That's not a short joke, is it? Because I feel that would be beneath you."

This time he laughed. "I'm only saying...for someone that has done such extensive damage to my operation, I expected...more. You don't seem powerful enough to open a water bottle let alone bring a worldwide multi-billion-dollar child trafficking ring to its knees."

"This operation feels anything but damaged and brought to its knees, Mr. Coff." Brianna replied. "But if you think that I've done any of those things in my own power, then you're not as smart as you look." She watched his reaction and saw that he appeared to be intrigued with her. Good. "Jesus Christ is the source of my strength."

He didn't as much as twitch at her statement, but he did lose that charming smile. "That is most unfortunate for you, Ms. Bowers." He took a step toward her. "Most unfortunate indeed. You see, trusting in a... deceased God is not only bad form...it's downright embarrassing for you."

"Well, you're the one who said there was extensive damage to your operation...that hardly sounds like the workings of someone dead," Brianna said, taking a step closer to him and feeling quite courageous at the moment. "And I can assure you, sir, that Jesus Christ is anything BUT deceased!

In fact, whatever god you're serving...I can promise you...is trembling at His very name!" She took another step toward him and gave him the biggest smile she could muster. "So, why don't we skip all the my God is better than you're God and you go ahead and kill me or whatever you have planned! Unlike you, Mr. Coff, when I die...I will continue to live!"

"Have a seat Ms. Bowers," he said, pointing her back to the bed. "There's something I would like for you to see." Once she was seated, he stood over her, causing her to lean back. "And just so you know, I have absolutely no intention of killing you, Brianna Bowers...I'm going to destroy you." He glanced at the first guard who took the cue and hit a button on the laptop. There on the screen appeared Jonah...who was hanging, chained up with his hands over his head. He looked as if he'd been severely beaten. His face was hardly recognizable.

Brianna gasped. "What have you done!? Why!? It's me you want to hurt…"

"Exactly, Brianna Bowers...YOU are the reason he is being tortured. YOU are the reason his sister will die. YOU are the reason Nadia, and her little sister will die!" He stepped toward her again and grabbed her under her chin, lifting her off the bed. He turned her face to the screen, and it changed to the outside of a house...Officer Ramsey's house. Again, she gasped. "That's right, sweetheart, we found your parents.

All my men are waiting on is for me to tell them to go and they will kill both of them AND the cop's entire family and it will be ALL YOUR FAULT!!!” He shoved her back down on the bed. “Not to mention, it's also going to be your fault when I kill that little brown whore your supposed to be here to save...Maria Sanchez...you’ll get to watch that one first!” He laughed and turned away from her.

Brianna was sobbing uncontrollably. Where was God??? How was this happening??? “Please, just kill me!!!” she begged.

“I told you!” he said, crossing to the other side of the room. “I’m going to destroy you!” He turned and watched her lying there crying. He smiled. “Tell me, Brianna Bowers...where is this powerful God of yours now?” She turned her face from him. “How about I show you mercy then...since he appears to be too busy. Look at me!” he yelled. She obeyed. “I am willing to let each person I’ve mentioned go, unharmed...minus what we’ve already done, of course...if you do just one thing for me.”

“What!?” she asked. “I’ll do anything!” Instantly millions of disgusting and vile images passed through her mind of things he would probably want her to do. “Please, just let them all go! I’ll do ANYTHING you want!!!”

“Perfect... then deny Jesus Christ as God...and I’ll put you out of my misery!”

SYDNEY, AUSTRALIA

There were over 60,000 people in attendance for the Dragon Slayers event in Sydney at the massive outside venue.

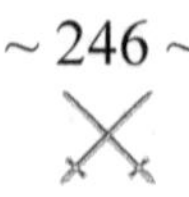

The skies were clear, and the temperature was absolutely perfect, with a slight breeze coming off the water. The music was pumping, and the light show was dancing off the trees in the distance.

Gabi led the praise from her keyboard as Matt played the drums, with Andy and Eddie on guitars. Mark, Scotty and several members of the crew were just off stage, hands lifted in praise, enjoying the music. They were in the middle of a song that Matt had written called Source of My Strength, and Gabi was really getting into it, jumping up and down. The crowd was loving the new song and singing along.

"Never gonna stay down! Never gonna give up! Never gonna lose this fight! With Jesus on my side, the darkness gonna bow! "Cause I'm standing in the light! You are the source, God! Standing at arm's length! You are the source, God! The source of my strength!"

The crowd started jumping as they hit the chorus and all of a sudden Gabi jumped back from the keyboard as if it had shocked her. She immediately bent over as if in pain and the band stopped playing. Mark peeked around one of the large speakers to see what was going on, something was definitely off. He motioned for Scotty to look at Gabi and the crowd went eerily quiet as she stood bent over at the waist.

All of a sudden, she raised up straight and let out an ear-piercing scream that was magnified because of the headset microphone she wore. Her face turned beet red as she screamed uncontrollably as if being tortured. Scotty ran to her and wrapped his arms around her….

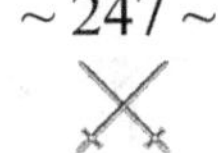

"Gabi! Baby, what's wrong!?" he asked in her ear. She threw off the microphone and pushed Scotty away, running to the front of the stage where she fell prostate on the floor.

Mark grabbed his microphone and headed out. "Every eye closed, heads bowed to the King of Kings!" he said, as he walked out to stand near Gabi. "Guys, this is NOT part of the show that you are seeing right now…" He looked down at Gabi and could hear her mumbling under her breath.

"What you are in fact witnessing right now is spiritual warfare...Gabi is doing battle in the spirit realm on behalf of a very close friend that is under some serious attacks from the enemy! Her name is Brianna Bowers and I need every believer within the sound of my voice to drop to your knees right now and begin lifting her up to God!" Mark knew that they were live around the world and in several languages thanks to the wonders of modern technology, so he was quite aware that Brianna was about to be prayed for from every corner of the planet.

Thousands of people around the venue dropped to their knees and began to cry out to God. "Dear Heavenly Father, I lift up my friend, Brianna Bowers to You, right now!" Mark said. "God, we pray that You cover her with Your mighty hands of protection! That You would dispatch thousands of angels on her behalf to battle for her in the name of Jesus Christ!"

Gabi screamed again from where she lay on the stage. Scotty stood over her like a centurion guarding his keep. "NOOOOO!!!!!!" she screamed. "IN JESUS' NAME, I COME AGAINST YOU, DEMON OF HELL!!!" Gabi rolled over onto her back and sat up. Every eye and camera were on her. "TEUFLISCH IS YOUR NAME!!!!" She was spitting as she screamed...standing up now, with her eyes closed. "YOU GET AWAY FROM MY FRIEND AND GO TO THE HELL YOU BELONG IN!!!!"

She had both hands lifted. "FATHER GOD!!!! I PRAY…." and she passed out on the stage, dropping like a bag of rocks. Scotty knelt down and checked on her, holding his hand over her forehead and praying.

Mark turned and nodded to Matt, who began a slow worship song.

"Worship Him, Christians!" Matt said, as hands were lifted all over the venue.

As Mark and Scotty knelt over Gabi and prayed, Mark saw the battle lines being drawn by the enemy. He literally saw millions and millions of demons marching across the land with the carcasses of children being left in their wake. There was a serious attack happening...but where was God's army!?

CODY, WYOMING

Jonah's brain was extremely foggy. He remembered his food being brought in... a ham sandwich and a glass of milk. He'd been so hungry. The next thing he remembered was being chained up in this warehouse-looking building and someone beating him over and over with what appeared to be brass knuckles on their hand. They had beaten his face until he could barely see.

He tasted blood and felt as if his jaw was shattered. He couldn't remember ever being in this much pain. It even hurt to breathe...they'd hit his ribs several times and once he could've

sworn, he'd heard them crack. He knew they were videotaping him, but he had no idea why. All that he knew was...he hoped he would be able to see Brianna one more time before he died. He also hoped he could be the hero in her story, but given his present situation, he doubted that would happen.

Then, a bay door at the other end of the massive room opened and a forklift drove in. It had a pallet with something on it and was coming straight toward him. He couldn't make out details because of his eyes being so swollen shut. As it got closer, he saw that it was cages with...people in them? "What the…" The pallet was set down about twenty feet in front of him.

There were two cages with what appeared to be a person in each...he couldn't make out their faces, but the one he could see appeared to be a child. The other cage was behind that one and whoever was in it seemed to be lying down. The forklift turned and went back out the door it had come through. Moments later it returned with another pallet with two more cages. Jonah didn't even try and focus in on who it was. He closed his eyes because it hurt so bad to have them open. He heard the pallet as it was set down…then he heard the gasp.

"JONAH!? OH MY GOD! JONAH!!!???" his sister, Jaclyn screamed, shaking the cage walls as she tried to get to her brother. "ARE YOU ALIVE!!!???" She was frantic as he did his best to move and show her, he was still alive. "What have these monsters done to you!?"

"Bind her hands," Joshua said, stepping away from Brianna to give the guard some room.

~ 250 ~

"I don't understand why you won't just kill me and get it over with," Brianna said as the guard pulled her arms behind her back and used the zip tie to shackle her hands. "With me out of the way, you can just continue your operation of child molesting and pedophilia, you disgusting pig!"

Joshua walked back over to her, lifting his cell phone for her to hear. "Yeah…" he said to someone on the other end. "Kill everybody in the house...then burn it to the ground."

"NOOOOO!!!!!" she screamed, bending over in grief, knowing that her refusal to deny Christ had just cost her the lives of her parents and possibly Officer and Mrs. Ramsey. "JESUS!!! NOOOO!!!" Joshua shoved her back onto her bed as she continued to wail. She glanced at the screen and saw two men going up to the house. They approached the front door and knocked. Just as the door began to open, the guard closed the laptop and smiled at her.

"Goodbye mommy and daddy," he said in his European accent. "Brianna sends her love!" Both guards laughed.

"Bring her to the warehouse," Joshua said. "We've only just begun to have fun!"

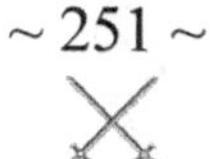

GATEWAY, FLORIDA

Mrs. Ramsey and Mrs. Bowers had been working on dinner together, while chatting about how nice it would be to have little ones running around and wondering who would get grand babies first. They were also reminiscing about when their kids were little and all the adventures they'd had together. The barbecue ribs, mashed potatoes, and corn on the cob were all placed on the table, and they called the men to wash up and come eat.

As Officer Ramsey walked out of the restroom from washing up, there was a flash of light at the end of the hall. He turned and walked down there to investigate when he saw something move in his bedroom. "Hello?" he said as he cautiously stepped into the room. There, to his surprise, stood Gabi Morgan...who should've been in Sydney, Australia with his son, Matt. Presently though, she was standing in his bedroom in full battle armor, gripping a sword. "Gabi!??? What in the…"

She held a finger to her mouth. "They're coming," she whispered. "Get your gun." And with that, she vanished.

"What just happened!?" he asked out loud and at that very moment, there was a knock at the door. The hairs on the back of his neck stood up as he spun in that direction.

"I'll get it!" his wife called from the kitchen.

"NO, Honey!" he called, running to the front of the house. He motioned for everybody to stay back. "Take the women to the back, Glenn! Do you have your pistol?"

"Always," Mr. Bowers said, patting his side. "But…"

"Lock and load…" Officer Ramsey said, grabbing his 9mm from his holster near the door.

CHAPTER 27

CODY, WYOMING

After about thirty minutes of talking with Maria about her mother and how she was going to be back home real soon, the door opened. A large man in a black suit entered and grabbed Maria by the arm. He gave Dustin a dirty look as he snatched the girl up.

"You don't have to be so rough, you big oaf!" he stood up from the bed and the man shoved him back down and pulled Maria out of the room so fast it made her scream out in pain.

That's when the thin British man, Bennet, entered the room with a burly looking guard. He motioned toward Dustin and the guard headed for him.

"Please stand up, Mr. Knight," Bennet said. "Your presence is now required in another room."

The guard pulled his hands behind his back and zip tied them together. "What is the meaning of this!?" Dustin exclaimed. "Take your hands off me!!!" He attempted to wriggle away but it was useless, for the guard had a firm grip on his forearm.

"If you insist on making this difficult, Mr. Knight, I could arrange to have you transported in a steel cage." Bennet said, in a quaint way that made it feel like it was perfectly normal to carry a human being around in a cage.

"You people are sick!" Dustin said. "I want to leave this place immediately! Where is Seth!? Where is my manager, Seth Stevens!?" he yelled as the guard escorted him from the room.

It had been a quiet ride on the elevator for Brianna, the two guards, and Joshua. She was mostly praying for the safety of her parents and the Ramsey family...for God to intervene in a mighty way. When the doors finally opened, she realized he hadn't been kidding about a warehouse. It was literally a massive warehouse lined with tons of shelves that contained crates, boxes, and what appeared to be a hundred-year supply of food and water. One of the guards kept hold of her arm as they led her across the polished concrete floor. In the distance she saw a forklift carrying what looked like a metal cage on a pallet. There were several people gathered around at that end of the room.

"Has Dustin been brought in yet?" Joshua asked the other guard that had been in contact with others through his headset.

"They're bringing him now, sir," the guard replied, and Brianna saw someone else being brought in with their hands bound.

As they drew closer, she saw Jonah hanging by his wrists from the thick chains. She tried to pick up the pace but was held back by the guard's firm grip.

"Easy, honey," he grunted in her ear.

That's when she noticed what was going on. There were several people gathered around Jonah and what appeared to be about five metal cages with people in them, spread about six feet from each other. She recognized Secretary-General Gunther Schmidt of Interpol...but wasn't sure who the others were...until she noticed Nadia in the cage to the far right. "Oh, Jesus! Nadia, are you okay!?"

"Brianna! Thank God you are still alive!" Nadia replied. "I'm so sorry it has come to this!"

"I told you to shut up!" a guard said to Nadia, kicking her cage. "Speak again and pay the price." Brianna wondered what the price was until she saw the electric cattle prod in his hand.

Brianna found it difficult to see her friend having been forced to be in a cage. She looked down the line and couldn't tell who the others were, but assumed the small dark-skinned girl with her back to Brianna was Maria. Two of the others were adults, but one appeared to be unconscious. One of them had to be Jonah's sister. She whispered a prayer for each of them.

They led her around in front of the cages and stood her between the man with his hands bound that had just been led in, and Jonah. She and Jonah shared a grim smile.

"Good," Joshua said. "Everyone is here." He smiled and looked around. "I have a lot of people waiting for me in the next room, so we're going to make this quick." He walked over and stood between Brianna and the cages. "First, let's make introductions...This is Dustin Knight...rising pop star that apparently doesn't want it bad enough." He put his hand on the shoulder of the man next to Brianna.

"I'm NOT sleeping with a child, you p...." Joshua slapped him on the back of his head.

"Not only will you be nothing more than a one hit wonder!" Joshua said. "But you can live with knowing this was YOUR fault as well..." He turned to the cage directly in front

~ 255 ~

of them and pointed to the little girl. "Has everyone met Maria? Nine-year-old little tramp from Jacksonville who still thinks her mommy is coming to get her!" He smiled at Brianna.

"My mommy IS coming to get me, you mean, mean man!" Maria yelled.

Joshua looked down on her and kicked her cage. "No, baby...Mr. Dustin's actions have caused us to have to end our need for you..." He nodded to one of the guards who turned around and picked something up. "You see, Dustin...every action has a reaction and I'm afraid this one is on you." The guard handed him a gas can and he turned and began pouring the liquid over Maria and saturating her entire cage.

"NO!!!" Brianna screamed at the top of her lungs and tried to stop him, but a guard held her back as another one held back Dustin. Jonah too was grunting and yelling for them to stop.

Maria was crying. "Please stop! You're messing up my dress! I want to look pretty for my Mommy!!!" Then suddenly she stopped screaming and looked over to her right as if someone were there. Brianna stopped fighting as well...she too could see Him. He was smiling at Maria as He removed His hat and knelt down next to her, sliding his fingers through the slats in the cage.

Joshua struck the match and tossed it in the cage. It immediately burst into flames, consuming Maria's little body. Each of the others in cages were screaming, even the woman who'd been unconscious was now freaking out. Dustin was screaming. Jonah was screaming. Even the guards turned their heads, so they didn't have to watch...It was the most horrible thing that any of them had ever witnessed. Pure evil.

But Brianna noticed that the little girl, Maria, never screamed. She just held hands with the Holy Spirit, looking into His eyes, as her body burned. Tears poured down Brianna's face as she watched their faces. Then...He looked up and nodded...and right there over the cage appeared someone that Brianna hadn't seen in over a decade...Topher, the messenger angel. He lifted Maria's spirit from the cage, smiled at Brianna, winked...and was gone.

Then...Brianna noticed something...there were tears in the eyes of the Holy Spirit. He continued to kneel there as her tiny body burned...his fingers still lacing hers. Brianna looked over at Dustin who was now on his knees convulsing...wailing… screaming. When she looked back, the Holy Spirit was gone.

"Why!?" Jonah screamed. "Why would you do that to a child!?"

"Jonah!" Joshua said. "I'd almost forgotten about you!" He walked over and stood in front of the severely beaten man. "What a sweet story...yours and Brianna's. Meeting like you did...probably one you could share with your grandchildren...if I weren't going to kill you today." He laughed. "I believe you've seen your sister is with us..." He leaned in close to Jonah's ear. "But have you seen who else we've brought...or can you even see?"

"What are you talking about?" Jonah attempted to open his eyes and look around.

"Why don't you tell him who you are!?" Joshua said, kicking the cage of the blonde woman who'd just woken up.

~ 257 ~

"What is going on here!? What are you doing!? Jonah!? Is that you, Jonah!?" she shook the cage door trying to get out. "Let me out of here!!!"

"Lacey!?" Jonah yelled.

"Oh my God, Lacey!?" Jonah's sister, Jaclyn yelled. "I didn't realize that was you!"

"It seems that Lacey here," Joshua said. "Was in the wrong place at the right time. What a bonus that she was walking up to your sister's house the moment my men were stuffing her in a van. We got two for the price of one...and she just might be pretty enough for me to make some money on, at auction." This made him smile. "Nah, I think I'll kill her…" He began to pour gasoline all over her head.

"NOOOO!!!!" They all screamed, but it seemed futile at this point. It seemed that their fate had already been sealed.

SYDNEY, AUSTRALIA

"Keep praying, church!" Mark said, motioning for one of the stage hands to come out to him. The teenage boy walked out, and Mark whispered in his ear for him to go get Maria, his wife.

Scotty was still kneeling next to Gabi at the front of the stage and literally hundreds of teenage girls had come forward to pray for her. They were lining the front of the stage and into the aisles.

Mark was pacing back and forth across the stage, eyes closed, hands waving over his head. He knew what was about to happen, but he wasn't sure to what extent it would happen.

There was suddenly a hand on his arm, and he jumped and opened his eyes. His beautiful wife was standing there with the 'you got work to do' look on her face. He smiled at her.

"Go," was all Maria said, and Mark McGee's body crumbled to the ground. She looked over and Scotty too had fallen over. She bent down and picked up Mark's microphone. "There is a spiritual battle going on tonight, folks!" Our leaders are at war! Worship Him! Worship the King of ALL Kings!" She nodded to Matt to kick the worship up a notch.

"Come on, church!" Matt said. "Lift your hands all over this building! We have come into this place and gathered in His name to worship Him!"

CODY, WYOMING

Jonah couldn't believe how this was playing out. That man had indeed burned a child alive and was now pouring gasoline on his ex-girlfriend, and there was nothing he could do about it. His strength was gone. He felt as if there was no blood in his arms and hands. He could no longer open his eyes...not that he wanted to see what was about to happen. All he felt was hatred for the man that they called Joshua. He envisioned killing him in sick ways. He wasn't sure which way he would choose, but he knew he would do it slowly.

Of course, it was all folly. There was no hope left. There would be no escaping this madness. These people would kill each one of them and then go to some grand party and never think of them again. "Bree," he managed to say, though he didn't look to see if she'd heard him. "Bree...where is God?" Then, someone placed a hand on the back of his shoulder.

~ 259 ~

"Let your eyes be open," a man's voice spoke softly into his ear.

Jonah's first thought was that this man must be really tall because with the chains lifting him up, his ear level had to be at least 6'6". His second thought was that whoever it was had apparently not seen Jonah's face with his eyes swollen shut. How could he see?

"I didn't tell you to see, Jonah," the man said. "I said let your eyes be open." With that he squeezed Jonah's shoulder and immediately a bright light flashed in front of Jonah.

That's when he noticed that he COULD see...though his eyes were still shut. He wasn't, however, seeing Joshua and Brianna and the cages...he was seeing…. "Dear God…" Before Jonah, was what appeared to be a type of amphitheater or something. It was as big as the sky and higher. That wasn't even the scariest part...it was what appeared to be millions and millions of demonic looking creatures…all cheering Joshua on. There was, in the front of all of them, standing beside Joshua, an extremely large demonic creature with massive horns like a ram. Now that he was focused, he COULD see Joshua and everyone else below him. Brianna was even there...and she was watching Jonah and smiling.

Brianna had struggled to stop the guard as he'd poured gasoline all over Jonah's ex-girlfriend. The guard behind her had quite the firm grip, though she'd definitely made him work for it. As soon as she'd given up, she'd whispered a prayer to heaven for God to intervene. That's when she'd heard Jonah mumble her name. She'd turned to acknowledge him and noticed that his eyes were closed. Then he'd asked something

about God that she couldn't understand. Just as she was about to tell him to trust God, she'd seen him stiffen and his face had changed...he was practically glowing. She immediately knew that he was having a one on one with her old friend. "Draw him to Christ, Holy Spirit," she whispered.

Jonah started to panic more than ever now. A sob escaped his mouth as he focused in on the millions of foul creatures that were cheering on the pure evil that was being done. There was absolutely no hope for them. They would all be dead within seconds. Then...the man behind him began to whistle...Jesus loves the little children...it calmed his nerves and brought a peace like he'd never felt.

The whistling continued for what felt like another minute. Jonah could see that Joshua was still talking but had not killed Lacey yet. He seemed to be moving in slow motion. Was Jonah in some kind of trance or something? Then, the whistling stopped. The hand on his back squeezed his shoulder again and the entire scene changed.

There was a man being beaten...he was strapped to a pole by his wrists, down on his knees, as a soldier flayed his back open with each hit of the whip. There was an enormous puddle of blood beneath the man and Jonah wondered how much more he could take. His ribs were showing as chunks of flesh flew with each swipe.

"Dear God, save him," Jonah muttered. "Take away his pain!" That's when he fell over, and the soldier stopped beating him. They lifted him to his feet and led him from the courtyard. Moments later, the scene changed again...to the same man being

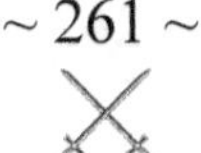

placed on a wooden beam. It was then that Jonah realized what he was watching.

That man was Jesus Christ...and he was about to be crucified. That's when Jonah noticed the glow around his body and knew that Jesus had the power to stop it ALL at any second...but he let them nail him to that tree. "Why!?" Jonah asked to no one in particular.

That's when the old man behind him stepped around in front of him, removed his hat, and smiled at Jonah. "Why?" he asked, His piercing eyes tearing through Jonah's soul. "Because you couldn't handle it...because of His immense love for you...because He wanted to have fellowship with you, Jonah Westbrook...for all eternity."

Tears began to pour down Jonah's cheek...he sobbed. "Thank you, Jesus!" he said as loud as his broken jaw would allow. "Please forgive my unbelief!"

Joshua just had the gasoline poured on Lacey's cage where it had completely saturated her. He held the match in his hand and was attempting to strike fear into the hearts of all the others. That's when he heard the idiot hanging behind him begin sobbing. He turned and smiled at him...and noticed that Brianna was doing the same. It was at that moment that he realized what was happening. Teuflisch had warned him. "NO!" he slapped the man in the face as hard as he could...but Jonah just smiled an extremely crooked smile.

"Good luck removing that smile," Brianna said. "You can kill his body...but God gets the rest."

Joshua shoved Brianna to the ground. "SHUT UP!!! I'M ABOUT TO KILL ALL OF YOU!!! YOU HAVE LOST!!!"

"What about THEM?" Jonah asked the old man, who turned around and faced the hundreds of millions of demons that had returned into Jonah's view.

"What about them?" the Holy Spirit asked. "There are more FOR you than there are against you, Jonah Westbrook."

CHAPTER 28

Jack Watson was not a patient man in the best of times. He made a living out of dealing and working with some of the roughest and worst scumbags on the planet, so he was used to waiting on people because of incompetence. He single-handedly coordinated the kidnapping, transporting, and storing of children on a daily basis, so he knew what it was like to have things not go as planned.

He was used to being let down by his subordinates as well as he was used to letting down those above him. It didn't make it any better though. Especially when it was your boss making you wait after he put you in charge of getting hundreds of extremely rich clients to be comfortable in a climate of complete discomfort.

He had gotten everyone settled into their seats about forty-five minutes ago by telling them that Mr. Coff would be out shortly, and the proceedings would begin. Now, here he was, standing in front of a group of billionaires, politicians, elites, and downright rich perverts...not to mention the thousands that were streaming in from all over the world. They were getting quite restless, and for good reason. Even the nicely dressed and primped children that were seated behind him on the stage were beginning to squirm.

"Mr. Watson!" a Middle Eastern Sheikh on one of the monitors snapped. "This has gone well beyond rude and quite honestly, it's embarrassing!?" Others that could hear him agreed.

He glanced over at Chi, who stood patiently next to the stage with her hands clasped in front of her and showing no

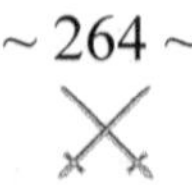

feelings whatsoever. "Once again, I apologize for Mr. Coff's tardiness, gentlemen...but please, if you will be so kind as to give him a few more moments...I'm sure he has his reasons...as he's been looking forward to this night for some time now." He looked down at his watch and swore into the microphone by accident. He turned and stormed off the stage and went over to the door that led back to the warehouse. Two large guards were standing like statues in front of it. "Excuse me, gent..." A strong arm pushed him back.

"Joshua said to not allow anyone beyond this door," one of the guards said. Seeing Jack's horror at being pushed away, he added. "I'm sorry, but he was quite adamant about the order...so you'll have to discuss your displeasure with him, Mr. Watson."

"It's starting to look like I have plenty of displeasure to discuss with him!" Jack said, turning around and storming away.

Joshua placed the match against the strip that would light it once he swiped it across. Lacey was screaming and kicking at the cage door like a wild woman, begging for her life. With an evil grin, he turned to Brianna. "I'm feeling generous! I will give you ONE more chance to deny Christ, Brianna Bowers! Deny him and I will spare this wailing, screaming, pathetic soul. I'm sure Jonah would THANK you for saving his previous lover..." he chuckled and waited for her response.

Brianna looked up at Joshua with contempt in her eyes. "Joshua...I'm begging you not to do this! Please, pour your gasoline on me...kill ME!!!" She attempted to free herself from

the iron grip of the large guard, but her writhing was futile. "Please don't kill anyone else just to prove a point!"

"Deny your God, Brianna Bowers!" he said, lowering his face to hers. "Deny Jesus Christ as the God of heaven and ALL of this stops! It's all you have to do!"

"I WILL…"

"NEVER!!!" Jonah screamed from behind her. They both jumped as Jonah began to flail like a fish on a hook, his arms lifting him up and down as he strained against the thick chains. "THERE ARE MORE FOR US THAN AGAINST US!!!!! YOU FOOL!!!" He stopped his attempts and with both eyes wide open, looked directly at Joshua. "I've seen them…and boy are you in trouble." With that, Brianna smiled.

Joshua laughed a nervous laugh. "You're delirious, and I don't have time for this anymore." He struck the match.

Jonah raised himself up one last time and at the top of his lungs shouted, "JESUUUUUSSSS!" When he dropped back down, the chains shattered like glass to the floor.

The guard holding Brianna swung around and Joshua kicked him out of the way. He also punched the startled guard next to him in the face, knocking him back. Brianna slapped the match from Joshua's hand and then turned her eyes to the ceiling as she alone saw it open and billions of warrior angels swooped in to do battle in the spirit realm…that's when she saw something else that made her laugh… Mark, Scotty, Gabi, and hundreds of teenagers…that were over ten feet tall and in full armor, slicing demon after demon as their bodies were probably still in Australia somewhere, praying in the spirit.

"YES!!! THANK YOU, JESUS!!!" Brianna shouted and at that exact moment, hundreds of federal and local law enforcement agents stormed into the building, guns drawn and forcing everyone to the ground.

Secretary-General Schmidt attempted to run down one of the warehouse aisles but was quickly tackled to the ground and placed in handcuffs.

Brianna looked back up and saw that most of the demons had been routed and warrior angels were being posted at every entrance and exit. Mark, Gabi, and Scotty were already gone. Even though, just minutes ago, it had felt like all was lost...the battle had belonged to God.

Jack was presently in a heated discussion with a famous Hollywood director, when he noticed several guards take off running toward the back of the room. "What is going on!?" he shouted to one of them as several people began to get up from their seats and gather their things.

"RUN!!!" the guard said, just as the door burst open and police in full body armor ran into the room yelling for everyone to get on the floor.

People were falling over each other to escape the room, trying various doors, only to find federal agents on the other side of each. Agents were screaming for people to stop and tackling them when they didn't. Within minutes, several hundreds of powerful elites were lying on their stomachs with their hands bound behind their backs.

"Well, well, well," Agent Donnie Wright said as he approached one of the bound suspects who was on the floor

screaming obscenities and demanding to be let go. "Who do we have here!? Talk about the fox getting caught in the hen house! If it isn't the Secretary-General of Interpol himself! Hello, Mr. Schmidt!"

"I DEMAND you let me go, this instant!" Gunther screamed. "I AM NOT a part of this circus; I can assure you sir!!! LET ME GO!!!"

"Well, Mr. Schmidt, you're going to have to take that up with Interpol...it seems that you've been under investigation for some time now...how do you think we were able to find this extraordinary operation?" He looked around the room at all the people being questioned and booked. "Wow, isn't that the actor that's in that famous kid's show? What's it called?"

CHAPTER 29

All the bad guys seemed to be under control and in cuffs. Brianna scanned the room looking for someone in particular but didn't see him. Had he already been taken away? "Excuse me," she stopped an agent as he passed by. "The ringleader of this operation...Joseph Coff? Did you guys get him?"

The agent shook his head. "I'm not sure, Ma'am, but my supervisor, Agent Wright, is in the next room." He pointed toward a door where several people had been coming and going. It was apparently the room where the children were going to be auctioned off. She looked around and saw that Jonah was busy being doctored by his sister and consoling his ex-girlfriend, Lacey.

Nadia was giving a statement to several agents and holding her little sister in her arms. That's when she spotted Dustin...he was apparently a superstar of some kind. Right now, however, he was kneeling beside the spot where Maria had been killed...still crying. She walked over and sat down on the floor beside him. She placed a hand on his back, and he glanced toward her.

"It's my fault...that monster killed her because..."

"Dustin!" Brianna said, interrupting him. "Stop! Did you pour the gasoline on her? No, you didn't. Did you light the match and throw it? No, you didn't." She took his hand and squeezed it. "It wasn't your fault. From my understanding...you're one of the few good guys in this place. You were willing to give up fame and fortune to hold onto your morals. In my book, you're a hero!" She reached up and turned his face toward her. "And Maria knew that too."

He tried to smile through his tears. "She only wanted to see her mommy," he said. "Joseph lied to her and…"

"Just like he lied to you saying it was your fault...but guess what? He also told me he was going to kill her because I wouldn't deny Christ!" That thought gave her a sick feeling...her parents! She needed to check on her parents! How had she forgotten?

"So, you're a Christian?" Dustin asked her. "My grandmother used to take me to church."

"I am…" she looked around. She desperately needed to find a phone so she could call and find out something about her parents. "Excuse me for a second, Dustin…"

"Brianna Bowers, I presume!" someone said from behind her. She looked up at the tall agent in the dark blue suit with the badge on his lapel. He held out his hand to help her up. "Agent Donnie Wright! We have a lot to talk about now, don't we?"

"Agent Wright!" she squeezed him in a big hug. "Thank you so much!"

"Just doing my job…"

"I need to find out if my parents…" she began, and he held up a hand.

"They're fine...apparently Lieutenant Ramsey and your father are far better shots than the thugs sent to kill them."

"Oh, thank God!" Brianna said. "So, everybody's okay? My mom?"

"Everybody except the bad guys...the report said that each of them had been shot over two dozen times. Dead on arrival! Which, may I add, is the best way to serve up child predators."

Brianna found a chair and had a seat, breathing out what felt like a month's worth of tension. "So, how did you find us?"

"What?" Agent Wright said with a grin. "Do you think you own the rights to having a secret source?"

"Agent Wright, are you a believer?" Brianna asked with a huge grin on her face.

"Deacon at my church, thank you very much!" Agent Wright replied. "Been secret sourcing for over twenty years." He winked at Brianna and leaned down to whisper... "Our mutual friend told me to contact Interpol...and well, they'd been keeping tabs on old Gunther for quite some time."

"Well, thank you for getting here when you did," Brianna said. "I thought Jonah and I were gonna have to take this freak show down by ourselves."

Agent Wright smiled and squeezed her shoulder. "I have absolutely no doubt that you could've done just that."

Just then, Nadia walked over and with tears in her eyes, gave Brianna a huge hug. She sobbed into Brianna's shoulder. Agent Wright took that as his cue to move along and make sure all the bad guys had been rounded up.

"Agent Wright!" Brianna called to him over Nadia's shoulder. "Joshua didn't get away, did he?"

"Joshua Coff?" he asked with a concerned look on his face. "My guys assumed he wasn't here."

~ 271 ~

CHAPTER 30

Joshua had always believed in being prepared for anything, in fact, it was the number one reason for his success. The very spot he'd been standing in the warehouse had been directly over a trap door, just in case he needed to make a quick escape. The release button for the door was on his keychain.

He'd known trouble was on the way the moment that buffoon had started talking to himself. In fact, Joshua had known immediately that he hadn't, in fact, been talking to himself...but the one responsible for all of Joshua's failings. He had learned to hate God at a young age...just after both of his parents had been killed in a car accident. It wasn't that he didn't believe in God, no, only a fool would be that stupid. He believed that God was real, yes, but extremely evil. Which was quite funny if you stopped and thought about it, because the god that he put his faith in, Teuflisch, was really the god of evil.

The word Teuflisch literally means evil or wicked in German. Joshua was no fool, mind you...he knew that Teuflisch was evil...but at least that's what he promised. That supposed God of Love...Jesus the hippie...said one thing and delivered another. Yes, Joshua knew that Brianna and her praying friends would eventually be his downfall if he didn't get rid of them...and in his arrogance, he'd stalled in killing her just to make her suffer.

Oh, how he wished he could be there to see how she was torn up over her parents' deaths. At least he had that going for him. She would always have herself to blame for that and the little girl's death. That made him smile.

Presently, however, he was speeding north on 120, in his brand new, rust orange colored Lamborghini Aventador. It appeared that he was the only vehicle on the road this evening, as he made his easy escape at the speed of 117 mph on the open road. He hated that this had happened, it would definitely be a monkey wrench in his overall plans and forced him to hide out in another country for a few years, but he was a billionaire. He had everything...money, cars, women, houses all over the world.

He was literally untouchable...even from that supposed God of Love. Again, he smiled. His hatred for God was what had driven his passion to live a life of opposition to that God. "I AM GOD!" he shouted in his car as he sped along miles away from the people who didn't even know he'd been there. His only regret was that he'd had to leave his precious sword behind. However, in two hours he would be airborne over the pacific on his way to his little hideaway near Batangas, Philippines.

What he didn't realize, however, was that the older gentleman in the seat beside him, had other plans for him. Quietly he had sat there, unnoticed, as Joshua sped up 120 in an attempt to escape the consequences of his actions. Finally, after giving Joshua enough time to think he was the master of his own destiny, He reached over and touched the side of his head.

In a flash of light, Joshua was standing in the midst of a large crowd on the side of a hill. By the sound of things, something big was happening. The crowd, mostly made up of men, were shouting what seemed like obscenities at whatever was going on. He wasn't sure what they were saying because they were shouting in an unfamiliar language to him. It felt like something from the middle east, but he wasn't sure.

He walked through the crowd, not sure why he was here, but figuring there had to be a reason and that reason must be whatever had these people so worked up. He finally pressed his way through the crowd and stood near the top when he let out an audible gasp...it was HIM! The one he hated...and he was hanging there on that cross, completely saturated in blood and sweat. Joshua could literally smell his stench. He covered his nose. There wasn't a part of his body that wasn't laid open. You could literally see his insides...his ribs...he hardly even looked human.

Then Joshua looked at the crowd. Some looked to have passion on the man, but most were hurling what must've been insults. They really hated Him. This Godman...this destroyer of lives...this liar...this evil, evil Godman...Joshua also hated Him. He found himself smiling at the plight of this man...getting what he deserved, no doubt. "I hope you burn in hell," Joshua whispered, as he saw the man writhing in pain. "And I hope everything you stand for burns with you...and every Christian...and every innocent child...and...."

Instantly, Joshua was back in the front seat of his brand-new Lamborghini Aventador, driving at top speed...living his best life...escaping the consequences of his actions. However, because of his little adventure at the cross, where he had decided to deny the ONLY one that had ever loved him, he didn't have time to realize that there was a large diesel truck parked in the road ahead of him. Despite its flashing lights and flares, Joshua's Lamborghini hit it at 123 mph and instantly evaporated on impact. Joshua Coff, one of the richest and most powerful men in the world...was no more.

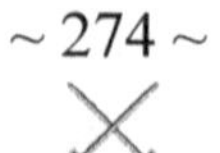

If you had been nearby when this happened...and you'd listened really close...you might've heard the faint sound of someone whistling an old children's church song…

"Jesus Loves the Little Children."

CHAPTER 31

"I doubted Him, Brianna," Nadia said, as she sobbed. "I thought He had abandoned us, and I doubted Him."

"Nadia," Brianna whispered in her ear, as they clung to each other. "He's a big God...He can take it. We all doubt Him from time to time...even me."

"I don't even believe that...please Brianna...pray for me...now...I want to know God like you know Him...I want Him to be my best friend...please." Nadia was crying as she'd never cried in her life. Her little sister sat a few feet away, being looked at by an EMT...watching.

"Father God!" Brianna started. "I lift up my friend, Nadia Skutnik, to You right now. Your Holy Spirit has been drawing her to You for some time now, Father. God, she is coming to You willingly...begging for a personal relationship with You."

Nadia nodded and moaned yes into Brianna's neck.

"God, I pray that You give her a passion to serve You...to get into Your word...to pursue a relationship with You as only best friends can. Help her, Father! Help her, Jesus! Help her, Holy Spirit! Pour Yourself into my sweet friend! Show her YOU!" She squeezed Nadia very tight, and Nadia responded with a hug of her own. "In Jesus' name I pray! Amen!"

"Amen, Brianna Bowers," Nadia replied. "Amen!" They squeezed each other one more time and broke their embrace. Both noticed a heavily bandaged Jonah standing next to them at the same time and smiled at him. Nadia leaned in close to Brianna and whispered... "You could do worse..."

"Get outta here, you!" Brianna said with a laugh and shoved her away. Nadia walked over to be with her sister.

"You good?" Jonah asked forcefully. His entire head was bandaged...along with his ribs, arms, hands…

"Better than you, apparently," she replied with a smile. "How's Lacey?"

"She'll live," he said, and stepped closer to her. "There was a point in the past however long we were here...that I thought, I would never...you know...see you again."

"Jonah…"

"Let me finish," he replied, interrupting her. "I've become quite...smitten with you, Brianna Bowers. Before you go getting all self-righteous and all...I've accepted Jesus into my heart and I'm as awesome as you, now." He smiled and she could tell that it hurt him to do so.

"Smitten, huh?" she asked. "Nobody has ever told me that they were smitten by me."

"Well, they have now," he said, as he took a seat on a nearby chair.

"I think it's awesome that you've accepted Jesus and all, Jonah...but I'm sorry." She walked over and stood directly in front of him. He looked down at his feet and she saw him take a deep breath. "But...you will NEVER be as awesome as me."

Jonah looked up and smiled at her, letting out a sad little laugh that sounded more like a grunt. He held out his arms and she let him pull her into a hug.

"I'd be lying if I said I weren't smitten by you as well," she added.

✗

"Ms. Bowers, I'm sorry...but we thought you might want to be the one to take this call," a young federal agent said, holding a cell phone out for her to take it.

"Who is it?" Brianna asked, taking the phone from him.

"A Carmen Sanchez, ma'am," he whispered. "She wants to know if her daughter, Maria, is alright…"

EPILOGUE

GATEWAY, FLORIDA (2 days later)

Brianna was sitting on the back deck of her parents' house, a glass of sweet tea in one hand and her cell phone in the other. Jonah had just left the night before to be with his parents in California. His dad was out of the hospital and doing well and his mother was frantically trying to take care of him. Jonah just wanted to be there for them and his sister for a few weeks. She and him had agreed to take things slow...neither of their lifestyles left much room for a relationship right now. Brianna just wanted to chill for now...maybe help her dad with another restoration of Bruce...the poor guy was full of bullet holes on one side.

"So, you guys were just praying for me and what? Your bodies just vanished from right there on the stage?" Brianna asked Gabi, who was on a video call with her from Tokyo, Japan.

"No, silly!" Gabi replied, with a laugh. "Basically, we just left our bodies and ended up there with you, doing battle. It was crazy!"

"Yeah, Officer Ramsey said you almost gave him a heart attack when you showed up here to warn them," she said with a chuckle, trying to imagine it.

"Well, I'm just glad they were all okay!" Gabi replied.

"So, how are you guys?" Brianna asked. "Are you still packing out stadiums?"

"This is the first one since Sydney, but yeah...it appears to be sold out," Gabi said. "Apparently the videos of Mark and

Scotty's bodies dropping to the floor and me acting all crazy went viral and caused quite the controversy."

"And we know how people love a good controversy!" Brianna said with a laugh.

"What's funny is, the controversy is more within the church than outside the church...God's people are the hardest to convince He's real sometimes!" Gabi turned as if someone else had entered the room. "Come say hi to Brianna!" she said and turned the phone for Brianna to see Matt Ramsey smiling at her. Matt had always been a great leader, being much larger than most boys his age when he was in school. He'd gotten all his friends involved in music and most of them were now the band for the Dragon Slayers conventions.

"Hey, Brianna!" Matt said, cheerfully. "It's so good to see you...you know you gave us quite the scare!"

"Yeah, sorry about that!" Brianna replied, taking a sip of her sweet tea.

"You know, I understand you're following your calling and all...but you really should start praying that the Holy Spirit would get you another job." He was joking, but Brianna knew that he meant it.

"Well, it's funny you say that!" Brianna replied.

"OH, REALLY!?" Matt and Gabi said in unison.

"Yeah, it has been made crystal clear to me by the Holy Spirit that I will no longer be involved with the human trafficking ministry at all." She held her glass up in a cheer fashion and smiled. "I'll miss helping those poor children, but I won't miss the evils that I had to deal with."

"That's awesome, Brianna!" Matt said. "You deserve a little break from the horrors of this world! Any idea what you'll be doing now?"

"No idea whatsoever...I've been informed to wait...the answer will be revealed soon. However, Carmen Sanchez, the woman whose daughter died…is praying about taking over my ministry. She said she wants to spend the rest of her life helping mothers like herself."

"That's so powerful, Brianna," Gabi said. "I can see God all over that."

"Well, I've got some big news myself!" Matt said.

"Oh yeah? Do tell!"

"I am going to be stepping down from the band here at Dragon Slayers and moving back to Gateway!" He seemed quite excited.

"No way, what are you going to be doing here?" Brianna asked.

"I've been asked to be the worship leader there at Lighthouse Christian Center!" he exclaimed. "Besides, I want to be closer to my family… you know, with what went down and all...I could've lost them."

Brianna knew that Matt had suffered a lot of losses in his life, including his best friend, Billy. "That's awesome, Matt! I'm sure you will be missed by your band, but I know God has big things for you here! Ooh, maybe Dustin Knight could help with the band, since you're leaving! He has given his heart to Jesus and wants to do something big for God!"

"Give him my number," Gabi said.

Just then, Brianna's phone began to buzz with an incoming call. "Hey guys!" she said, sitting up in her chair. "I'm getting a call from one of our old friends, and I should probably take this."

"Oh yeah?" Gabi asked. "Who?"

"Jason Green, or should I say Pastor Jason Green!" she replied. "I'll talk to you guys later!" She clicked off the video call. Jason had been Mark's best friend in Pittsburgh before he'd moved to Gateway. During their whole dragon adventure, Jason had been pulled into the middle of it. He'd ended up getting saved, getting seriously involved in ministry in Pittsburgh and then going to Bible college with Mark and most of the gang. He'd even been involved in Dragon Slayers Ministry for a few years before becoming a pastor somewhere up in the mountains of Tennessee. Brianna hadn't talked to Jason in a few years. She clicked on the call. "Jason Green?"

"Hey, Brianna," he said, sounding quite tired. "How are you doing?"

"I'm doing well, Pastor Green, are you okay?"

"I heard about what went down up in Wyoming...that was some crazy stuff. Child traffickers...people are sick."

"So, what do I owe the honor of this call?" Brianna asked, noticing his avoidance of her first question.

"Brianna…" she could hear him sigh. "This is gonna sound crazy...but I need you to trust me."

"I'm already scared," she said, teasingly.

"I'm pastoring in a small town called Pennington Springs, Tennessee," he said. "And we've got something going on up here that I think is, well, I could really use your help."

"What is it, Jason?" she asked, noting the sincerity in his voice. Jason had always been the wild and crazy one in the group. When he was serious...it was time to be serious.

"I just need you to trust me, Brianna...can you do that?" he asked. "I need you to come up here as soon as you can...and I'll explain everything when you get here."

"Okay, Jason," she replied. The Holy Spirit HAD said that her new calling would be revealed soon. "I'll book a flight as soon as I can."

"Thank you so much...for trusting me."

Brianna clicked off the call and headed into the house. This whole new adventure thing was exciting...and terrifying.

PENNINGTON SPRINGS, TENNESSEE

Jason clicked off the call and closed his eyes. "God, forgive me." A tear rolled down his cheek as he turned around and walked back up the trail. He'd gone to the closest place he could find with cell service. The mountain was quiet tonight. He reached the top in a matter of minutes and headed toward the small run-down cabin in the distance. He tried to avert his eyes as he got closer but found it was better to look and NOT step on the scattered body parts of the latest victims. Seven total tonight. Bodies just torn apart...limb from limb. He held a rag over his mouth and fought the urge to gag. Stepping inside the old shack, the detectives turned to acknowledge him.

"Well?" the older, heavy set Detective Horne, asked.

"She's coming…" Jason said, glancing up on the wall of the room they were in. The room where the brutal killings had taken place. With the shirt of one of the victims, the killer had painted on the wall in blood… "BRING ME BRIANNA BOWERS"

Coming Soon

Unholy:

The Chronicles Of Brianna Bowers

Check Out These Other Exciting Stories By

Billy Stancil:

Mark McGee and The Gateway To God

Mark McGee and The Valley of The Shadow of Death

Mark McGee and The Journey To The Dragon's Lair

...Greater Is He That Is In You,

Than He That Is In The World.

1 John 4:4 KJV

www.ingramcontent.com/pod-product-compliance
Lightning Source LLC
Chambersburg PA
CBHW071218210726
48293CB00002B/487